TOM PLAYFAIR
OR MAKING A START

Dear Will,

Please enjoy this captivating story book!

Growing up is hard but if you look in the right place, God will bless you and you will grow up to become a great man!

With love,
your cousin,

Sophia

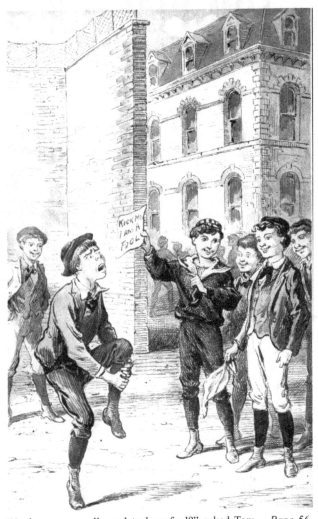

"And are you really and truly a fool?" asked Tom.—*Page* 56.

Tom Playfair
OR MAKING A START

By

Fr. Francis J. Finn, S.J.
AUTHOR OF PERCY WYNN, HARRY DEE, ETC.

Reprinted from the Twelfth Edition

TAN Books
Charlotte, North Carolina

Copyright © 1891 by Benziger Brothers, New York. Reprinted from the Twelfth Edition by TAN Books in 2000.

ISBN: 978-0-89555-670-7

Library of Congress Control No.: 00-131556

Cover illustrations by Margaret Ethier; reproduced courtesy of the Headmaster of St. Mary's Academy and College, St. Mary's, Kansas, publisher of the former *Crusade* Magazine, in which the illustrations first appeared.

Cover design by Peter Massari.

THE TOM PLAYFAIR SERIES
"Father Finn's Famous Three"

Tom Playfair—or Making a Start   ISBN 978-0-89555-670-7
Percy Wynn—
   or Making a Boy of Him   ISBN 978-0-89555-671-4
Harry Dee—or Working It Out   ISBN 978-0-89555-672-1
The Set of 3   ISBN 978-0-89555-687-5

Printed and bound in the United States of America.

TAN Books
Charlotte, North Carolina
www.TANBooks.com
2011

PREFACE

THE vicissitudes of the "Tom Playfair" manuscript would alone make a story. How it was written over seven years ago, for the sake of a college class, and with no ulterior thought of publication; how portions of it gradually found their way into print; how the writer hesitated for years whether to consign the remaining parts to the book publisher or to the wastebasket; how the cordial reception of "Percy Wynn," and the kind words concerning "Tom Playfair" from critics and from readers inspirited him to take the venerable manuscript—done at all manner of odd times, in lead pencil and ink, upon all sorts and conditions of paper—from his trunk, and subsequently devote no small part of his vacation days (July, August, 1891) to its revisal; how the valued advice and kind words of literary friends served him in the revision—are not all these things indelibly impressed upon the author's memory?

And now he ventures to offer this story to the boys and girls of the land, in the hope that it may afford them healthful pleasure.

Advancing the figure learnedly styled *hysteron-proteron* from sentences to volumes, he has published "Percy Wynn" first, although Percy's adventures are subsequent to Tom's. The reason for this procedure may be gathered from what has been said of the "Tom Playfair" manuscript.

St. Maure's is a pseudonym for a certain college in the West. Besides inventing incidents, the author, to suit his purpose, has on occasion taken liberties with the local surroundings; but in the main he has adhered to the prototype.

It is almost needless to say that the real college never suffered from the effects of a thunderbolt; in fact, the "cupola," upon which turns a catastrophe recorded in these pages, was erected, not by an architect, but by a few strokes of the pen.

Near this Western college there is a village—a thriving, happy community. This village the author has eliminated from these stories. The village of St. Maure's, which takes its place, is a fiction.

In drawing, with certain necessary reserves, upon his three years' experience at this Western college, the author has, perhaps, made too little of one striking feature—the manly piety of the students. In all his experiences there he could *count upon his fingers* those who, while in attendance, had evidently changed for the worse; and they were marked exceptions.

It is hard upon seven years since the writer last saw "St. Maure's." Then it was just on this side of its pioneer days. Now it is a college with a history of which it may well be proud. The "old church building," the little boys' dormitory and washroom, the long, low frame structure used as an infirmary, are gone; new and nobler piles have arisen in their place so that the college of today, as Peggotty remarked, I believe, of her nephew, Ham, has "growed out of knowledge"; and yet the sweet spirit of faith and prayer has abided unchanged amid all changes.

The author has not seen these changes he is blessed in believing. Nor can he doubt, aside from all testimony, that the same spirit pervades them all. *The Dial*, a college paper conducted by the students, reaches him every month; and he can read in the lines and between the lines that the college of today and the college of seven years ago are one in that closest and most sacred of moral unions—a true, devout, Catholic spirit.

Francis J. Finn, S.J.

October 19, 1891

CONTENTS

ix

CONTENTS

Chapter I

*IN WHICH THE HERO OF THE STORY IS
REPRESENTED IN A DOUBTFUL LIGHT*

"TOMMY!"

No answer.

"Tommy—do you hear me? Get up this moment, sir. Do you think this house is a hotel? Everyone's at breakfast except yourself."

Miss Meadow, Tom Playfair's maternal aunt, stood without the door of Master Playfair's sleeping apartment. She paused for a moment, partly to gain her breath (having come up three pairs of stairs to arouse Tom) and partly to await some reply from our sleeping hero.

The silence, however, was simply emphasized by the ticking of the great clock in the hall.

"Tommy!" she resumed at length, in a higher key, "do you hear me?"

Her strained ears caught the dull sound as of someone turning lazily in his bed. "Now you're awake, sir, jump right up, and dress

1

for your breakfast."

"Sho! scat!" came a yawning voice from the room.

"Dear me!" cried poor Miss Meadow, "the boy doesn't mind me in the least."

"What's the trouble, Jane?" queried Mr. Playfair, who just then issued from his room.

"I can't get that Tommy out of bed. He's growing worse every day, George. Last week he was late for school five times."

"I'll fix that, Jane," said Mr. Playfair. And he took one step toward Tom's sleeping-room, when the door of that apartment opened a few inches, discovering a young face peering anxiously from beneath a mass of tangled hair.

"Pa," said the apparition, "I'm dressing just as fast as I know how. I heard you, auntie, and I'm coming right away."

Then the door closed. Tom, it must be explained, had been composing himself for another nap, when the whispered dialogue between his aunt and his father had brought him out of bed with most unwonted celerity. The wily lad deemed it best not to wait for an order from his father. Hence the apparition.

"If you are not at the breakfast table in two minutes, sir, you shall hear from me," and with these sternly delivered words Mr. Playfair conducted Miss Meadow to breakfast.

Little more than a minute later, a stout, healthy, dark-complexioned lad of ten emerged from his room ready and eager for the labor and heat of the day. His rosy face and jet-black hair gave token of a hasty toilet. His shoes were partially buttoned, his sturdy legs were encased in a pair of bright red stockings and rather tight knickerbockers, and his chubby cheeks wore an air of serenity, which coupled with his naturally handsome features made him a pleasing sight to all lovers of the genuine American boy.

Hastily descending the stairs (which he did by taking from three to four steps at a bound), Tom very quickly presented himself in the dining room, and ignoring the presence of the cat, in the teasing of which he spent a considerable portion of his valuable time, he seated himself at table, and fell to with great good will. But trouble was brewing.

Besides Mr. Playfair and Miss Meadow, there was at table a young man, brother to Tom's aunt, and the bane of our hero's life. Mr. Charles Meadow was not a bad young man, but he had, despite this negative good quality, a large and constantly increasing stock of small faults, one of which was an inordinate delight in teasing and browbeating Tom. It is fair to say, however, that in the indulgence of this fault Mr. Meadow did not always come off with flying colors. Tom contrived to gain a victory now and then, and thus added a zest to the domestic war, which would otherwise have been too one-sided to be interesting. Strangely enough, Mr. Playfair held himself, in general, strictly neutral; and it was only when the campaign gave signs of unusual bitterness that he felt himself called upon to interfere.

On the present occasion young Mr. Meadow had been awaiting with ill-concealed anxiety Tom's appearance.

"Oh, so here you are at last, are you?" he began as Tom seated himself at the table.

In the tranquillity of a healthy appetite applied to its proper purpose, Tom ignored the enemy's hostile flag.

"Look here, young man," continued Mr. Meadow, "were you at my room again last night?"

"How could a fellow get in your old room when you had it locked?" queried Tom with virtuous indignation.

"Never mind the 'how,' but did you go into my room last night?"

"Say, Aunt Jane, please put a little more sugar in this coffee. You never *do* give me enough."

"What I want to know," pursued the unrelenting uncle, "is, whether you went into my room last night."

"If you stayed at home, and went to bed early, instead of running round the town nights," answered Tom, still desirous of shifting the battle-ground, "you wouldn't be asking such questions."

At this moment Mary the cook entered the dining room with a plate of pancakes.

If Tom had a preference, it was for this dish.

"Whoop!" he cried, and his eyes glistened.

A smile of triumph passed over Mr. Meadow's countenance; just as Tom was about to help himself liberally to the food of his preference, his persecutor took possession of the plate, and having helped Mr. Playfair and Miss Meadow to several cakes, he placed the rest upon his own plate.

Tom waxed angry.

"Oh! you think you're funny, don't you? Maybe you don't use hair-dye for that straw-colored mustache of yours—I spelled it on a big bottle."

Mr. Playfair smiled, Miss Meadow tittered,

Mr. Meadow blushed deeply. Recovering himself, he returned to the charge.

"Aha!" he cried, directing his forefinger at Tom. "So you *have* been in my room?"

It was Tom's turn to blush; he was fairly caught.

"How did you get in, sir?" continued Mr. Meadow, pursuing his advantage.

"Button-hook," answered Tom, with the falling inflection.

"Exactly—that's just what I thought, and that's just the way you ruined the lock of the pantry last week."

Mr. Playfair's face took on an air of concern; he glanced severely at the culprit.

"Well," drawled Tom, "I guess it isn't fair to lock up ripe apples. They don't give a fellow any show in this house."

"Tommy!"—an electric shock seemed to convulse our little pantry-burglar at the low, stern tones of his father's voice—"Tommy, have you been forcing locks with a button-hook again?"

The roses in Tom's cheeks grew out of all bounds, till the "roots of his hair were stirred"; he dropped his knife and fork, and with a despairing expression hung his head.

"This is getting too bad," Mr. Playfair continued. "I don't like to say it, but such conduct is more fit for a young thief than for a little boy whom his father wishes to make a gentleman." At the word "thief" there was a subdued boo-hoo, followed by the sound of heavy breathing.

"You may well cry, sir," pursued the parent, "for you have every reason to be ashamed of yourself."

"I j-j-just d-d-did it for f-fun," he sobbed.

"Oh, you're exceedingly funny!" broke in Mr. Meadow with infinite sarcasm.

This last remark filled his cup of sorrow to overflowing; stifling an incipient sob and muttering that he "didn't want no breakfast," he departed into the welcome solitude of the hall. The word "thief" still rang in his ears, and sigh upon sigh bursting at short intervals from his passion-racked bosom testified his appreciation of the term.

Presently Mr. Meadow, on his way down town, where he held the honorable position of assistant bookkeeper in a St. Louis hardware store, issued from the dining room. At the sight of him, Tom's grief hardened into the sterner form of anger.

"You'll pay for this, Mr. Give-away," he muttered, shaking a diminutive fist at Mr. Meadow. "I'm going to see Miss Larkin today—I will, I *will*!—and I'll just tell her all the mean things you say to me, how your mustache is dyed—see if I don't—I'll spoil your chances there."

Mr. Meadow, who *had* a soft spot in his heart (devoted almost exclusively to said Miss Larkin), was taken back not a little at this threat.

"You young scamp," he roared with more earnestness than dignity, "if you go near that young lady with any of your wretched stories, I'll give you a cowhiding."

"Ugh! you give-away!" cried Tom with ineffable disgust.

"So, sir; *that's* the language you use to your uncle," said Mr. Playfair, who as he opened the dining room door had caught these words. "Go up to your room, sir, and don't leave it till nine o'clock. Jane," he continued, looking into the dining room, "please tell Tommy when it is nine."

Mr. Playfair left the house with a stern cast of countenance. Tom was scarcely five when his mother died. The boy was good— but the want of a mother's care and refining influence was very evident. Then too, Mr. Playfair reflected, the child stood in great danger of having his disposition ruined. Petted by Miss Meadow, he was growing selfish; teased by Mr. Meadow, he was becoming bold.

"Yes," he muttered, "I shall have to take some decisive step, or the boy will be spoiled."

Chapter II

IN WHICH TOM BY A SERIES OF MISADVENTURES BRINGS DOWN THE WRATH OF HIS FATHER IN SUCH WISE THAT THE AUTHOR, FOR FEAR OF FORFEITING TOM'S CHANCES OF BECOMING A HERO IN THE READER'S EYES, DISCREETLY VEILS WHAT ACTUALLY HAPPENED WHEN JUSTICE WAS ADMINISTERED

THE mournful wail that swept at dismal intervals through Mr. Playfair's house touched the sympathetic chord of compassion in the heartstrings of gentle Aunt Jane. Stealing softly up to Tom's room, she entered on tiptoe. Master Tom, his hair dishevelled, and the channels of grief plainly traced upon his cheeks, was lying prone upon his bed. The sight of her compassionate face opened a new flood of tears.

"Don't cry, Tommy," she said softly.

"I wish I was dead," cried that young gentleman.

"Now, now, Tommy," exclaimed the horrified and too credulous aunt, "don't talk that way: it is sinful, and I'm sure you don't mean it."

"I'll bet I do," he howled. "And I wish I

was b-b-buried too under the ground. And I'll tell you what, Aunt Jane, I'll run away."

"Oh, Tommy, how can you say such wicked things? Come, now, can't I bring you up some breakfast?"

"Don't want any breakfast. I'll run away, and sell newspapers, and have a jolly time."

"Dear, dear, where did you get all these notions?" queried Miss Meadow, whose confiding spirit received these exaggerated expressions of grief as so much gospel truth. "Tommy, what do you say to some buttered toast, and a bit of cake?"

In spite of himself, Tom could not help showing, at this stage, some interest in sublunary affairs.

"No," he said, sitting up in bed, "but I'd like to have some pancakes."

"They're all gone, Tommy, and it's so much trouble to make them."

"Well, then, I don't want any breakfast," he said, throwing himself back on the bed, and relapsing into sobs.

This last exhibition of tactics won the victory. Miss Meadow descended to the kitchen, and put herself to the elaborate work of making pancakes for the world-worn youth of ten.

Upon her departure, Tom smiled in a manner not entirely devoid of guile; and the smile running counter to his tears formed a sort of facial rainbow.

Presently Aunt Jane appeared with the pancakes, and other delicacies, and very shortly, indeed, Tom fell to in a manner most encouraging to behold.

"I say, Aunt Jane," he said, speaking with as much distinctness as the crowded state of his mouth would allow, "you're a real genuine, old fairy-grandmother, you are."

He intended this for a magnificent compliment, but Aunt Jane did not look particularly gratified. To a Miss of thirty the epithets "old" and "grandmother" were rather suggestive.

Perceiving that he had made some mistake, Tom added:

"I'll tell you what, Auntie, I won't bother your pantry, or scare the cook for—well, for a week." He spoke as if he felt how handsome his offer was.

"That sounds better," said Miss Meadow. "So you'll be a good boy now, won't you?"

"Honor bright, Aunt Jane." And Miss Meadow, with this consolatory assurance gladdening her heart, departed to attend to her domestic affairs, having first given him his liberty.

Availing himself of this, he was presently engaged in the back yard in constructing a chicken-coop.

"Halloa!" said a voice directly behind him.

"Halloa yourself; is that you, Jeff?" he made answer, as a boy of about his own age, with a dollish face, and clad in soft garments, met his view.

"Got any chickens yet?" asked Jeff, ignoring Tom's question as being superfluous.

"Not yet, but I guess I'll trade off my base-ball with Tom White for one." And master Tom picked up a pine board which he proceeded to split into smaller sections. In the midst of this interesting operation, a chip flew up, striking Jeff rather sharply upon the lobe of his left ear.

"Confound you!" shouted Jeff, rubbing the injured member with pathetic earnestness.

"You needn't curse," said Tom resentfully.

"That ain't cursin'," retorted Jeff in a sharper key.

"Well, it's vulgar all the same," insisted Tom, unwilling to give in entirely.

"It isn't."

"It is."

"I tell you it isn't."

"I tell you it is."

"I guess my pa uses it."

"*My* pa doesn't, and he ought to know."

Their voices "took a higher range."

"See here, Jeff Thompson, do you mean to say that your pa knows more than mine?"

"Yes, I do."

Tom seemed to think that the conversation had reached a point where argument should be advanced by other means than mere verbal expression, for he suddenly struck out straight from the shoulder, and before his astonished opponent could hold up his hands to ward off the blow a sturdy little fist came into forceful contact with Jeff's nose.

As stars gladiatorial flashed before Jeff's eyes, his yell of anguish broke upon the silence.

"I'm killed!" he shrieked, as the blood gushed from his injured member.

The fast-flowing stream frightened Tom exceedingly.

"Oh, Jeff!" he cried, clasping his hands, "I didn't mean to hurt you so much—cross my heart, I didn't," and he rubbed his thumb so as to form an invisible cross upon the right side of his sailor jacket, supposing, in his ignorance, that he had precisely located his heart.

"Go 'way, don't talk to me," said Jeff, suspending a howl to deliver this important communication. "I'll never speak to you again."

"Oh, Jeff, don't stand bleeding!" implored Tom. "Come 'long to the pump and I'll help you wash yourself."

"I won't go to the pump!" roared Jeff. "I'll just stand here and bleed to death, and you'll be hung for a murderer."

This threat, coupled with the sight of the flowing blood, filled Tom's soul with horror.

"Good gracious! Jeff, I believe you *will* die, if you keep on bleeding."

"Do you think so?" inquired Jeff, paling a little, for he was not so *very* anxious for death.

"Yes, Jeff, I—I'm afraid you're gone, and you'll be cold and stiff, and a big policeman will come and grab me, and a judge will hang me in a black cap—Oh, gracious!" And at this dismal prospect Tom blubbered.

"I guess I'll go to the pump," said Jeff. And two mournful little lads sought together the cooling waters. Despite the wholesome application of the water, the bleeding still continued. Their looks of dismay deepened. Suddenly Tom's face lighted up.

"Oh, Jeff! I've got it! I heard Aunt Jane read in an almanax that if you hold your arm up when your nose is blooded it will stop."

Forthwith, Jeff's right arm reached madly toward the sky. To the intense gratification of both parties the bleeding soon began to subside.

"I say, Jeff, hold up both arms, that ought to make it stop twice as fast."

With equal docility, Jeff struck the new attitude. The bleeding was now almost imperceptible.

"And, Jeff, what's the matter with your leg?"

"How?"

"Suppose you hold that up too."

There was a returning twinkle in Tom's eye, which Jeff failed to notice.

"How'll I do it?"

"Lean up against the pump, and I'll fix the rest."

Jeff obeyed, and Tom catching hold of the patient's right leg lifted it up, up, up, till Jeff shrieked with pain.

"Drop it, you goose!"

"You needn't get excited. I didn't mean to hurt you," said Tom, apologetically, and he lowered Jeff's leg a few inches.

It was a funny sight—Jeff leaning against the pump with his two arms raised perpendicularly, and his leg supported at a right angle to the rest of his body by his sympathetic friend. The bleeding soon ceased, and Tom showed his sense of the humor of the situation by giving the leg such a twist that Jeff shrieked louder than ever.

"You're a mean fellow, and I won't speak to you again," vociferated Jeff when he had recovered speech.

"You oughtn't to sass a boy in his own yard," said Tom argumentatively.

"Who's going to stay in your old yard?" and Jeff in high dudgeon made his way into the alley.

Tom now devoted himself for the next five minutes to the construction of the chicken-coop. Presently wearying of this lonely occupation he clambered over the fence into the alley in search of some companion. To his great disappointment not a single boy was to be seen except Jeff Thompson, who was poring interestedly over a kite. The loneliness which had come upon Tom caused his heart to soften.

"I say, Jeff, got a string for that kite?"

"You needn't mind about this kite,"

answered Jeff, without raising his eyes.

"Because, if you haven't," went on Tom in gentle tones, "I'll lend you mine."

Jeff's countenance softened somewhat. Tom, seeing his advantage, followed it up.

"Oh, Jeff, you ought to see my new flint!"

"Where'd you get it?" This with awakened interest.

"Bunkered it off Sadie Roberts; come on up, and I'll show it to you."

This ended all hostilities; and within five minutes Jeff and Tom had entered into a solemn contract to be "partners" thenceforward and forever.

An hour or so after this binding contract, Aunt Jane called up at Tom's room to ascertain what was keeping that young gentleman so quiet. His tranquillity was easily explained; neither Tom nor Jeff was there. Miss Meadow made a careful examination of the house, paying special attention to Mr. Meadow's room, and the pantry; but finding not even a trace of her graceless charge in these places, she hurried into the yard. Her eyes swept anxiously over the limited view. The yard was deserted.

"Tom!" she cried.

"Yes'm."

"Good gracious! where in the world are you?"

"Up here."

Miss Meadow raised her eyes, then gave a shriek of horror; on the slanting roof of the house Tom was busily attending to a dove-cot with one hand, while the other was held by Jeff, who was standing on the top rung of a ladder, his little nose, "tip-tilted like the petal of a flower," just appearing over the opening in the skylight.

"Tommy, get down out of that this very instant. Good gracious! do you want to slip off and kill yourself?"

"I want to put some feed in for my doves. I don't care about falling and killing myself," came the tranquil answer.

"Tommy, I want you to get down from that dangerous position instantly."

"Oh, Auntie, just one minute; I'm all right."

Miss Meadow was ready to cry with anxiety. "Tommy, if you don't obey me this very—"

Miss Meadow paused on seeing the look of animation that suddenly appeared upon Tom's features.

"Did you hear it, Jeff?"

"What?"

"It's the fire bell—hurrah!" and with a quick spring through the trap-door Master Tom disappeared.

"Now, he thinks he's going off to the fire," soliloquized Miss Meadow; "but out of this house he shall not stir one step." And she hastened in, constraining her mind to the proper degree of firmness. But alas! as she passed through the kitchen and dining room into the hall, four sturdy little legs twinkled down the front door steps; and two treble voices raised to their highest yelling key completely drowned her command to come back.

Miss Meadow sank into a chair and wiped her eyes. It was mortifying to confess even to herself, but she had to admit that Tom was fast slipping beyond her control. The mild, timid little lady was no match for the wild, impetuous, thoughtless boy. If Tom could have understood the pain and anxiety his conduct had wrought in her gentle bosom, he would have thought twice before taking so abrupt a departure. But her tears (so far as he was concerned) were as dew upon the naked rock; and, shouting with excitement, he hurried away through the streets to the scene of the fire.

The dinner hour came, but no Tom; and the poor lady with aching eyes peered long through the parlor window hoping to catch some glimpse of the returning adventurer. As the quarters passed on, Miss Meadow became more grieved.

"I must give up," she said to herself. "The boy loves me, I am sure; but I cannot take the place of his poor dead mother. He does just what he likes. Unless something decided be done, he will grow up to be self-willed and undisciplined. Thank God! tomorrow's a class day. But even at school he is not under the proper charge. Miss Harvey teaches well; but in Tommy's hands she is powerless."

At length, wearied with waiting, and vexed with the disagreeable train of thought Tom's recent escapades had occasioned, she endeavored, with poor success, however, to eat a little dinner. As she was about to leave the table, a light but slow tread was heard without. The tread drew nearer; the door opened, and Tom, his stockings bespattered with mud, his shirt-collar crushed out of all shapeliness, his hat gone, and an expression of shame upon his dirt-smeared features, entered the room.

"Well, sir," began his aunt, who, in spite of the joy she felt at his reappearance, was determined to be severe, "how are you going to account for yourself?" Tom hung his head, fell into a close consideration of his feet; and, having no hat to twirl, began pulling his fingers.

"Aren't you ashamed of yourself?"

Tom appeared to consider this a difficult question.

"Do you hear? Aren't you ashamed of yourself?"

"Yes'm," this in a subdued tone, and after due reflection.

"Now, sir, you needn't think to escape a flogging. Let's hear your story, and then I'll attend to you in your room, where you may remain fasting till supper."

Healthy boys as a rule are not pleased with the prospect of losing their dinner; nor is the number great of those boys who entertain no prejudices against flogging. Tom saw that matters had come to a crisis; and that nothing but a masterly stroke would win the day. Quick as thought the young general had planned out his campaign. Advancing to his aunt's side in all humility, he suddenly caught her hand, and said:

"Auntie Jane, I'm sorry," and before Miss Meadow could become aware of his intention, he threw his arms round her neck and kissed her.

Under the warmth of this greeting, her icy sternness melted away, and flowed off in a gentle stream of kindness.

"Poor boy! you must be tired and hungry, too. Indeed you don't deserve any dinner. But sit down; I haven't the heart to see you go to your room in hunger."

Tom was not slow to avail himself of this permission; and while Miss Meadow, her bosom agitated by a conflict between duty and affection, helped him to the various dishes, Tom plied knife and fork with no small earnestness.

For the rest of the afternoon he distinguished himself by his conduct. In fact, he was trembling on account of the wrath to come. His unusual excursion would be reported to his father, and then it would require more than Tom's address to avoid serious consequences.

Nor were his forebodings without foundation. When Mr. Playfair heard from Miss Meadow's lips the account of his son's doings, he compressed his lips tightly, knit his brow, and then, after some serious reflection, called for the culprit.

"Sir," said the father sternly, "you have gone the limit of your tether."

Tom did not know what "going the limit of one's tether" meant; but entertaining the idea that it was something very horrid indeed, he set up a dismal wail.

"Sir, you need to learn obedience and respect to your elders. Next September, just five months from now, you start for St. Maure's boarding-school, and remember this—if you give any trouble there, I'll not allow you to make your First Communion for another year. Now, sir"—

But as Tom Playfair is to be the hero of this veracious story I cannot bring myself to put on record what his father said further; still less have I the heart to chronicle what Mr. Playfair did. Tom was very noisy on the occasion. Up to this hour he had known the force of his father's hand only from the friendly clasp. But over that occasion, which Tom never forgot, and over the ensuing five months, you and I, dear reader, drop a veil which shall not be withdrawn.

Chapter III

*IN WHICH TOM LEAVES FOR ST. MAURE'S, AND
FINDS ON THE ROAD THITHER THAT FUN
SOMETIMES COMES EXPENSIVE*

THIS interval of five months taught Tom several years, as it were. The prospect of preparing for his First Communion, and of going to a school where he would be thrown upon his own resources, put a touch of earnestness, hitherto lacking, into his life, in such wise that there came a change so perceptible as even to attract Mr. Meadow's notice.

During the vacation, strange to say, Tom gave so little trouble that Aunt Jane entertained serious fears for his health.

About thirty minutes past seven, on a Monday evening in September, Master Tom, enveloped in a linen duster which reached nearly to his heels, looking rather solemn and accompanied by his uncle, aunt, and father, stood silent in the Union Depot of St. Louis.

Bells were ringing, engines were puffing, hissing, and shrieking, tracks were rumbling and quivering; cars were moving in and out; newsboys, hackmen, and depot officials were shouting, porters were hurrying in every direction throwing trunks and other baggage, now here, now there, in a manner most confusing to the inexperienced eye; women and children were standing near the ticket offices, or sitting restlessly in the waiting-rooms, some indulging in a hasty lunch, many looking hopelessly lost: while the multitudinous electric lights flared and sputtered over the whole scene.

As train after train moved away for its long journey, and Tom realized that he too would soon be on his way to another part of the world, his heart grew heavy.

"I say, Pa," he suggested, "I guess I don't want to go."

Pa smiled.

"Mr. Don't-Want is not a member of our family," volunteered Mr. Meadow very smartly.

Tom shot an indignant glance at the speaker of these cruel words.

"Keep up your courage, Tommy," whispered Aunt Jane, quietly pressing a silver dollar into his hands. "It's for your own good, dear, and in ten short months you'll come back a little man."

The prospect of ten short months, and the resultant of a little man afforded him small consolation, but the silver dollar had a reassuring effect. Absenting himself from the family group, he immediately expended one quarter of his aunt's gift on a paper of caramels and a cream-cake; and he was thinking very seriously of laying out twenty-five cents more in the purchase of a toy pistol, when a crowd of boys of all ages and sizes came pouring into the depot.

Tom gazed at them in amazement.

"I say," he said, addressing one of the boys about his own age, "what's broken loose?"

Instead of answering this question, the boy stopped and considered Tom attentively. "Don't you belong to our crowd?" he at length said.

"What crowd?" asked Tom.

"The St. Maure's fellows."

"What!" cried Tom in amazement, "are all you fellows going there too?"

"That's what they say."

"Why, then, things aren't so bad as I thought they would be. I say, let's be partners. My name is Tommy Playfair: What's yours?"

"Harry Quip."

"Here, take some candy," said Tom, opening his package.

Harry embraced both offers. Henceforth he and Tom were "partners."

While the two were thus exchanging small-boy courtesies, a clean-shaven gentleman, somewhat beyond middle age and attired in a clerical suit, walked up to them.

Harry raised his hat, and endeavored to compose his features.

"Well, Harry," said the newcomer, "who is this little friend of yours?"

Tom, perceiving that the eyes of the gentleman were fixed upon him, became nervous, and in endeavoring to bolt a caramel which he had recently placed in his mouth, nearly choked himself.

"This is Tommy Playfair," said Harry.

"Oh, indeed! so this is the boy that runs after fire-engines, is it?"

"Only did it four or five times in my life, Father."

"And gets himself on top of slippery roofs."

Tom only remarked:

"Please, father, I won't do it again."

Upon this the reverend gentleman who had charge of the boys laughed cheerfully, shook his new acquaintance's hand, and, cautioning both to take their places in a car which he pointed out, hurried away to see to the safety of the luggage.

"What's his name?" inquired Tom.

"That's Father Teeman, he's prefect of

discipline at the college."

"Discipline!" echoed Tom, with a vague idea of a cat-o'-nine-tails running through his head; "what does that mean?"

"It means that he does the whipping."

"Whew!—But he doesn't look so savage."

"He doesn't have to. But just wait till he catches you cutting up. He'll thrash you so as you will prefer standing to any other position for a week after."

Tom was appalled. His companion, could he only know it, was exaggerating grossly for the sake of enjoying the newcomer's surprise and terror.

"Does he thrash a fellow often?" was Tom's next question.

"Well, I should say so! last year I got whipped nearly twice a day, and there was scarcely a week that I didn't go to the infirmary to lay up for repairs."

"Gracious!" ejaculated Tom. "I won't stand it. Harry, you and I are partners. I'll tell you what let's do. Nobody's watching us. Let's slip out. I've got a dollar, and we can support ourselves on that: and when we get broke, we'll sell newspapers."

Harry had no idea of encouraging Tom to run away. In his school-boy idea of a good joke, he merely wished to put him in a state of dismal suspense. So he said:

"Oh! you needn't get scared! There's lots of fun out there."

"I don't see any fun in getting strapped once or twice a day."

"You won't get a strapping at all, maybe. I was such a dreadful hard case, you see; that's why I got it." Notwithstanding this avowal it is but just to remark that Harry Quip's features, in their normal state, wore a very mild expression.

Still, Harry's explanation did not succeed in disarming Tom's fears. If there were to be any wild boys at St. Maure's, Tom, like Abou Ben Adhem, had substantial reasons for believing that his name would lead all the rest. He was about to press his proposition of running away with still greater earnestness, when he heard his name called.

"Coming directly, sir. I say, Harry, you keep a seat for me next you on the car," and Tom pattered off to bid adieu to his father.

"Well, my boy," said Mr. Playfair, catching Tom's hand, "I am about to put you into good hands. But you must be careful. You will now be thrown among all kinds of boys— bad, good, and indifferent. Remember, that on your choice of company depends in great part your piety. Teachers may instruct, priests may exhort, but if your company be bad you will be no better. And don't forget that every day you are preparing for your First Communion. That should be *the* day of your life. If you make a good First Communion, you're sure to get on well; so look out for your company, and try to be as good a boy as you can. Now, my dear child, be watchful on these points. As to the rest, I hold no fear. Here's something to keep your courage up—but don't spend it all at once."

Tom took the advice in good part, and the five-dollar bill with effusive enthusiasm. Then kissing his father, he turned to Aunt Jane. The kind lady could not repress a few sobs.

"God bless you, my boy!" she faltered. "Be sure and write every week; and I'll pray for you every morning and every night as long as you're away." And she handed him a basket laden with his favorite delicacies. Tom's eyes filled at these exhibitions of his aunt's kindness.

"I've been awful mean to you, Aunt Jane, lots of time; but I didn't intend anything, you know; and I'm sorry. And when I come back I hope I'll be better—honor bright."

Even Mr. Meadow, yielding to the solemn influence of a parting scene, had purchased his nephew a red-covered book, concerning an impossible boy, who met with all kinds of impossible adventures in an impossible country.

"Chicago-ooo-and Alton Railroad; all aboard for Kansas City!" shouted a voice.

"That's for you, Tommy," Mr. Playfair said.

They all moved towards the cars indicated. A negro in the official garments of the railroad met them half-way.

"Is he a college boy, sah? Step jes dis way, sah. I have de high honaw of taking chahge of all of them. Come on, young gemman. Now, up you go." And without giving our hero an opportunity of making a farewell speech, he quickly raised Tom upon the platform, and, in a manner quite gentle, yet effective, pushed him into the reclining-chair car.

"Here you are, Tom!" shouted Master Quip, who faithful to his promise had kept his friend a seat beside him.

Tom hastened to occupy the vacant chair, and seated himself as the train began to move out from the depot, while the boys gave three vigorous cheers.

"Ah! I like this," said Tom, throwing himself back in his seat, and yielding to the luxury of the hour.

"Jolly, isn't it?" Harry observed. "Take a

smoke," and he offered Tom a cigarette.

"Well, no," said Tom with some hesitation.

"Why not?"

"Well, I'll tell you," answered Tom, in a burst of confidence. "I hate anything like humbug. And if I was to smoke now, it would only be to look big. You see I've got no liking for it. I've smoked once or twice up in papa's hayloft, but it's always made me feel bad. So you see I don't like it; and I'd be a humbug if I pretended I did."

This was one of the longest speeches Tom had ever made; and it produced its impression.

"Well, you've got true grit, Tom. And I like you the better for what you've said. I like a smoke myself once in a while, but I'm pretty sure that half the little chaps who smoke do it to look big."

"I'd rather be little than big," said Tom.

"Why?"

"Oh, pshaw! a man's got to shave, and has to dress stylish, and can't play, nor eat candy in the streets, and lots of things."

"That's so."

"Yes; and then half of them get stuck up. And they wear stiff hats, and are afraid to run, and don't play any games at all."

"Yes," assented Harry; "and then when

chaps grow up, they've such a lot of worry about bringing out their mustaches."

Both considered the subject pretty well exhausted.

"I say," continued Tom, "they're all boys in this car."

"Yes; it's been chartered for our crowd."

"Do you know them all?"

"I know some of the old boys."

"Who's that fellow with his coat collar turned so's to hide his ears, and his hair stickin' up like bristles, trying to smoke a cigar as if he was used to it?"

"That's Johnny Shoestrings."

"*Who?*"

"Johnny Shoestrings. That's his nickname, you know; he's such a slouch. I can't think of his right name."

"Who's that boy with hair like a carrot banged all over his forehead, and a pug nose, and an awfully big mouth?"

"That's Crazy Green."

"*Crazy* Green?"

"That's what everybody calls him. He hasn't got any sense, and doesn't know how to behave decent. In fact, I think he's a real bad boy."

"Do all the fellows have nicknames?" asked Tom.

"All the old boys have, except one."

"Who's that?"

"His real name is Black, and it fits his color so well we thought we'd let him keep it."

"Who are those five fellows down there, who look like each other's sisters, they're all so timid and pretty?"

"Newcomers," answered Harry.

Tom's eyes were fascinated by this group; and, not being satisfied with the information Harry had vouchsafed, he went to the other end of the car where he could interview them personally.

Having first satisfied himself by taking a deliberate survey of the five, much to their uneasiness and manifest discomfiture, he opened the conversation thus:

"I say, halloa!"

The largest of the group, a boy about fourteen, answered timidly:

"How do you do, sir?"

"I ain't a sir: my name's Tom Playfair. What's your name?"

"Alexander Jones."

"Whew! five Joneses. Are any of you twins?"

"Harry and Willie are twins, sir."

"There ain't any triplets among you, are there?"

"No, sir; not this time," answered Alexander Jones, who in his timidity was accidentally facetious.

"Well, good-by; take care of yourselves." And bestowing a genial grin upon the Jones brothers he returned to his seat.

The train, having now crossed the great bridge that spans the Mississippi and passed out of the city of Alton, was speeding along through the open country. Without it was pitch dark, and the sable solemnity of the night was enhanced by an occasional light that flashed before the eyes of the passengers at the windows, and then as quickly disappeared.

"I say, what kind of a place is it?" asked Tom, resuming his conversation with Harry.

"What place?—the gravy station?"

"Is that what you call it?"

"Yes; they feed us on corn-bread and gravy."

"And don't you get any meat?"

"Oh, yes! they give us meat on Christmas; and at New Years every one gets a small piece of pie."

"Gracious!" cried Tom, absently placing his hand upon his stomach. "But I suppose you have lots of holidays?"

"Not so many, I can just tell you; and then even we've got to stay cooped up in a little yard that isn't large enough to swing a cat in."

"They're not going to treat me that way. When no one is looking I'll slip out every chance I get."

"If you do," said Master Quip, who was bent on scaring Tom to the utmost, "you'll get collared by a prefect and then posted."

"What do you mean by 'posted'?"

"Why, a great big prefect bangs you up against a tree-box, or a post, or a stone wall; and tells you that if you move from it before three hours are up he'll petrify you."

Tom groaned.

"I guess my fun is all over," he muttered in a faltering voice.

"Oh, we have fun sometimes, you know."

"How is that?" asked Tom anxiously.

"Why, we go out walking in ranks—two abreast—on recreation days, with a big prefect walking in front and another big prefect behind us. Then we walk six miles or so; that is, we keep on walking till most of the little tads aren't able to stand any longer. We sit down, then, and rest for five minutes, before we start to walk back again. And while we are sitting down to rest, we are allowed to talk, you know."

"Why, can't you talk while you're walking?"

"Not much," said Harry emphatically.

"And do you mean to say," cried Tom excitedly, "that after resting five minutes, they're all able to walk back again?"

"I didn't say any such thing."

"Are they left behind, then?"

"No, indeed; they always have a big hay-wagon along; and when a fellow can't walk they tumble him in. But he's got to be mighty tired before that happens."

"So," said Tom, after a moment's reflection, "that's what you call fun?"

"Certainly; it's the jolliest kind of fun."

"I suppose you fellows consider a funeral a good joke." Tom did not know that he was sarcastic.

"You're talking now," said Harry. "Whenever a boy dies we get off night studies."

"Does a boy die often out there?"

Harry ignored the literal meaning of this question as he answered:—

"Well, no; not as many as we would like. Only two or three a month."

"What do they die of?"

"They don't die at all; they get killed by being hit over the head with a loaded cane."

Tom jumped up from his seat.

"Take it back," he said, with considerable fierceness.

"Take what back?" inquired his astonished friend rising from his reclining position.

"You've been telling me yarns. Take it back, will you, or you and I aren't partners any more."

"Well, I'm willing to take it back. I only did it for fun, just wanted to rattle you a little. You needn't get mad about it."

Whither the conversation would have drifted it is impossible to say; for, as the train stopped just then at a station, Harry and Tom, with that natural curiosity to see and know all things which is the proud pre-rogative of the American boy, dashed out upon the platform. So satisfied were they with this new position, that they resolved to keep it for a time indefinite, and accord-ingly squatted down on the side steps. They were not long there, however, when Father Teeman ordered them inside.

"Harry," suggested Tom when they had gained their proper positions, "let's have a little fun."

"What are you thinking of now?" asked Harry.

"Let's play conductor."

Harry glanced around the car dubiously. It was now after ten o'clock; and most of the boys, wearied with the excitement of the day, were asleep.

"What's the use," he said, "nobody's awake."

"All the better."

"Well, how'll we do it?"

"Did you see that lantern on the platform of the car?"

"Yes."

"Well, that's the idea. Come on."

Accompanied by Harry, Tom sallied forth, obtained possession of the lantern, and again walked into the car. Stealing up to a boy who was locked in slumber, he thrust the lantern into his face and, in as deep a voice as he could assume, said:

"Tickets, please."

"I haven't got it," cried the boy, jumping up and rubbing his eyes. I gave mine to Father—"

He broke off when he perceived the grinning face of an unknown boy behind the lantern, and in great rage he levelled a blow at the joker. Tom very naturally held up his hands to protect himself, not taking into account that a lantern was in one of them. Crash! out went the light, down clattered the glass in a hundred fragments. He had guarded himself very well; but the lantern was the worse for it. The youthful conductors stood aghast.

"Let's put the old thing back," said Tom.

"Yes; and we'd better hurry," counselled Harry.

But before they could carry out their purpose, the porter came hurrying in.

"Young gemmen, who done tuk my lantern from the platform?" And as he spoke he glanced sternly at the discomfited culprits.

"I did," said Tom. "Here's the old thing; looks like it's exploded, don't it?"

"Oh, muffins!" cried the porter, "it's ruined, and I'll be discharged. You young bantams, what did you go and spile my lantern for?"

Tom, remembering the words of Scripture that a soft answer turneth away wrath, put his hand into his pocket, came out with it filled, and said:

"Here, old fellow, take some candy."

"Sah! I doesn't want none of your candy. Unless I can get a lantern at the next station I'm ruined. Can't you pay for it? 'cos if you don't, I'll report you to the company."

"How much do you want?" asked Tom sadly.

"Foah dollars, sah," said the negro, smiling, and muttering that he "knowed they was gemmen."

"I'll give you fifty cents," said Tom.

"Does you want to ruin a poor man?"

"How does a dollar suit you?"

"Can't afford it, sah, for less than two dollars."

"Well, I'll give you a dollar and a half; and we'll call it square."

"Seein' you're such a puffick gemmen, I'll take it, sah." And the negro went his way rejoicing in a neat bit of profit.

"Boys," said Father Teeman coming upon them from behind, "suppose you go to sleep, or at least give the others a chance to rest. Get your chairs, and keep them."

"I don't want any more fun tonight," said Tom ruefully.

"Neither do I," said Harry.

And the two innocents falling back in their chairs soon slept the sleep of the just.

Chapter IV

TOM ARRIVES AT ST. MAURE'S AND MAKES THE ACQUAINTANCE OF JOHN GREEN UNDER CIRCUMSTANCES NOT ENTIRELY GRATEFUL TO THAT INTERESTING CHARACTER

"LOOK out, Tom; that's Pawnee Creek." Tom thrust his head out of the window and saw a small picturesque stone-bridge passing over the ghost of a stream of water.

He had hardly time to catch one glimpse of it, when his hat blew off, dropping straight down into the bed of Pawnee Creek. He drew in his head mournfully.

"I guess travelling is pretty expensive," he growled. "There's twenty-five cents for caramels, one dollar and ten cents for railroad candy that made me sick, eighty-five cents for oranges, a dollar and a half to that porter for his old lantern, and a new hat to Pawnee Creek."

"Oh, you can get your hat back easily enough. It's only a short walk from the College. Now, keep your eyes open one minute," continued Harry, "See," he added a few minutes later, "see that road leading along by the hedge? Many's the time I've taken a walk on it. Halloa, there's the good old white fence. Now we are passing the College grounds."

Tom had scarcely time to take a fair look at the fence, when the train came to a standstill in front of a large four-story brick building with the words "St. Maure's College," crowning its brow.

Fronting the building was a spacious garden, diversified by several winding and shady walks; fronting the garden was a high white fence, and fronting the high white fence were some hundred and odd boys, with a few pro-

fessors, awaiting the old scholars and new
from the train. But Tom took no notice of
all these things; his eyes, ears, feelings—his
whole being seemed to be concentrated on
the Professor standing nearest him. The long
black cassock and cincture were something
new to him; and so great was his astonishment that the loud cheers of the boys, the
fierce whistling of the locomotive, the sharp
cry of "All aboard," followed by the departure of the train, might, as far as he was
concerned, have happened at the other end
of the world.

Harry, who had left him to shake hands
with some of his friends, found him, a few
minutes later, standing in exactly the same
position.

"Wake up, Tom," he cried, slapping his
friend on the back.

This touch snapped the charm.

"I say, Harry," he at length burst out, "for
goodness' sake, look at that fellow with the
gown on. Isn't *he* a sight?"

"Oh, what a greenhorn you are!" said Harry,
with an easy air of superiority; "that's not
a gown, it's a cassock, and the man in it is
your boss: he's the prefect of the small boys."

Tom's face expressed about two closely
written pages of astonishment.

"Does he always wear that—that thing?"

"Yes, come on up, and I'll introduce you."

"But does he really wear it all the time?"

"That's what I said."

"Gracious! I'm glad of that. I'd like to see him catch me, if I want to run. Pshaw! he looks for all the world like an old lady."

"You'll find out, pretty soon, whether he can run or not," retorted Harry a little sharply; "and as to being an old lady, you'll change your mind mighty soon if you try any of your tricks on him. Mr. Middleton," he continued addressing himself to the subject of these remarks, "here's another St. Louis boy, my friend Tommy Playfair."

The prefect, with a smile and a word of welcome, cordially shook Tom's hand, at the same time bestowing such a clear, penetrating look upon the chubby upturned face that, as Tom afterwards declared, "Mr. Middleton seemed to see clear through his sailor shirt way back to his shirt-collar on the other side."

"You're a wild colt, I suppose."

"Not so very wild, sir," said Tom in his gentlest tones.

"Is he lively as you, Harry?" asked the prefect.

"I'm not going to be wild any more, Mr.

Middleton," returned Harry in all meekness.

Indeed the subdued air that had come over Harry, now that he stood in the presence of his prefect, was something wonderful.

"Well, Harry," continued Mr. Middleton, "you may take care of your new friend yourself for the present; I see some newcomers over there who appear to be very timid and ill at ease—they are quite lost." And he hastened away to do the honors to the five Jones boys.

Tom and Harry, left to themselves, sauntered leisurely up the garden walk, the former all eyes for his new surroundings.

"What's that long, low, frame shanty to our right?" asked Tom.

"That's the infirmary; when you get sick you go there and lay up for repairs."

"It looks kind of snug."

"Yes; but when a fellow's getting just well enough to enjoy the jam and buttered toast, they turn him out. This large four-story brick building in front of us is the house where the fathers and prefects have their rooms. The lower floor of it on the east side, though, is the refectory for us little boys. You know there are two yards, two refectories, two study-halls, and two washrooms and four dormitories, so as to keep little boys and big boys apart; the large room just above the refectory is our study-hall; now come on over to our washroom and we'll wash and brush up before dinner."

They turned to the right on reaching the railed steps leading up to the brick building, and passed between the infirmary on one side and on the other a substantial three-story structure of stone, which, as Harry informed Tom, was the classroom building.

Continuing straight on, they passed through a double gate—generally ajar, by the way—and found themselves in an open playground about four hundred feet long by two hundred wide.

"This is the small boys' yard," volunteered Harry.

"Yes?" queried Tom plaintively. "Does a fellow have to stay around here all the time?"

"All the time, if he doesn't behave himself. But come on; let's hurry in before the rush."

Beside the gate, at their right, and next to the classroom building, stood a two-story frame house, the upper floor of which was a dormitory and the lower a washroom.

On entering, a novel scene presented itself to Tom's eyes. With the exception of one plain and two shuffleboard tables, and a few benches, the main body of the room was devoid of all furniture or other obstruction. But lining the four walls all around was a series of small boxes with hinged doors, each box divided into an upper and lower partition, used for the keeping of soap, brushes, toilet articles, and the like; and above the boxes were scattered towels, soap, and tin basins in all manner of ungraceful confusion; the towels, for the most part, dangling from a water-pipe, ornamented with here and there a faucet. At the time that our two friends entered there were a few boys in the room, engaged at their ablutions, while a prefect, notebook in hand, was giving each boy on his entrance one of the many boxes.

"Howdo, Mr. Phelan," said Harry, tipping his hat and shaking hands with his superior.

"Why, Harry! So here you are again."

"Yes, Mr. Phelan, I'm like a bad penny."

"In one sense, yes," said Mr. Phelan; "but you're too modest. I'm delighted to see you again. And I see you have a new friend. Who is this?"

"This is Tommy Playfair, Mr. Phelan. And I say, can't I have my old box again, same as last year—it was near that window, you know—and can't Tom Playfair have the one next to me? I'm the only boy here that he knows."

Mr. Phelan, who had, in the meantime, taken Tom's hand with a smile of welcome, assented to Master Harry's requests.

"Thank you, sir," said Harry effusively; and he conducted Tom to box number twenty-nine, near the window he had pointed out in the making of his petition.

"This is number twenty-nine—my box, Tom—and here's your's next to mine, number thirty."

But Tom was not satisfied.

"That little bit of a box for me!" he exclaimed.

"Why, of course," Harry responded. "You don't want the earth, do you?"

Without making any answer to this important question, Tom walked over to the prefect.

"I say, Mr. Phelan, can't I have another box, besides the one you've given me?"

"Why? What have you to say against the box I gave you?"

"Oh, that's all right! but I want two boxes."

"Indeed! what do you want two boxes for?"

"Well, you see, I want one for my books, you know."

"Oh!" said the prefect, breaking into a

smile, "you'll get a desk in the study-hall for them!"

"Oh! that's it—is it?" and Tom, satisfied with this information, rejoined Harry Quip, who with his eyes bulging out of his head had been watching Tom's proceedings in utmost astonishment.

In the mean time the washroom had been rapidly filling. Every other moment witnessed the appearance of new faces. Among those that entered, some, notably the Jones boys, were timid beyond description; others, like Tom, were quite tranquil and self-possessed; others again were rather bold and undoubtedly noisy. This latter class aroused Tom's curiosity.

"I say, Harry," he inquired, "who are those fellows in here that talk so loud, and lift up their shoulders when they walk around, and go on as if they owned the whole place?"

"Sh! don't talk so loud, Tom," said Harry, with unaffected seriousness. "They're a few of the old boys. You see they're perfectly at home. They're apt to be pretty hard on new-comers."

"Are all the old boys that way?" was Tom's next question.

"Well, not all. But a great many are."

These questions and answers afford con-

siderable insight into the economy of boarding-school life. We hear and read a great
deal about the easy confidence—nay boldness—of old servants, old clerks, and the
like; but what are they all compared to the
old student at boarding-school? As a newcomer, he may be the most timid, the most
meek of mortals. The first few weeks of his
changed life he may rarely speak above a
whisper. But with the rolling months, as he
picks up a friend or so, evidences of ease
and natural bearing insinuate themselves
into his address. At the end of the term he
departs, it may be, a quiet, gentlemanly boy.
But, vacation over, lo! he returns as one of
the owners of earth and sky—with all the
assurance and arrogance attributed by the
American press to a plumber in mid-winter.
Every look, every tone, every gesture pro-
claims in terms unmistakable that he is an
old boy; that he knows more about life in
any phase than a newcomer; that he is up
to every conceivable turn of school-boy fortune; that a new boy, how naturally gifted
soever, is but an inferior sort of creature;
and that, in fine, there is nothing, humanly
speaking, in the heavens above or the earth
beneath, or in the waters under the earth,
that can compare with that supremest of

mortals—the old boy. It would be an injustice, however, to let the reader suppose that *all* old boys belong to this class. Not so; quite a goodly number are as polite, unpretending, gentlemanly, and sensible as the most refined newcomer.

Johnny Green was an old boy of the former class.

For the last five or six minutes he had been making himself very conspicuous in the washroom, by talking in a raised voice—whenever the prefect was out of hearing—of the way he had "got ahead of the old man," as he irreverently termed his father, of the great and disgusting number of "new kids" that had already appeared in the wash-room, and of their uncommonly disagreeable appearance, which Master Green put down as being "rather green."

Having completed his toilet, which consisted chiefly, and indeed almost exclusively, in so arranging his hair as to conceal almost entirely his freckled forehead, John Green stationed himself at the narrow door of the washroom, where he amused himself, at such odd times as the attending prefect's preoccupying duties allowed, by tripping up various little newcomers, as they chanced to leave or enter.

Tom and Harry were now going out; and Green was anxiously awaiting his new victim. Harry advanced first, and, being an old boy, was allowed to pass unmolested; then came Tom, who, by the way, had been watching Master Green's little practical joke for fully five minutes. As Tom was verging upon the threshold, Green put out his foot; suddenly a howl arose from the bully's mouth.

"Why, good gracious!" exclaimed Tom, turning on his steps, "did I walk on your foot? But really, what a big foot you've got!"

"You wretched little fool!" roared the bully, who was now hopping about with a combination of earnestness and liveliness, exhilarating to see; "you've stepped on at least five of my corns."

"That's too bad," Tom made answer, with his face screwed into its most serious expression. "But all the farmers say there's going to be a large corn crop this year."

With this consolatory reflection he passed on arm in arm with Harry Quip, who was struggling, but with sorry success, to keep a straight face, leaving the discomfited Master Green to continue or conclude his dance as he pleased.

Adjoining the end of the washroom there was—and is yet, doubtless—a small shed, under whose protecting cover were a turning-pole, a pair of parallel bars, a few other articles of gymnastics, and a line of benches. Upon one of these latter our two friends seated themselves, calmly awaiting the welcome sound of the dinner bell. But the calm—how history repeats itself!—proved to be the forerunner of a storm.

Scarcely had they composed themselves in their seats, when John Green, who was wearied of dancing, and was anxious to meet Tom in a place beyond sight of all prefects, turned the corner. Leisurely leaning his head on his left arm, his left arm on one of the parallel bars, and placing his right hand on his hip—he had made a special study of this special attitude during vacation—he fastened a stern gaze upon Tom. Notwithstanding, our hero seemed to be oblivious of Green's presence.

"I say," began the bully, when he realized that both pose and gaze had shot wide of the mark, "are there any more like you at home?"

"I don't know, I'm sure," answered Tom with suavity; "but if you wish, I'll write home and ask."

At this retort three or four newcomers who were sitting nearby, and had been gazing about listlessly, broke into a titter. The bully glared at them ferociously, whereupon their faces fell into length again, and a far-away look—the symptom of home-sickness—came into their eyes. Harry had laughed too; but his laugh met with no rebuke; he was an old boy, and in consequence was entitled to the privilege.

Encouraged by the power of his eye, Master Green turned it in full force upon Tom, and again addressed himself to that unterrified youth.

"What's your name, Sonny?"

Tom's face assumed a troubled expression; he passed his hand over his forehead and through his hair—then, after a pause, made answer:

"Can't remember it just now. My memory's bad when the weather's warm. It's an awful long name. It took the priest over five minutes to get it in, the day I was baptized."

Another titter from the listeners, and a loud laugh from Harry. But Green was too astonished at the coolness of the newcomer to check this outburst.

"I suppose," continued Green, with excessive irony, "you think you're funny?"

"I guess I do," answered Tom blandly. "All the family say I am; and when I was home they'd never let me go to funerals, for fear I'd make 'em laugh in the solemn parts."

A prolonged giggle and a louder laugh.

"You're terribly smart," exclaimed the withering Green, who, forgetting his pose, was now quite stiff and bolt upright.

"Smart!" echoed Tom, "why, now you're hitting the nail right on the head. The fellows at the school I 'tended last year said they wouldn't come back if I did, because I always carried off all the premiums; and that's why I came here."

"You'd better shut your mouth or I'll hit you one," vociferated the bully, drowning the laughter evoked by this last retort; and as he spoke he pulled up the arms of his coat, revealing in the act a pair of cuffs with many flashing cuff-buttons.

"Oh! if you're going to strike," pursued Tom with all the placidity of a midspring zephyr, "I think I had better shut my mouth, or you might poke your fist down my throat, and then I'd be sick for life."

In this quick rejoinder there was to the spectators gazing upon Green's clenched fists a certain obviousness of point; consequently it aroused mirth in all the listeners and rage in the heart of the bully.

"You're a coward!" he foamed.

"That's what *you* say," said Tom.

"And a sneak."

"That's what *you* say."

"And a mule thief."

"I never stole you."

This was too much for Green; he made a spring at Tom. But Harry caught his arm.

"Hold on, Green," said Harry. "Just take a boy of your size."

Harry and Tom, it should be remarked, were each a year or two younger than Green.

"Let go of me, will you?" shouted the bully.

"No; I won't."

Suddenly John Green became very quiet, jumped upon the parallel bars, and began swinging up and down; Mr. Middleton had just turned the corner. Harry broke into a whistle, while Tom maintained his blandness to the end. Before hostilities could be renewed the bell rang for dinner.

"You took him up in great shape, Tom," observed Harry on the way to the refectory. "Where did you get that cool way of saying things?"

"Oh, I used to have a great many rows with my uncle; and he got me so's I couldn't get excited."

"All the same, you'd better keep your eyes open. Green will pay you back for your talk before long. Anyhow, if I'm around, or any decent old fellow, you'll be all right. He's a coward and a mean boy, and if he caught you alone he'd be sure to take it out on you. But he won't tackle us together."

They were now at the door of the refectory; as each student entered Mr. Middleton assigned him his place at one of the ten tables, each of these being laid for twelve.

To their regret, Harry and Tom were placed at different tables. Dinner passed off quietly. Before thanks had been returned, Mr. Middleton announced that each boy should, immediately on leaving the refectory, go to the room of the prefect of studies, where he would learn his class and obtain a list of the books which he should procure from the procurator, or (being translated) the buyer.

Tom and Harry, who contrived to have their interview with the prefect of studies at the same time, were both assigned to the class of Rudiments—a class where the student is prepared to enter upon the study of Latin. They managed to get their books about the same time, too; and so, to their undisguised delight, Mr. Middleton appointed them seats next to each other in the hall of studies.

"Tom, this is just glorious!" exclaimed Harry, as they emerged from the study room.

"We're in the same class; and we're right next to each other for studies. But look here!—while you were getting your books, and I was outside waiting for you, I heard something. Do you know the first thing Green's going to do to you?"

"No; what?"

"Why, the first chance he gets today he's going to pin a paper on your back with

'KICK ME

I AM A FOOL'

on it. He's waiting his chance now in the yard, I think."

Tom stood still, and gave himself up for a few seconds to reflection; then he resumed his walk and observed:

"We'll fix him, if he tries it, Harry. I'll tell you what: we'll let him go pretty far with his joke. I won't notice him. But when he gets behind me, and is pinning it on, you take out your handkerchief—will you? Of course you'll be standing in front and facing me."

"What'll you do?"

"You'll see. He won't enjoy the joke very much anyhow."

No sooner had the boys entered the yard, than they noticed that John Green was eyeing them closely.

"He's waiting his chance," whispered Harry.

"Just so," answered Tom. "Say, let's go down by the handball alley."

Harry acquiesced, and both made their way to the further end of the yard. Harry, with his hands in his pockets, leaned against the body of the alley so as to take in the whole playground, while Tom, also hands in pockets, stood facing Harry, commanding a view of nothing save what was included in the two walls of the alley. Green, in the meantime, was following in their wake with stealthy steps; even Tom could divine this from the expression on Harry's countenance. At length Green had secured a suitable position for pinning on the placard. He stooped. Forthwith Harry drew out his handkerchief.

"Talking of jumping," exclaimed Tom at once, "how's this?" and he gave a sharp backward kick with his right foot.

Green received the full force of this on his shins—the tenderest part of him, perhaps, by the law of compensation; for his head was within a little of being actually impregnable both as to blows and as to ideas.

On the moment, Green testified his presence by a prolonged howl.

"Good gracious!" Tom exclaimed, turning around and addressing Green, who with both hands was holding one knee, and hopping enthusiastically with the only foot he had at liberty: "Why how in the world did you come to be behind me? You're terribly unlucky—ain't you?"

A crowd of boys, who had been watching Green's ill-timed attempt to fasten on the placard, were now shouting and laughing, as they hurried down the yard to take in, in fuller detail, the victim's lively and novel dance.

"Does it hurt?" asked Tom compassionately, as he picked up the placard, which Green had allowed to fall to the ground.

"Does it hurt?" bawled Green, suspending his dance to give full effect to his answer. "Oh no! it doesn't hurt at all. It's awful pleasant, you fool!" And with this burst of eloquence, he resumed his dancing.

"I say, what's this?" enquired Tom, holding the placard at arm's length, and scanning it critically. "Is this your paper?"

"Yes; and I wish you and that paper were in Halifax."

The intense devotion of this sentiment was beyond doubt.

"But," pursued Tom, "you've got 'kick me' written on it. So you've got what you want. And are you really and truly a fool?"

This question so angered Green that he lost sight of his pain. Releasing his injured leg, he made a savage rush at Tom. But this time, too, his intentions were frustrated. George Keenan, a boy who had attended St. Maure's for several years, and who, judging by his modesty, didn't seem to know it, caught the aggressor's arm with a grip which elicited another howl.

"Let him alone, Green; he served you right. You've no business to be picking on boys under your size every chance you get. And look here—you'd better not touch him when John Donnell or I am around." And George walked away.

The bully was too crestfallen to face his fellow-students. Scowling and shame-faced, he hobbled off to the infirmary to get his leg "painted" with iodine.

George Keenan, who has here entered upon the scene, merits a few words. He was a model boy; not the kind of a model boy that figures in many tales for the young; but such a model as you may expect to meet with occasionally, nay—God be thanked for it—oftentimes in real life.

At baseball, running, handball, football, and all manner of athletic games, no one was more skilled than George. He was small, undergrown for his years, and slightly made; still his strength was unquestioned. And yet no one had ever known George to exert his strength for mean or low purposes, no one had ever known him to use his influence for aught save what was ennobling. He was everybody's friend—with him the bad were, for the nonce, good; and the good were better. Withal, he was cheerful, jocose, and a bit of a wag. He made his way through life with the brightness and wholesomeness of a sunbeam. Nor is George, among the general run of boarding-school students, an isolated character.

In every well-conducted boarding school there are hearts as warm and minds as noble. These boys are themselves the least self-conscious of mortals. Though they know it not, they are doing work, and good work, too, for the Lord and Saviour whom in the nobility of their hearts they love with manly tenderness.

Chapter V

IN WHICH TOM IS PERSUADED TO GO TO SLEEP

NO doubt many of my readers have been asking themselves what manner of hero is Tom Playfair. Couldn't the author have selected a better, or at least a more refined character? This Tom is bold, given to slang, rather forward, self-willed, and—but stay, reader, let us get in a word. We throw up our hands, and grant the full force and truth of all these naughty adjectives. Indeed there are faults, and great faults, to be found in Tom. There are many flaws in the crystal. But what then? These little flaws, after all, are not irremediable. Tom may be a real gem—even if it be that the gem is in the rough. Some of his flaws, indeed, are simply untrimmed virtues. His boldness is an exaggerated manliness—certainly it has nothing of the bully in its ring; his slang is that ineffectual struggle for humor so noticeable in many young people; and in them, at least—we speak not for maturer sinners in this line—pardonable; his forwardness is the exaggeration of what we all love and hold fast to—American independence. But enough on the score of excuses. Let us hope that the edges may be rounded;

that the gem in the rough may sparkle unto the admiration of many, that the exaggeration of American virtues may be subdued to that golden mean which we all admire so much and practice so little.

Tom's dialogue with the shin-worried Green, while drawing our hero into prominent notice, gained him a host of admirers and a few friends.

As he and Harry were taking a stroll about the yard, shortly after Green's departure in quest of that boarding-school-boy panacea, iodine, he was accosted by a little lad in knickerbockers, his expression a mixture of timidity and wistfulness.

"Well, my son," said Tom, who was about half an inch taller than the stranger, "what can I do for you?"

"I'm so glad you didn't let that Green get ahead of you. He's mean; he pinched me for nothing, and asked me whether my mother knew I was out—and—and I don't want to stay here. My baby sister"—here the little man began to cry—"won't know me when I get home."

"He's homesick—got it bad," whispered Harry in a kindly tone.

"Here," said Tom; "take some candy."

The youngster accepted the candy, and

tried to cheer up; he ceased crying, though he gave vent at intervals to deep sighs.

"Come and sit down here," continued Tom. "Now, what's your name?"

"Joe Whyte. My pa is a doctor in Hot Springs, and he's got lots of money, and rides round in a horse and buggy."

"It must be fun riding round in a horse," observed Harry. "Does he do that often?"

Joe relented into a smile.

"Haven't you any friends here?" pursued Tom.

"No; and I want to go home," sobbed Joe, in a fatal relapse. "The boys are all mean here; and nothing is good."

"Oh, you don't know 'em well enough yet," said Tom; and he added with ingenuous modesty, "Harry and myself are good fellows. You just wait, Joe, till you grow up to be a man, and then you won't have to go to boarding-school, you know. Then your papa will die, and you'll have all his money, and go riding round in a horse and—"

"Boo-oo!" interrupted Joe, appalled by this ill-directed bit of word-painting. "I don't want my papa to die."

"Don't get so excited," put in Harry. "He isn't going to die now."

"I don't want him to die at all," blubbered

the wretched victim of homesickness. "I want to go home right now, and see him and mamma and Sissy and little Jane and all of 'em."

"I tell you what," said Tom; "let's be friends, and then you won't be lonesome. What do you say, Joe?"

With one hand rubbing his eyes, Joe extended the other first to Tom, then to Harry. Each of these young gentlemen shook it warmly.

Master Joe's case is a fair specimen of the malady which attacks almost invariably the new boy—homesickness. Like measles, whooping-cough, or sea-sickness, few escape it and, still true to the likeness, it seizes upon its victim with various degrees of malignity. Under an ordinary attack, the patient feels fully convinced that life outside the home-circle is not worth living. Games, meals, even candies lose their zest. Like the quality of mercy, homesickness is "mightiest in the mightiest"; the large boy when afflicted with it is a piteous sight indeed.

After five o'clock supper, the students took recreation till six, when a bell summoned them to the hall of studies. Here they were at liberty to sort and examine their books, and write their parents assurance of their safe arrival.

Tom on entering noticed that the older boys, instead of seating themselves at once, were all standing in silence. Following their implicit guidance, he too stood beside his desk, and fixed an inquiring look upon Mr. Middleton, who from a raised platform commanded a view of the entire study hall.

While Tom was still wondering why the old boys were so slow about sitting down, the prefect made the Sign of the Cross and recited the *"Veni Sancte Spiritus."* This beautiful prayer concluded, all addressed themselves to their work.

Instead of beginning to study, Tom sat for some time curiously watching the movements of those about him. The old boys, with scarce an exception, were inscribing their respective names in their new books, the newcomers were rummaging in their desks in a vain attempt at appearing easy and self-possessed. Mr. Middleton seemed to have his eyes on every one.

Presently a professor entered the study hall, and Mr. Middleton retired. This professor was the regular study-keeper.

Tom gazed at the new official for some moments, and then turned to Harry.

"I say, what's the name of that man?"

"Sh!" said Harry.

Throwing a look of disgust at his admonitor, Tom turned to Joe Whyte, who sat at his left side, and repeated the question.

"I don't know," returned Joe.

"Say, what are you going to do this hour?"

"I'm goin' to write home and ask them to take me away from this place."

"Oh, don't be in a hurry about that!" whispered Tom; "after a few days you will begin to know the fellows better and—" Just then a hand was laid upon his arm, and Tom on lifting his eyes saw the study-keeper before him, looking rather stern than otherwise.

"Keep silence in here, Playfair," he said, "no talking; take out your books and paper and go to work."

"Say, Mister, how did you come to know my name?"

The study-keeper bit his lip to restrain a smile and moved to another part of the hall. The secret of his knowing Tom's name was very simple.

A map is made of each boy's place in the study-hall, washroom, refectory, dormitory, and chapel. One glance at the map will inform the presiding officer whether each boy be at his post, and, in consequence of this system, a boy cannot absent himself from college for any period beyond an hour at the most without being missed.

Thus admonished, Tom opened his desk, took out his writing materials, and after great effort, much blotting of paper, soiling of fingers, and intellectual travail, delivered himself of the following letter:—

St. Mars College,
Sept. 5, 188-.

My dear Aunt Jane:

I take my pen in hand to let you know that i am well, hoping this leaves you the same. St. Mars is a pretty jolly sort of a place; and i am not one bit home sick; lots of new kids are. Tell Jeff Thomas I will write to him soon. Who is takin care of my pijins? Tell papa my love. Is my rooster with the long tale all rite? My money is nearly all gone. I had an axident on the car comin here, and I had to pay the porter for an old lantern. Good bye. I am goin to study rite hard.

Your lovely nephew,
Thomas Playfair

While he was addressing the envelope destined to carry away this choice bit of literature, he felt someone poking him in the back. On turning, he perceived a hand extended from under the desk behind him, holding a bit of paper. Tom received the note. It read as follows:

MISTER PLAYFAIR:

Say will you fite me at recess, behind the old church building.

Yrs.,
JOHN GREEN

P.S. You're a sneak.

To which Tom elaborately replied:

DEAR MISTER GREEN:

How did you come to be called green? and why do the boys call you crazy? How is your knee? does it hurt much? You don't spell well. *Fite* is wrong; it ought to be *fight*. You are biger than i am and older. Insted of fighting you ought to study your speling book. Fightin' is low and i don't want to and you ought to be ashamed of yourself. When you rite home give my love to your papa and mamma.

Yrs.,
THOMAS PLAYFAIR

After passing this note, he took a leisurely survey of the study-hall, stretched his arms; then concluded to go out. Taking up his cap, which, by the way, he had borrowed from Harry Quip on losing his own, he walked toward the door. Just as he was opening it, his progress was arrested by the study-keeper's voice.

"Playfair, go back to your seat." This in a very imperative tone.

"I'm going out, sir," said Tom, pausing with

his hand on the doorknob to impart this information.

"Go back to your seat."

With a look of patient unmerited persecution Tom returned to his place, casting wrathful glances on the way at several who were grinning at his mistake.

A little later the bell rang; and all repaired to the yard to enjoy a few minutes of recess.

This over, they recited night prayers in common, and retired to their dormitories for the night.

The novel sight of a hundred boys undressing as one struck Tom as being rather funny than otherwise. Indeed he was so absorbed in a humorous survey of this spectacle that he stood stock still, grinning broadly and incessantly for some minutes. A hand upon his arm called him down from his humorous heights. It was Mr. Middleton.

"Playfair," he whispered, "have you anything on hand just now?"

"No, sir," answered Tom, wondering what would come next.

"Well, then, you had better undress, and get to bed." And Mr. Middleton resumed the saying of his beads, as he continued his route up and down the passage formed between the beds.

"Pshaw!" growled Tom. "A fellow can't look cross-eyed here, but he gets hauled up for it. I don't see any harm in looking around." And sadly he proceeded to pull off his sailor-shirt. He had just succeeded in getting this garment free of one arm, when he perceived Harry Quip some ten or eleven beds further off. Harry caught his glance and smiled. The smile brought sunshine back into Tom's heart; suspending further operations on the sailor-shirt, he playfully put the thumb of his right hand to his nose, and made the popular signal with his fingers.

Instead of taking this friendly and jocose demonstration in the spirit in which it was given, Harry's face lengthened into dismay, while his eyes glanced apprehensively in the direction of Mr. Middleton. Tom, following the movement of Harry's eyes, turned and— yes! there it was again—saw Mr. Middleton bearing down upon him.

"Well, I'm switched," he thought, as he slipped out of his clothes with marvellous speed, "if he isn't makin' for me again." And leaping into bed he buried his face in the pillow.

"Young man," whispered Mr. Middleton, bending down over him, "we want no levity in this dormitory."

"No what, sir?"

"No levity."

"What's that, sir?"

"Sh! don't talk so loud. I mean you mustn't talk, whisper, laugh, or make signs. Do you understand me?"

"Yes; but—"

"That'll do; go to sleep now; and if you have any objections to make I'll hear you in the morning."

"He's a nice one," grumbled Tom to his pillow. "He won't give a fellow any chance to explain."

Two minutes later he was sleeping a dreamless sleep.

Chapter VI

IN WHICH GREEN AND TOM RUN A RACE WHICH PROVES DISASTROUS TO BOTH

CLANG—clang—clang—clang—clang!

"Halloa! what's the matter?" cried Tom, in the midst of this clatter, as he jumped out of bed and rubbed his eyes.

The cause of the din was a large, iron-tongued bell, which Mr. Middleton was ringing right lustily.

Tom looked about him; all the students, with the exception, of course, of several of the old boys, who were quite accustomed to this unearthly sound, were up and dressing.

"It's a little too early for me," thought Tom; and, satisfied that the horrid bell had become silent, he turned in again. He was peacefully dozing off when a hand was laid upon him.

"Playfair, did you hear the bell?"

"Did I? I should think I did! That's all right, Mr. Middleton; but I guess I don't care about getting up just now."

The sentence was barely out of his mouth, when, as it appeared to him, there was a mild form of earthquake in the vicinity; and before he could realize that anything had happened at all, he was sprawling on the floor with his mattress on top.

"I say, what did you do that for?" he sputtered; but Mr. Middleton was already halfway down the aisle.

"If that's the way they treat a fellow the first day, what'll they do on the last?" he murmured. "I don't think this school is much account anyhow."

On rising, the boys were allowed half an hour for washing and dressing. Then came Mass, followed by studies and breakfast.

At nine o'clock—on this particular day—they had what is technically termed "*Lectio brevis*"; that is, the teachers of the respective classes gave their boys a short talk, and appointed lessons for the next day.

Tom was mildly surprised, and a trifle dismayed, when he discovered that his teacher for the year was none other than Mr. Middleton. But after listening in silence for some minutes to his professor's opening speech, he concluded that perhaps things might not be so bad.

The "*Lectio brevis*" was compressed into an hour, and the students had the rest of the day free.

Shortly after dinner Harry Quip, accompanied by a strange boy, approached Tom.

"Tom, here's a particular friend of mine, Willie Ruthers; and I'm sure he'll be a great friend of yours."

Willie and Tom shook hands, while Will murmured sheepishly, "Happy to see you."

"Won't you take some candy?" inquired Tom.

The candy was gratefully received, and the friendship of the two was firmly based.

"Have you been out walking yet?" asked Willie.

"No; and that's a fact; Harry, we ought to

go and get that hat of mine at Pawnee Creek."

Obtaining permission from the prefect, they set out on their walk along the railroad track, and in course of time discovered the hat partially embedded in the mud. When on their return they came near the college, Harry proposed that they should pass through the "Blue-grass." The "Blue-grass" is a favorite resort of the boys. It lies just beyond the college yard, and is well shaded with large, graceful pine trees.

It chanced on this particular day that the only occupants of the "Blue-grass" were John Green and three lads of similar taste.

Green caught sight of our trio from afar.

"Oh, I say, boys," he exclaimed, "here comes the funny man. Come on here, you young sneak," he added, addressing himself to Tom, "and we'll settle our accounts."

"Tom," whispered Harry earnestly, "let's run; those fellows with him won't let me or Willie help you; and Green has been acting like a bully since he's come back from vacation."

"I'm not going to run, unless I've got to," answered Tom; and he walked straight on, intending to pass by Green and his following. But Green put himself squarely in the trio's path.

"Where are you going, funny man?" he inquired.

"I'm going to St. Maure's this year. How's your shin?"

"You've got to fight me, you sneak," pursued Green, reddening with anger at the retort.

"But I don't want to fight, you see."

"I don't care a cent what you want. Put up your hands. I'll teach you to sass me. You can't get out of it!"

"Can't I though? Catch me!" and as Tom spoke he dashed away in the direction of Pawnee Creek.

It took some seconds for Green to realize this sudden and utterly unexpected change of front; then with a shout of wrath he gave chase.

Before leaving home, it may be explained, Tom had made a solemn promise to his Aunt Meadow not to engage at fisticuffs under any circumstances.

He was a good runner for his age; but he lacked the speed of his older and longer-legged pursuer. Although he had obtained a start of some twenty-five or thirty feet, he perceived presently that he was losing ground rapidly. For all that the serenity habitual to his chubby face did not diminish one whit;

and as he turned his head from time to time to make a reconnaissance, his expression was as tranquil as though he were racing for amusement.

The scene was an interesting one. Tom was followed by Harry and Willie, while Green was cheered on by his three cronies, who were also hot in pursuit.

Before Tom had got clear of the "Blue-grass" trees, he saw that he was sure of being captured, unless he could introduce some new feature into his flight. His invention did not fail him. Suddenly he wheeled sharply, and, assisted by a tree which he caught hold of, turned at a right angle to his former line of retreat.

In nimbleness Green could not compare with Tom; and so, before he could adjust himself to the change, our hero obtained a new lease of flight. All were now speeding towards the line of low bluffs which fronted the "Blue-grass," and divided it off from the prairie land beyond.

But it seemed quite evident that Tom could not hold out long enough to gain the bluffs.

Nearer and nearer panted Green. "He was coming along in short pants," Harry Quip subsequently remarked to some of his school-mates; who roused his indignation and cut short his narrative with their laughter over his remarkable bull—in his case, original. Well—nearer and nearer came the pursuer. The interval between the two was scarcely twelve feet.

"You're gone, Tom!" cried Harry.

"It's no use," added Willie Ruthers, as he ceased running, "you can't get away."

Tom was now within twenty yards of the bluff, while his pursuer was but six or seven feet behind. Suddenly Tom came to a full stop, turned, and as his pursuer shot on, whisked aside, and put out his foot.

Green took the foot offered him, and went right on, not as a runner, but more after the manner of a flying squirrel. He came down all-fours on a soft bank of earth, and in no wise injured picked himself up.

But before he was well on his feet, Harry Quip had come to the rescue with a suggestion.

"Tom, Tom!" he cried, running, as he spoke, at an angle toward the bluff, "run this way for all you're worth. We're near Keenan's cave; and if we can make it, we'll bar them out."

Long before Harry had ceased speaking, Tom was making for this prospective sanctuary. The cave in question was fronted by a rough, clumsy, wooden structure, in general appearance not unlike a storm-door.

Tom's eyes grew brighter. He felt sure of himself now. Once within the cave, Harry, Willie, and himself might bid defiance to all outside.

Nearer and nearer loomed the cave; one hundred and fifty feet more, and all was well. Green was far behind, and was not running as at first.

But alas! as Tom with his eyes fixed on the refuge was making bravely on, he struck his foot against a stone and fell violently to the ground. It was an ugly fall. But Green did not pause to make any inquiries. Throwing himself upon Tom, he proceeded to strike him blow after blow upon the partially upturned face.

In falling, Tom had incurred an ugly cut on the head. The pain was intense; more than enough to bear without the savage attacks of Green.

"Give up—will you?" roared the young savage.

"Give up what?" groaned Tom, who, dizzy and weak and suffering as he was, could not take his tormentor seriously.

The bully continued his brutal work. Tom's condition was becoming serious. Harry and

Willie, who had attempted to come to his assistance, were forcibly held back by Pitch and his companions.

"Now will you give up?" asked Green, again pausing.

Tom felt that he was fainting; lights flickered before his eyes, strange noises rang in his ears—for all that he had no idea of "giving up." Summoning all his strength, he said, almost in his natural tones:

"I think you asked me that before."

"Well, I'll punch you so's you won't know yourself next time—"

Green never finished his speech; a vigorous jerk at this juncture brought his jaws together with a snap, and sent him to grass with almost lightning-like rapidity.

George Kennan stood over him. But even when released, Tom made no move; he had fainted.

"Quip!" cried Keenan, "run over to our cave and get some water—quick!—Look at that, you low-lived bully," he continued, addressing Green. "Do you see what you've done?" And as George spoke he seized the terrified boy by the collar, and shook him with the energy of boiling indignation.

"He wouldn't give up," howled Green.

"Ugh!" growled George, casting an anxious

look at the pallid face of Tom. "If I had nothing better to do, I'd be glad to spend my life
in shaking you up. That's it, Harry," he continued, as Quip with a jug of water bent
over Tom, "throw it over his face; he'll be
all right in a moment."

George seemed to be quite absent-minded.
With his eyes fixed anxiously on Tom, his
hands and arms were working to and fro with
such energy that it was impossible to say
where Green's head was at any given moment.

He made no pause even, when, a second
later, Tom's face twitched.

"Hurrah! he's comin' to!" cried Willie
Ruthers, who had just thrown open Tom's
collar.

Willie was right. Tom opened his eyes; then
with an effort raised himself on his arm. He
gazed about him in a dazed manner, till his
eyes fixed upon the tear-stained face of Harry
Quip. He brightened at once, put his hand
in his pocket, and said:

"Here, Harry, take some candy." And Tom
arose, feeble but smiling.

"Green," said George, "before I let you go,
you must beg this boy's pardon."

"I'll not."

"You won't—eh?" and George annotated
this remark with a shake.

"Ow! stop! Yes! I beg your pardon."

"Much obliged," said Tom seriously.

"Now," continued George, "I want you to promise me not to interfere with smaller boys. Do you hear? We want no bullies this year."

"Oh yes!" cried Green, now shaken into a ball. "I promise, upon my word. Oh, George, please let me go."

George acceded to this earnest request, and Green hastened away to rejoin his friends, who, at the first approach of danger, had fled.

Morally speaking, Tom had won the fight.

Chapter VII

IN WHICH TOM USURPS MINOR ORDERS WITH STARTLING RESULTS

ONE Sunday morning toward the end of September, the president preached a sermon to the students, taking for his subject Our Lord's casting out of the devils. He proceeded to show how the Church has established certain forms of prayer, called exorcism, for the casting out of unclean spirits;

and he dwelt at some length on the pitiable condition of a soul possessed by the evil one.

Then, turning to the allegorical side of the subject, he declared that perhaps there were in that very students' chapel some who were in the toils of Satan; some who were profane, impure, unjust; some who had blackened their souls with mortal sin, and driven out the Holy Spirit from His proper temple.

So engaging was the style, so impressive the manner of the speaker, that all listened with eager attention. But no one was more interested than Tom Playfair. That young gentleman, it must be confessed, had scarcely ever heard a sermon during the decade of years that summed up his life. What little knowledge he had of his religion had been gleaned from an occasional flash of attention to his aunt's exhortations. Hence it is not surprising that Tom did not fully take in the speaker's remarks; it is not surprising that he confounded fact with fancy, the literal with the figurative.

Mass over, Tom remained in the chapel, and proceeded to make a careful examination of all the prayer-books scattered about on the benches. At length the gratified expression which came upon his countenance evinced that he had found what he desired.

Gravely seating himself, he read and pondered, pondered and read. Finally seeming to be satisfied with his researches, he closed the book and hurried away to the yard, where he at once sought out his three confidants, Harry, Willie, and Joe.

"I say," began Tom, "take some candy." Candy was Tom's pipe of peace. All accepted the peace-offering, whereupon the young chief unfolded his ideas in the following conversation:

"I say, did you fellows mind what the president said at Mass?"

"Yes; what about it?" inquired Harry.

"Why, just this—one of the boys in this yard is possessed by the devil."

"What!" exclaimed all in a breath.

"That is just what," returned Tom, in a decided manner. "Didn't he say that anyone who curses and acts vile is possessed by the devil?"

"That's so," assented Willie.

"Now, boys, I ask you—what fellow in the yard is it who curses and talks vile?"

"John Green," put in Harry.

"John Green," echoed Willie.

"Just so," added Joe.

"Well, now," resumed Tom, "I've been looking this thing up, and I guess we must—

what's that word the President used?"

"Exercise," suggested Willie.

"That's just it; we must exercise him."

"Chase him round the yard or something of that sort," said Joe, imparting to his voice a tone half of suggestion, and half of inquiry.

Tom rewarded this remark with a glance which was almost severe.

"Joe," he said, reproachfully, "exercise is something religious, and you oughtn't to talk that way. To exercise means to drive the devil out, and that's what we're going to do for Green."

"But seems to me," observed Harry, the best theologian of these youths, "we ought to get a priest to do it."

"I've thought of that, too," answered Tom, with an impressiveness which carried confidence. "But you see here's the trouble; no fellow likes to give another fellow away. And if we told a priest, we'd have to say all the bad things we know about Green. Anyhow, *we* can try our hands first, and if our praying don't do good, we can get a priest at it."

Strangely enough, these three boys began to look upon Tom's proposition in a serious light. Our hero had a boyish eloquence which persuaded where it did not prove. Had any other student of the yard made this proposal, Harry Quip would have laughed him into silence; but Tom was a born leader.

"Well, how are we to go about it?" inquired Willie.

"I'll tell you," answered Tom. "Fasting and prayers is what does it."

"Fasting?" echoed Joe.

"Yes; we must go without supper tonight."

The members of the little band looked at each other doubtfully.

"It's got to be done," said Tom, with decision. "I read about it in a prayer-book."

"And what else?" asked Harry.

"Then we've got to pray *over* him."

The prospect of these duties was inducing a feeling of awe upon all.

"What will we say, Tom?" whispered Willie.

"That's just the trouble; it's got to be in Latin, 'cause I saw in the prayer-book a lot of Latin prayers they use for exercising."

"Whew!" exclaimed Harry. "We can't get over that."

"Yes, we can," said the ever-ready Tom. "There's a lot of Latin hymns at the end of my prayer-book, and I'll practice saying them during the day. Then, when I read them out loud, all you fellows need do is to answer, '*Amen.*'"

"We can do that easy enough," assented

Harry. "But when is all this to come off?"

"That's another thing I've settled," Tom made answer. "At twelve o'clock tonight. You needn't look so scared. I'll keep awake till twelve, and then I'll call you fellows. You see, we must pray *over* him; and when he is lying in bed, we can do it as easy as not. I'll stand at his head reading the verses, and you three be ready to grab him, if he wakes, so as to make him behave while he's getting exercised."

"Oh, Tom!" suddenly exclaimed the ingenious Joe. "How can you read at twelve o'clock without a light?"

For the first time during the proceedings Tom was nonplussed. The question of illumination had not occurred to him.

"Gracious! I didn't think of that. Let's all try and get up some scheme."

"Halloa! I'll tell you what!" cried Harry triumphantly, breaking in upon the silence which had ensued: "we can get some candlesticks out of the sacristy."

"You're a jewel, Harry!" exclaimed Tom, enthusiastically. "That'll make it more religious-like, still."

"What's the matter with a few surplices?" asked Willie.

"I don't know," mused Tom. "Do you think

it would make the thing more piouser?"

"Of course," rejoined Harry.

"Then we'll get surplices, too; and, Harry, I'll leave all that to you, because you know more about the sacristy than I do. Get 'em at last recess tonight. Hide the candlesticks behind the door going up to the dormitory. Each boy can keep his surplice under his pillow. Now, don't speak about this affair, and we'll put it through in style."

At supper that evening four little boys took nothing; and before retiring Harry procured candles and surplices, and bestowed them according to directions.

As Tom slipped into bed he felt confident of success. Indeed, he found less difficulty in keeping awake than might have been expected. With his eyes fixed on the presiding prefect, Mr. Middleton, he watched anxiously to see him retire. But Mr. Middleton sat at his desk, calmly reading, till a cold perspiration came upon Tom, who feared the prefect might stay up all night. Finally, to Tom's great relief, the prefect arose and set about preparing for bed; but before retiring he knelt beside his bed, and kept this position for an interminably long time, as it seemed to Tom.

"Pshaw," growled the impatient sentinel;

"this isn't the time to pray. He ought to do that when the boys are awake instead of watching 'em."

At length Mr. Middleton *did* go to bed, and there was silence for an hour. Then arose Tom, donned his garments, and, tiptoeing from bed to bed, aroused his fellow-conspirators.

All dressed, they stole noiselessly out of the dormitory. Presently a solemn procession enters. Tom, surpliced, and with prayer-book, at the head, followed by his three friends, each bearing a lighted candle. Solemn and silent they range themselves round the bed of the unconscious victim.

"Don't touch him," whispered Tom, "unless he wakes. But if he does, grab him, and hold him down till I'm done expelling the devil out."

"What if he shouts?" asked Joe.

"He won't shout," said Harry; "I'll see that he's quiet."

"Very well," said Tom. "Now, are you all ready?"

General assent.

"All right; here goes:

'Dies iræ, dies illa,
Solvet sæclum in favilla,
Teste David cum Sibylla.'"

Here Tom looked up from his book. General silence.

"Answer, will you—it's the end of the verse."

"*A—men*," came the solemn answer. The sleeping innocent did not appear to be affected in the least.

Tom went on:

"'Quantus tremor est futurus,
Quando Judex est venturus,
Cuncta stricte discussurus.'"

"*Amen*," was the prompt response. Green moved uneasily, and gave a groan.

"Go on, Tom, it's fetching him," observed Harry gravely.

"Oh!" cried Joe, "maybe it's the devil coming out. Do you think he'll hurt us?"

"Not if we behave properly," said Tom, though he paled a little. "Come on, now. Here's one that's got a sound to it:

'Tuba mirum spargens sonum
Per sepulchra regionum
Coget omnes ante thronum.'"

"*Amen*."

Green moved and groaned again.

"Grab him boys; he's waking!" exclaimed Tom.

As Green opened his eyes to find himself in the clutches of four white-robed figures, his terror knew no bounds. "What's the matter?" he gasped. "Am I dead?"

"No; but you will be," answered Tom, "if you don't lie still. Keep quiet, you goose, while you are being exercised."

Green's terror, now that he came to appreciate the situation, fast gave way to rage. He attempted to cry out, whereupon Harry Quip promptly stuffed a towel into his mouth. Green was a strong lad; and he made violent struggles to escape from the grasp of his persecutors. But his efforts seemed to be unavailing.

Suddenly there was a great crash. The bed had come to pieces. Panic stricken, Joe, Harry, and Willie rushed from the dormitory. Quick as thought, Tom extinguished the lighted candles, which the deserters had left on the field, and with a skip and a bound tucked himself snugly in his bed.

Nor was he too quick. Mr. Middleton, on coming to the scene of action, found Green standing beside his dismantled bed, looking the embodiment of guilt.

"Take that vacant bed over there, Green,

and we'll settle this matter in the morning."

"But, sir—" remonstrated the innocent victim—"but, sir—"

"That'll do now; go to bed."

And Mr. Middleton, glancing about the dormitory, took down the names of the absentees.

Next morning Tom confessed the whole affair, taking all the blame upon his own shoulders. Mr. Middleton was secretly amused at Tom's ideas of diabolical possession; nonetheless, he kept that young gentleman very busy for some time committing lines to memory; and with this exercise terminated Tom's career as an exorcist.

Chapter VIII

IN WHICH TOM GETS INTO MANY DIFFICULTIES, AND HOLDS AN ASTONISHING INTERVIEW WITH MR. MIDDLETON

TOM'S first five or six weeks at St. Maure's, like the course of true love in fable and history, did not run smooth. His troubles, some of which we have narrated, were not confined to the yard alone. They followed him into the classroom.

Tom thought, like many other students, that he would pick up the class matter by easy studying. But on this point his professor did not agree with him.

It must be confessed, too, that Tom was at times overbold in his manner of deporting himself in the classroom.

On one occasion, Mr. Middleton put himself to much trouble to explain a long and complicated sum in fractions. He went over the problem step by step in such wise that no one not absolutely feather-brained could fail of following the process. Mr. Middleton was the soul of earnestness in teaching; and so at the end of half an hour's explanation he was covered with chalk, while beads of perspiration—it was by no means a warm day—stood out upon his brow.

"Now, boys," he said, turning full upon the class, "do you understand it all?" The head of each and every boy nodded assent. Suddenly a hand went up. It was Tom's.

"Well, Playfair?"

"Yes, sir," said Tom soberly.

Mr. Middleton was puzzled.

"What do you mean, Playfair?"

"I understand it, sir."

Mr. Middleton smiled; there was a slight titter among the more thoughtless boys; yet somehow Tom felt that he was out of order; he was sensible in a dim way that Mr. Middleton's smile carried a reproof with it. But the words had been spoken, and were beyond recall.

A day or two later, Mr. Middleton was hearing recitations. Alexander Jones was called upon to answer some questions on the geography of Vermont.

"What is the nature of the land, Jones?" asked Mr. Middleton in a kindly manner.

Jones arose, one quivering bundle of nerves, his eyebrows twitching, his knees bending under him, his lips quivering, and his fingers in a fury of motion. He grew intensely pale and gave several gasps.

Mr. Middleton, with a few encouraging words, repeated the question.

"It's a con-continent," gasped Jones.

"I'm afraid you didn't catch my question," said Mr. Middleton. "Now don't be afraid. I'm sure you know it. Listen; what is the nature of the land? Is it rocky, or mountainous, or sandy, or what?

Poor Jones gasped again, but gave no answer. Here Tom (who knew nothing about the lesson) came bravely to the rescue. He was seated just behind Jones.

"It's mountainous," he whispered.

"It's m—mountainous," Jones stammered.

"Yes," said Mr. Middleton, as if expecting more.

"Go on," growled Tom, "and tell him it's rocky."

"It's rocky," repeated Jones.

But even this answer did not seem to satisfy Mr. Middleton.

"Tell him it's sandy," continued the prompter.

"It's—it's sandy."

But Mr. Middleton, for some unknown reason, failed to come to the rescue of the hapless boy. He still waited.

"Hang it," growled Tom, unwittingly speaking so loud as to be heard by the professor and the entire class, "tell him it's very mountainous, very rocky, and very sandy."

"It's very mountainous, very rocky, and very sandy," blurted forth Jones, and as a burst of laughter saluted his remark he sank back into his seat miserably conscious that he had cut a very ridiculous figure.

"Playfair, after class," said Mr. Middleton sententiously.

"I didn't do anything," exclaimed Tom with virtuous indignation.

But the professor very wisely ignored this disclaimer, and continued the recitation.

In consequence, then, of bad conduct and faulty recitations, it was not an uncommon sight after class to see our little friend, book in hand, patrolling the yard, endeavoring to make up at the eleventh hour what he had failed in at the first. And so, naturally enough, Tom came gradually to imbibe a disgust for study and class-work, which in the course of three or four weeks culminated in an almost entire neglect of studies. Tom felt in his heart that he was acting wrong; but he was a thoughtless boy, and his sense of responsibility was but poorly developed. Yet he realized with growing unhappiness that, should he continue in his present courses, he would soon be at the foot of the class.

Mr. Middleton, indeed, had no trouble in divining the state of Tom's mind; but he resolved to wait till some favorable opportunity should present itself for turning the pupil from his ill-chosen path. The opportunity soon came. An incident in the yard brought it about.

It was a gloomy morning in early autumn. Tom was straggling along moodily from the refectory towards the yard, when he perceived lying upon the ground two ready-made cigarettes, dropped, probably, by one of the senior students in the rush and shock of a game of football. Quickly picking them up, he hurried to his yard and sought Harry Quip. Tom was rather out of spirits on this morning—he was totally unprepared in lessons, and he looked forward with unpleasant feelings to the day's recitations. There was unhappiness awaiting him in the line of duty. He would seek happiness in the line of mischief.

He found Harry without difficulty, and drew him aside.

"Look here, Harry," and Tom produced the two cigarettes, "what do you say to a smoke?"

"Halloa! what's up now?" Harry exclaimed. "On the road here you told me you didn't care about smoking, and I liked what you said first-rate."

"Yes; but just for fun," pleaded Tom.

Harry placed his hand affectionately on Tom's shoulder, and with his honest face and eyes beaming earnestness, said:

"Tom, old fellow, I'm afraid you're going wrong—just a little bit, you know. Of course there's nothing bad about smoking—but—but—well, I ain't no philosopher, but it's so anyhow."

This speech was incoherent enough. Harry had endeavored to tell the truth and at the same time spare the feelings of his "partner." But honest words are more than grammar and rhetoric; and long, long after, the sympathetic face and kindly voice of Harry haunted Tom, and helped him in the path of duty.

But at the moment he was in no mood to be softened. He added in extenuation:

"You see, Harry, I've got to do something or I'll die. Come on and take a few puffs."

"Nixie," responded Harry, shaking his head and grinning, "and I tell you what, Tom, don't you get in with the smokers on the sly. It doesn't pay."

Seeing Harry's determination to behave well, Tom respected it; and forthwith sought in his stead an old and tried smoker, John Pitch.

"You're just the fellow I wanted to see!" exclaimed John Pitch enthusiastically, when Tom had made his proposition. "You see the old church-building? Come on over to that corner between the walls of the handball alley. It's a safe place now. Mr. Middleton is taking his breakfast, and Mr. Phelan has to stay in the playroom—and I've got any amount of matches."

"Now," resumed Johnny a few seconds later, when they had nestled close together in the corner, "unless you want to get caught, don't blow your smoke out ahead of you, so's it can be seen. Every time you take a puff, turn your head round this way, and blow it here right through this chink into the old church. It's a great trick; I found it out myself."

Tom gave audible approbation to this advice, and proceeded to carry it out to the letter; and for some minutes the two smoked in silence.

"Isn't it immense?" John at length inquired.

"Isn't it though?" answered Tom, repressing a cough.

"Say," resumed John, a moment later, "can you make the smoke come out of your nose?"

"Oh! that's nothing," responded Tom; and he executed the required feat.

"You can't inhale—can you?" pursued John.

"Of course I can, if I want to; but I don't care much about it."

"Well, I'll tell you what you can't do; you can't talk with smoke inside of you and then blow it out after you're through talking."

"Neither can you."

"I'll bet I can."

"Let's see you do it, then!" exclaimed Tom with increasing animation.

In answer to this, John gravely inhaled a mouthful of smoke; then said:

"See! that's the way to do the thing," and blew it forth.

"Gracious, but that's immense. I want to learn that trick too; let's see you do it again."

Both were now absorbed—Tom, cigarette in hand, intently eyeing John; and John, cigarette in mouth, determined to heighten his disciple's admiration.

John now took two or three vigorous puffs, then inhaled the triple installment.

Just at this most interesting juncture, Tom's quick ear caught the sound of approaching footsteps.

"*Cave*, look out," he whispered, and as he spoke he dropped his cigarette by his side and crushed it under his foot.

But John was not so quick, his lungs were still filled with smoke, and his cigarette was still in his hand, as Mr. Middleton, the terror of smokers, turned the corner. But the young rogue was not without resource; he and his companion, as has been said, were nestled together, and the open pocket in Tom's sailor-jacket was convenient to the hand in which John was holding the cigarette. There was no resisting the temptation. Deftly, quietly, he dropped the burning cigarette into the yawning pocket. Unconscious of this, Tom, with his eyes full upon Mr.

Middleton, was inwardly congratulating himself upon his lucky escape. Not so John. Although free of the telltale cigarette, it could hardly be said that he was in a happy frame of mind. The smoke within him imperatively demanded an outlet; and there stood Mr. Middleton, confronting him with the evident intention of opening a conversation.

"Good morning, boys," the prefect began.

"Good morning, Mr. Middleton," answered Tom, who, aware of John's predicament, was resolved to do the talking for both.

"There's a strange smell about here," continued the prefect, with a peculiar smile.

"Yes, sir, there is," returned Tom gravely. "I wonder if there aren't some skunks in this old building. Some of the old fellows says there are."

"I hardly think it a skunk. But what's the matter with you, Johnny? Are you ill?"

The question was pertinent. John was now in a partial state of suffocation, his eyes were bulging out of his head, his mouth was closed tight, and his cheeks were puffed out as though he were a cornet player executing a high and difficult note.

It is superfluous to add, then, that John returned no answer. Tom made an awkward attempt to divert Mr. Middleton's attention.

A number of boys had just issued from the playroom; Tom made the most of it.

"Oh! Mr. Middleton, what's that crowd of boys outside the playroom up to? Looks as if there's going to be a fight or something."

"Johnny, you *must* tell me what ails you"; and Mr. Middleton, regardless of Tom's eager remark, fixed his penetrating eyes on John.

A moment of painful silence followed.

One moment and the victim of asphyxiation could hold it in no longer—a gasp and a choke, and out came the smoke.

"Dear me! you appear to be on fire inside," remarked the prefect.

"I guess you're pretty sick, Johnny," put in Tom, becoming bolder under stress of desperation. "Anyhow I hope it ain't catching. I've been sitting alongside of—"

He finished this interesting address with a shriek of pain, as he suddenly jumped to his feet and clapped both hands to his bosom—smoke was streaming from his pocket.

"It looks as if it *was* catching," remarked Mr. Middleton. "You are on fire outside."

With some rubbing and slapping—accompanied by a round of hopping and wriggling—Tom saved his jacket pocket from utter destruction; then as he grew calmer he threw a reproachful eye upon John.

With a smile the prefect walked away, leaving them to conjecture the nature and extent of their punishment.

During six o'clock studies that evening, Tom was summoned to the room of Mr. Middleton.

"Well, Tom," began the prefect when the culprit had presented himself, "how are you getting on?"

Tom became lost in the contemplation of his feet.

"Take a seat," continued Mr. Middleton, indicating a chair. "I want to have a talk with you. Now, my boy," he resumed when Tom had seated himself, "I have had a good chance to watch you in class and in the yard, for some weeks, and I have come to the conclusion that you are a very stubborn boy. Isn't that so?"

"Yes, sir," said Tom mildly.

"You don't seem to mind anything I tell you. Day after day, it's the same old story, bad lessons, careless exercises, and then when I call you to account, your manner shows that you have little or no intention of doing better. Do you deny that?"

"No, sir," answered Tom, beginning to feel

very uncomfortable and very wicked.

"And don't you think that a stubborn disposition is a bad thing for a little boy?"

"Yes, sir."

"Well, I don't," said Mr. Middleton.

"You don't!" exclaimed Tom in surprise.

"Not entirely. Columbus, Washington, St. Francis Xavier were in a sense stubborn men. Indeed, I think all truly great men must have a fair share of stubbornness in their composition.

Tom's face betrayed no less astonishment than interest.

"Columbus," continued Mr. Middleton, "by stubbornly clinging to one idea in spite of rebuffs and disappointment, discovered a new world. Washington in the face of most disheartening difficulties—difficulties from friends and from foes—held to his purpose, and created a nation. If Columbus had not been stubborn he would have given in; and America might have been undiscovered for years and years after his death; if Washington had been less stubborn, perhaps our country might have never achieved her freedom. Did you ever read the life of St. Francis Xavier?"

"I don't read pious books very often, sir."

"Well, he was just such another man—

stubborn as could be. When he was a young student nothing would satisfy him but to become a great philosopher. So he studied away, week after week, year after year, till he became one of the learned doctors of his age. Then when St. Ignatius converted him, he became just as stubborn in converting souls to God, as he had before been stubborn in acquiring philosophy. Nothing could divert him from his new work. Labor, pain, hunger, abandonment of home and friends— all were bravely endured to this end; and Francis Xavier became the great apostle of modern times."

"Well, it seems to me, Mr. Middleton, that if stubbornness were a good thing, it wouldn't make a boy act wrong."

"Oh, it may," answered Mr. Middleton with a smile, "if it be misused. Isn't bread a good thing?"

"Yes, sir."

"But it wouldn't be good if you were to pave the streets with it. Stubbornness is good too, but only when used the right way. Stubbornness is merely the sign of a strong will—a strong determination. If you exert your stubborn strength of will to doing what is good, you are all the better and nobler for your stubbornness. But if you exert it for a bad purpose, then you are so much the worse. And what a pity it is that boys misuse so good a gift of God! Why, my dear boy, I have known not a few college students who bent all their energies to getting off their lessons without being punished, and who with the same energy might have acquired such an education as would have reflected honor on themselves. And you too, Tom, must guard against misapplying this energy, this determination, this perseverance, this stubbornness—you see it has many names—to wrong purposes. It is a gift to you from God Himself; and you must show your gratitude by using the gift aright. Do you remember when Green attacked you, how steadfastly you bore his blows till you fainted?"

"I guess I do."

"You were determined not to give in. Now take your lessons the same way. Don't let trouble, weariness, memory-work scare you; just hold on tight to your lessons. Never give in or yield to them; make them yield to you. Then, indeed, you will see that your stubbornness is a gift of the good God. By the way, you intend making your First Communion this year, don't you?"

"Yes, sir; I'm awful anxious to make it. I'm going on eleven, sir"—here the boy's lips quivered, and he caught his breath—"and—and—well, whenever I think of Holy Communion, I—eh—think of my mamma, sir. She died when I was only seven. But I remember how she was always speaking to me about my making a good First Communion."

While speaking these words, Tom repeatedly shifted from one foot to the other. This was his expression of strong emotion. And he had reason to be affected. For, as he spoke, the sweet, pure face of his departed mother came back vividly to his memory, and while her deep, dark, tender eyes kindled into love, her lips moved in a last prayer for the weeping child whom she strained in a dying clasp to her bosom; moved in a prayer that Mary the Virgin Mother might guide the ways of her darling son. Then the strain relaxed, the sweet eyes closed, a shadow seemed to pass over the pallid face, and, as he covered the stilled features with kisses, he knew that his mamma was with God. Poor motherless boy!

Mr. Middleton was touched. From Tom's halting words and shifting of position he had caught some glimpse of the little lad's heart.

"In general," said the prefect quite gently, "a boy is a great loser if his mamma dies before he grows up. The reason often is that he forgets. But you do not forget, Tom."

"Sometimes I do, Mr. Middleton; I've been forgetting a heap more than I ought to."

"Well, Tom, I have great confidence in you."

Mr. Middleton said these words in a tone so impressive, so earnest, that Tom felt more and more humbled.

"I haven't done anything to deserve it, sir."

"But you *will* do much to deserve it, or I am sadly mistaken in you. Now, I'm going to tell you a secret, Tom; but mind you keep it to yourself. Three weeks ago, I received a letter from your father in which he asked me to give him a report of you."

Tom's cheeks lost their color.

"He said that you had given much trouble at home, that you seemed to be very thoughtless even for your age, and that he doubted strongly about your fitness to make your First Communion this year."

Tom caught his breath.

"And he added that, unless I could assure him that you were giving perfect satisfaction, he would defer your First Communion till you were twelve."

The listener turned away his face and gazed through the open window.

"I answered your father's letter half an hour ago."

"O! I'm a goner, then." Tom's expression was really pathetic.

"Listen to what I've sent him.

DEAR MR. PLAYFAIR:

In regard to your son's conduct, it is too early in the year to say anything definite. But from the data already afforded me by what I have seen of him in the classroom and in the playground, I feel quite certain that he will develop into a thoroughly good and noble boy.

Yours sincerely in Xt.,
FRANCIS MIDDLETON, S.J.

Tom's lips quivered, and a softness came into his dark eyes; he made no attempt to speak. The firm, noble head bowed low. He could have fallen at Mr. Middleton's feet.

"Now, Tom, I'm quite sure that I have not been deceived in you. Perhaps I was over harsh with you at first—"

"No, you weren't. Hang it," blurted forth Tom, "if you'd kicked me once or twice, I'd feel better now."

Mr. Middleton held out his hand; Tom caught it in a fervent grasp.

"Now my boy, we will forget the past. Take a walk in the yard for a while, and think over what I have said. Then make your resolutions carefully, and ask the blessing of the Sacred Heart."

Tom departed, carrying a new range of ideas in his little brain; up and down the yard he paced, buried in thought. The seed had fallen on good ground. Finally, going to the chapel, he knelt for a long time before the tabernacle and prayed with all the earnestness of his soul, that he might turn over a new leaf. Nor was his prayer unheard; from that hour Tom became a more faithful student, a more earnest Christian.

It was twelve of the night, when Harry Quip was aroused from slumber by a hand which was shaking him in no gentle manner.

On opening his eyes, he discerned by the dim light of the dormitory lamp Tom Playfair.

"What's the matter, Tom?"

"I say, Harry, isn't Mr. Middleton a brick?"

"Oh, go to bed," growled Harry, turning over and burying his face in the pillow.

Tom complied with this sensible advice, and lay awake for full three minutes, building golden visions of the great day now assuredly near at hand.

Ah! if he only knew what difficulties were to arise, and under what tragic circumstances he was to make his First Communion, I am quite sure that he would have lain awake for at least six minutes.

Chapter IX

*IN WHICH TOM CONCLUDES THAT VINEGAR
NEVER CATCHES FLIES*

FOR the ensuing two or three weeks the current of events at college flowed on with scarcely a ripple. Every day Tom seemed to gain new friends. Indeed, with the exception of John Green, he had not a single enemy among his playmates; and even Green's enmity had grown less demonstrative.

As a fit preparation for his First Communion, Tom had resolved to put himself at peace with the whole world. He now regretted that he had made a laughing-stock of Green on the occasion of their first meeting; and he was on the alert to do something towards closing the breach between them.

A slight change in the routine of school-life gave him the desired opportunity.

Towards the end of October, it was found necessary to make some repairs in the western corner of the small boys' dormitory. In consequence, seventeen of the students occupying beds in that part were assigned temporary accommodations in the attic of the main building, a structure towering high above all its fellows.

It was Wednesday afternoon when Mr. Middleton announced the names of those who were to change their sleeping quarters. Tom, Harry Quip, Alexander Jones, John Pitch, Green, and others with whom our story has not to do, composed this privileged number.

To add a zest to the privilege, he allowed the happy seventeen to explore their improved dormitory immediately after class, and very quickly after class the brick building resounded to the tramp of multitudinous feet scampering nimbly up the stairs as though on a mission of life and death.

"Whoop-la!" cried Tom, as he burst into the great room, seamed and ribbed overhead with heavy beams. "It's like the attic of a haunted house, only bigger—isn't it, Green?"

"It's an immense place for fun," responded his companion. "Look at all the corners and hiding-places. We can play 'I spy' here, if we don't feel sleepy."

"Yes," assented Tom, "and at night we might climb out on the roof and count the stars. Did you ever count the stars, Johnny?"

"Naw; did you?"

"I tried it one night at home, when I was lying in bed and couldn't sleep. I got as far as fifty-seven, and then I went off sound asleep. But there are lots more than fifty-seven."

"I guess there's over a trillion," said Green reflectively.

Both felt that their remarks had fairly exhausted their astronomical researches.

"Come on," said Tom, "let's get out on the roof."

As he spoke he pointed toward a ladder which led up to a cupola, rising some seven or eight feet above the roof of the building. This cupola gave access to the roof by means of a small door, which opened at the side and was secured from within by a strong bolt.

Followed by Tom, Green ran up the ladder, shot back the bolt, and made his way upon the roof.

"I'd like to live on a roof," said Tom tranquilly, as he walked over to the eastern verge, and gazed down upon the yard below.

"Come back, you idiot," cried Green, in what he considered his most persuasive accents, "you'll get dizzy and keel over."

"I'll bet I won't," answered Tom. "Don't you think I've ever been on a roof before? This one isn't steep like ours, but it's a heap higher. I say, how'd you like to stand on top of that lightning rod?" and Tom motioned with his index finger toward the tip of a rod, which rose above the cupola.

Green ran over, caught hold of the rod and shook it.

"I wouldn't like it at all, unless I wanted to break my neck; it's loose. What'll you bet I can't pull it down?"

"It isn't ours, Johnnie."

"I'd just as soon pull it down as not," continued Green. Nevertheless, he relinquished his hold upon it, and turned away.

Tom had occasion to remember this episode subsequently, though at the moment both he and Green dismissed the subject so lightly.

Some seven or eight others now found their way to the roof, and the conversation, made up in great part of "ohs" and "ahs," had become quite general and very noisy, when Mr. Middleton appeared and sternly ordered all down.

Tom and Green were the first to descend, followed by the others in Indian file. The last to re-enter shut the door behind him, but neglected to bolt it. The omission passed unnoticed.

"I say, Mr. Middleton," observed Tom solemnly, "I thought you didn't believe in slang."

"Indeed! I wouldn't advise people to use it in ordinary."

"Well, sir, you gave us bad example."

"How?"

"You told us to 'come off the roof,' sir."

And satisfied with his little joke, Tom was about to hurry away, when he was arrested by Mr. Middleton's voice.

"Well, sir."

"You'll have to do penance for that joke, Tom. I want four or five willing boys to bring over pillows and bedding; the workmen will attend to the beds and mattresses. You might get Quip and Donnel to help you."

"All right, sir; that'll be fun." As Tom spoke, he saw an eager look upon Green's face. "And I say, Mr. Middleton," he added, "can't Johnny Green help us? He's willing."

"Of course," was the cordial answer, accompanied by a kindly look at Johnny.

Poor Green! There was a real, wholesome blush upon his face as he blurted forth some disjointed words of thanks.

"Well," commented Mr. Middleton to himself, as the lads went pattering down the stairs, "that Playfair has unconsciously taught me another lesson. I mustn't forget to notice the hard cases now and then. Unless I'm mistaken, Green will be in a better mood for a week."

"He's a good fellow," Green observed, as

they were trotting across the yard.

"Isn't he?" said Tom.

"And so are you," added Green, growing very red as he spoke.

Tom laughed; he had succeeded. His only enemy was won over.

Tom had brought a diary from home having made a promise on receiving it to write something in it every day. That night at studies, he opened it for the first time, and made this his first entry. It happened to be the last also.

OCT. 30TH.—Since coming to college I have notised that viniger never catches flys. Today I am eleven years old. This year I am going to make my First Communion. His name is Green. I don't believe there is anything near a trillion stars.

———————————

Chapter X

IN WHICH TOM GIVES GREEN A BIT OF ADVICE, WHICH, AIDED BY A STORM, IS NOT WITHOUT ITS EFFECT

ON the afternoon of the following day, Tom, Harry, and Alexander Jones were engaged in an earnest consultation.

"I don't think he'd allow it," said Harry.

"What do you think, Alec?" asked Tom.

"I'd be afraid to ask," responded Alec.

"Well, he can't more than refuse, and I guess I can stand that. Yes, fellows, I'm going to ask."

And without further ado, Tom walked over toward Mr. Middleton, who was acting as umpire in a game of handball between Donnel and Keenan.

"Well, Tom," said the prefect, as he caught the anxious eyes of our hero fixed upon him, "what do you want?"

"If you please, sir, I'd like permission to take a walk with Harry Quip and Alec Jones."

"Certainly; you are all on the good conduct list. Be back half an hour before supper."

"And, Mr. Middleton, can't Crazy—that is, can't Johnny Green come along with us?"

"He's not on the conduct list. You know the rule."

"Yes, sir; but he hasn't had a chance to go out since the first week of school."

"That's not a sufficient reason for his going out now."

"But, Mr. Middleton, yesterday you told me you'd make it all right with me for carrying over the bedclothes and things. Let Green come along, and I can't ask for anything I'd like more. You know, sir, we haven't been friends up to yesterday." And Tom gazed at the prefect wistfully.

"Tom," answered Mr. Middleton, after a few moments of consideration, "please tell Green that I'm very glad to have an excuse for letting him out, and that I hope he'll have all the privileges of the conduct list next month."

"Thanks, Mr. Middleton; I know every word you said just then by heart, and I'll tell it to him exactly as you said it." And touching his cap Tom hurried away.

"Say, Green, won't you take some candy?" he inquired of that young gentleman, whom he found engaged in furtively carving his name on a corner of the little boys' building.

Green closed his knife very promptly, and accepted the candy with silent enthusiasm.

"How'd you like to take a walk, Green, with me and Quip and Jones?"

"I'd like it well enough to walk with any-body," came the rough answer. "But I'm not allowed outside this wretched yard." And Green went on to express his injured feelings in a manner too realistic for reproduction.

"You needn't swear about it anyhow,"

interrupted Tom, "and besides, Mr. Middleton has given you permission."

Green opened his eyes.

"What?" he gasped.

Then Tom repeated Mr. Middleton's message.

"Just my luck," observed Green, gazing ruefully at the letters he had cut. "If he sees those initials I'll lose my conduct-card again. I can't behave, to save myself."

Tom pulled out his own knife, and forthwith began working upon Green's carving.

"There!" he said presently. "If anybody can make J. G. out of that now he'll have to be pretty smart. Come on, Johnnie, and we'll have a fine walk."

Accordingly the four were soon outside the college grounds, an event which Green celebrated by putting a huge quid of tobacco into his mouth.

It was a gloomy afternoon. The morning had opened with a black mass of clouds low down upon the eastern horizon. With the progress of the day, they had been accumulating and spreading westward, growing thicker and blacker in their advance, till nearly half of the firmament was now veiled from the eye.

"That's an ugly sky," observed Harry.

"There's lots of wind in those clouds," added Tom. It looks as though we'd have a big storm tonight."

"So it does," assented Alec, who did little else in ordinary conversation beyond contributing the scriptural yea and nay.

"I ain't afraid of storms," said Green.

"There's nothing wonderful about that," commented Tom. "What would you be afraid for?"

"Some fellows get scared when they hear the thunder," explained Green; "but I don't mind it one bit."

"I do," said Alec. "When the thunder begins, and I'm in bed, I always put my head under the blankets and pray."

"That's 'cos you're a coward," said Green loftily. "I don't fear going to bed in the dark nor nothin'."

"In other words," remarked Quip, with a solemn roll of his big eyes, "you aren't afraid of anything."

"Naw—I ain't afraid of nothing."

"You're not afraid to blow, that's sure," put in Tom, in a matter-of-fact tone. "All the same, Johnnie, I rather think you'd be scared if you knew you had to die right off."

"I don't know about that," answered Green. "I don't expect to go to Heaven anyhow."

"You don't?"

"Naw; I gave up trying to be good long ago."

"At least, you might try to make the nine First Fridays that Father Nelson talked to us about in the chapel," suggested Tom.

Green stared at him heavily.

"He said, you know," continued Tom, "that there's a promise of grace to die well for any fellow that makes 'em."

"I heard him; but once a month is too often for me."

"Just think," added Harry Quip, "tomorrow's the first Friday in November. Make a start, Crazy; it won't hurt you to try."

"I guess I'll not begin yet," answered Green, as he proceeded to roll a cigarette.

"It would please Mr. Middleton a heap," Tom observed.

"Yes, indeed," put in Alec.

"And it would do you any amount of good," added Tom. "Come on, Johnny; you sneaked out of going to Communion last time the boys went. You needn't stare; I had my eyes open, and I saw you dodging. It's my opinion that you've been dodging ever since you came back to college."

"Say, you didn't tell on me, did you?"

"Not yet," answered Tom diplomatically—

he had never entertained the idea of reporting Green to the authorities; "and I won't mention it either. Now you'll go tomorrow, won't you?"

There was a short silence.

"Yes," answered Green at length, and speaking with an effort, "I'll go."

Making their way through the woods which girded the river, they presently arrived at a clearing upon the bank.

"Isn't it growing dark awful fast?" exclaimed Harry.

"Just look at those clouds; they're beginning to move faster and faster; and they're coming our way too," cried Tom.

"Let's run home," suggested Green.

Borne on the wings of the storm, the dark masses in the east were advancing gloomily, rapidly, like a marshalled army. The wind which carried them on could be faintly heard, breaking upon the dread silence which had come over the scene round about them, as the ticking of a watch at midnight upon a nerve-shattered invalid.

Fascinated by the sweep of clouds, they stood, these little boys, with their eyes lifted toward the heavens.

"Ah!"

This exclamation which seemed to break

from all simultaneously was evoked by a sudden change in the moving panorama. For, as they stood gazing, there dropped from the bosom of these clouds thin, dark veils reaching from earth to sky.

"What is that?" cried Green.

"I don't know, I'm sure," answered Tom. "I never saw anything like that in St. Louis. Maybe it's rain moving this way. Anyhow, the storm'll be on us in a moment. Just look how it's rushing towards us. It's too late to start for the college. Where'll we go to?"

And as they set about answering this question the clouds came nearer and nearer. The whistling of the breeze that one moment before had seemed but to emphasize the silence, had risen to an angry scream.

The four lads wavering and irresolute, not knowing whither they should go for shelter, presented a striking tableau as they paused there in the open.

Tom stood with his legs apart and firmly braced. His hands were clasped behind his back; and with his hat tilted so as to show a shock of thick black hair over his forehead, and his mouth pursed as though he were about to whistle, he raised his eyes in an unblinking gaze upon the angry clouds. Next to him was Alec, pale, silent, with an awe-stricken look upon his fair face. He had put his arm through Tom's, and clung to our little friend as a drowning man to a plank. Tom was Alec's hero. Harry Quip was on the other side of Tom, the usual grin still lingering upon his merry face, and his hands thrust deep in his pockets. Green, who stood in advance of these, had become intensely pale. His fingers were quivering, his breath came in gasps, and he glanced over and over from sky to companions, from companions to sky.

The first drops of rain began to patter about them, while the wind keeping time with the movement of the rain sent the trees before them bowing and swaying in a weird dance, all the more weird for the unnatural darkness that had fallen upon all nature.

"Hadn't we better run?" asked Tom.

"Yes," said Green, eagerly. "Come on."

"I'm afraid, Tom, I can't run," said poor Alec. "I feel weak and dizzy, and I'm so frightened."

"Harry and John, go ahead," said Tom. "I'll stay with Alec."

"No you don't, Tom" said Quip. "If you stay, I stay."

"Come on, Quip," implored Green, "they can look out for themselves."

"Go on yourself," said Harry, speaking with some asperity. "You can take care of yourself, if you want to."

"But I don't want to be alone in this storm."

"Then stay here," came the curt answer.

"Halloa!" cried a voice, "why you're smart boys for your age; you've chosen about the safest place around here." And John Donnel, out of breath with running, emerged from the woods and placed himself beside Green.

"We came near running away," said Tom. "We thought we could run through the woods and find some house to stay in till the storm blew over. We're mighty glad to see you, John."

"It's lucky you stayed here. If the wind gets any worse the woods will be a dangerous place—flying branches and lightning and what not!"

During this conversation, short as it was, rain and wind had grown worse.

"Ugh! we'll be drenched to the skin," said Tom. "Why, halloa!" he added, "Alec is sick."

Alec had pillowed his face on Tom's bosom, and before the exclamation was well out of Tom's mouth, the poor child fainted.

"Here, give me the boy," shouted Donnel (shouting had now become necessary as the ordinary tone of conversation). "I'll fix him in a trice." And John, as he spoke, took Alec in his arms, carried him to a soft bit of earth, and depositing him gently, threw open his collar.

"Halloa, Green, what's the matter?" bawled Tom, attracted by the strange motions of the frightened boy.

"I can't stand here; I've got to run," came the answer.

Donnel raised his face.

"Stay where you are," he said sternly; "if you want to die young, run through those woods."

As he ceased speaking, there came a dazzling flash of lightning, followed almost instantaneously by a terrific clap of thunder.

With a wild cry, Green dashed for the woods.

"Stop him, Tom," cried Donnel, jumping to his feet, "stop him; he's lost his wits."

Donnel, though many yards in the rear of both, had set forward in hot pursuit. As for Tom, he scarcely needed Donnel's bidding. Green had not fairly made a start when Tom was at his heels.

Terror, they say, lends speed. But poor Green seemed to be an exception to this as to many other rules. He slipped several times, and once was within a little of losing his balance and falling to the earth. Indeed it seemed as though Tom, who was running at his best, would catch him before he reached the woods. But as Green drew nearer the dangerous shelter, he regained something of his customary speed; and Tom, who had thus far gained upon him, began to lose his advantage; Donnel, meanwhile, was lessening the distance between himself and Tom at every step.

At length Green, in passing a tree that stood like a sentinel, guarding the main body of the woods, slipped again, and before he could well recover himself, Tom had come within five feet of him. Then, just as the thoroughly frantic boy broke into his regular speed, Tom sprang into the air, alighted on Green's back, and bore him to the ground.

And while they were still rolling upon the drenched earth, there was a sharp crack, like the report of a pistol discharged at one's ear, a strange *swishing* sound, a crash as of many branches beating against each other; and, twenty feet before them, there came crashing to the earth a giant oak. As it fell, a twig struck Tom in the face.

In an instant, though dazed and bewildered, Tom had sprung to his feet. But Green rose only to his knees; he was quivering with fear and beat his breast.

"Spare me! spare me!" he cried. "I'll go to Confession this very night."

"Get up, will you?" bawled John Donnel, his voice rising high above the noises of the elements, as he caught Green by the shoulders, and dragged him to his feet. "If you don't move away from here, you'll not have a chance to make a Confession." And without further words, John dragged him back into the open. Tom followed quietly; even his face, it must be said, had paled a trifle.

And there they stood motionless as statues, silent and awed for two or three minutes; there they stood till in the swiftness of its might the wind had flown by them, till the clouds had moved on to the western horizon, and left the sky above them perfectly clear, till, in fine, the storm had ceased with a suddenness befitting its violence.

"Well, it's over and all is well," said John Donnel.

"I guess we had better run for college, John," put in Tom, "and change our things, our we'll get rheumatism or small-pox, or something ugly. What's the matter, Green?"

Green pointed a quivering finger at the western sky.

"It is coming back. Those clouds have stopped moving."

"I guess we can beat 'em," answered Tom. "John, I'm awful glad you came. We'd have lost our heads, if it hadn't been for you. How did you come to be around?"

"I was hunting for snakes with Keenan, and we got separated; you can rely upon it that George is safe in college by this time. Now boys, for a run home. Are you all right, Alec?"

"Yes, sir," said Alec, who had risen to his feet while the race between Green and Tom had been going on, "but I'm afraid I can't run very fast."

"Here, put your arm through mine," said John.

"And your other arm through mine," added Tom, whose color had fully returned.

In a very short time, indeed, they were changing their garments in the dormitory.

Green uttered not a word till he was about to leave the room. Then he said:

"Tom, if you hadn't jumped on my back and pulled me over, I'd be dead now. Ugh!"

"Yes," replied Tom, adjusting his tie with more than wonted precision; "and if I hadn't tumbled over with you, I'd have been killed too. I was scared that time, I can tell you. But, of course, you weren't scared." Tom grinned as he waited for an answer.

"Scared! I should think I was. Say, Tom, I was lying to you fellows about my not being afraid."

"You needn't tell us that," said Tom bluntly.

"But I'm going to change; see if I don't." And Green left the dormitory and went straight to the chapel, leaving Tom and Alec alone.

"Well, Alec," began Tom, who divined from the timid lad's face that he wished to say something, "do you feel shaken?"

"A little, Tom. Did you hear what Green said just after the storm?"

"What did he say?"

"He said it was coming back."

"Oh, well! you know he was most scared out of his wits."

"Tom, it *is* coming back."

"Nonsense."

"Well, I feel as though something were about to happen. Won't you please pray for me?"

And Alec caught Tom's hand and gazed into his countenance with a sweet pathos inexpressibly touching. A beautiful face it was that met our hero's, nonetheless beautiful for the modesty which nearly every minute of the day veiled the eyes, and sent the blood purpling the pale cheeks. Now, however, Alec's eyes were wide open and fixed, oh, so appealingly, upon Tom's. And Tom, as he returned the gaze, was impressed with something which he could not define, but which brought home to him for the first time, that he was in the presence of a boy of extraordinary holiness and purity.

"Why, of course I'll pray for you, if you want me to. What's up?"

"Tomorrow, Tom, I finish making the nine First Fridays."

"Well, I don't see why you want any praying for. I need it bad. I've done a lot of things that I hadn't ought to."

"Yes; but you've done a lot of good, too. I was so glad, Tom, when you spoke up to Green. You know how to talk."

"That's what I've got a tongue for. But it was that falling tree which fetched him. He'll behave decently for a week, I reckon."

Poor Alec looked as though he would say more; but words and courage failed him. He again caught his friend's hand, pressed it, then hurried form the dormitory with that indefinable expression which Tom had noticed before.

Tom continued sitting on his bed for some moments longer.

"I didn't know that Alec Jones," he soliloquized as he rose. "I thought he was a little girl, but he's a mighty good girl anyhow."

And with a grin on his face, he left the dormitory.

Chapter XI

THE NIGHT OF THE FIRST FRIDAY IN NOVEMBER

IT was ten of the night, and, though so late in the season, quite warm and extremely oppressive. Above, the clear sky was gemmed with stars. In the west hung a thick, black cloud; it had been motionless all the day.

There was a hush over the dormitory. The feeble light of the lamp at the entrance was utterly insufficient to limn the countenances of the slumberers lying beneath the cupola; and so it would have been difficult for any one to perceive that Tom Playfair, whose bed stood directly beneath the cupola, was wide awake. With the single exception of the night when he undertook to exorcise Green, who, by the way, was now his right-hand neighbor, nothing like this had ever happened to him before. To his left lay Alec Jones; beyond him Harry Quip, and, last of the row, John

Pitch. These five were grouped under and about the cupola. The other occupants were at the further end of the room, separated from this row of five by a space of some thirty odd feet. It will be convenient for the reader to keep these details in mind.

Tom, as I have said, was awake. Perhaps a sense of novelty reconciled him to the situation; for he lay very quiet. The subdued breathing of the sleepers was the only sound to break the stillness; without the winds were hushed, and no cry of man or bird or beast broke upon the brooding calm of the night.

For fully half an hour, Tom, from their different modes of breathing, endeavored to place the various sleepers. He easily picked out Harry Quip's, and, with more difficulty, John Pitch's. At this point he grew weary of this new study, and cast about in his thoughts for some fresh diversion. It was hard upon eleven o'clock, when he concluded to arise, go to a window, and count the stars.

As he was setting foot upon the floor, a silvery, sweet voice, with a sacred pathos in every tone, broke, or rather glorified, the silence.

"My Jesus, mercy!"

The invocation came from Alec.

Tom bent down and gazed into the dreamer's face. Even with the feeble light, he could perceive lines of terror upon the slight, delicate, innocent features.

With a gentleness which, on recalling the incident afterwards, surprised Tom himself, he lightly patted the upturned cheek; and forthwith the face grew strangely calm; a smile, tender yet so feeble that the facial muscles scarce changed, passed over it, and from the lips came the whispered, "Sweet Heart of Jesus, be my love."

With his hand still resting on the sleeper's cheek, Tom stood gazing upon the radiant face in mute admiration.

"Amen," he whispered softly to himself. "If ever I get to talking in my sleep, I hope I'll do it that style."

He removed his hand; Alec opened his eyes.

"You're all right, Alec," explained Tom, bending low so as to whisper into the boy's ear. "You got a hollering in your sleep, and I just passed my hand over your cheek. Go to sleep again. Good night." And he held out his hand.

"Good night, Tom." And Alec drew his hand from the coverlet to clasp Tom's, displaying, as he did so, his rosary twined about the fragile arm. Then very gently Alec fell into a calm slumber. Looking on such a face, it was hard to imagine that the world was full of wickedness and sin.

Tom waited till he felt sure that Alec was sound asleep. Then he murmured to himself:

"I guess I'll count the stars now."

Walking over a-tiptoe to one of the western windows he looked out. He counted no stars that night. For the dismal, black cloud was now in motion, advancing ominously, swiftly, in a direct line toward the small boy standing in his nightshirt at the window.

"Whew!" whistled the would-be star-gazer. "Green and Alec were right after all. It *is* coming back."

Even as he spoke, the awful whisper of the approaching storm could be heard; a whisper that lasted but for a moment, when it changed to a sigh, deepened into a groan, which grew louder, more violent, more threatening every second.

"It's getting chilly too," murmured Tom to himself. "I guess I'll hop into my pants."

And very quickly indeed, he was fully dressed—sailor shirt, knickerbockers, stockings, everything save his tie and his shoes—and, with his usual calmness, returned to the window to watch and wait upon the turn of events.

The patter of the rain upon the roof could now be distinctly heard, while far off from the east came the muffled thunder of some distant storm. In attempting to take another look from the window, Tom happened to touch a wire fastening for the window-curtain.

"Ouch!" he muttered, withdrawing his hand very quickly; and perhaps for the first time since his mother's death, he became thoroughly frightened. A queer feeling had passed through his whole body. What could it be?

There was something wrong about things, and the mystery frightened him. He had received a sharp shock; but he knew nothing of electricity.

The beating of the rain, while Tom was still pondering, became louder and louder, and the boys began to move uneasily in their beds; many, indeed, were now half awake. The wind, too, was howling about the house in a fury of power.

Tom had just reached his bed, when a loud banging noise brought everyone in the room from the land of sleep; and a gust of rain came sweeping in, thoroughly drenching Tom's bed. Ah! that neglected bolt. The door of the cupola had flown open, and was now flapping noisily against the lightning-rod.

As with noisy recurrence it opened and

shut, Tom caught a glimpse of the stars on the clear eastern horizon, and almost directly overhead that black, sinister cloud, hanging like a curse over St. Maure's.

Even while he was taking in this strange aspect of the heavens, the water had formed into several pools upon the floor. Quip, Jones, Green, and Pitch, all of them with appalled faces, had grouped themselves beside Tom. No wonder they were alarmed; the frightful banging of the door, coupled with the fierce beat of the sheeted rain, was an overtax on the nerves of the boldest.

"Oh, Tom!" chattered Green, "I'm glad I went to Holy Communion this morning."

"So'm I," answered Tom. "Say, boys, I'm going to shut that door, even if I do get a ducking. Good-by." And he made a dash at the ladder.

Unmindful of the rain which almost blinded him, he succeeded at length in securing a hold on the door. But pull and tug as he might, the wind, now at its height, held its own; till at last, in a sudden lull, the door yielded to his efforts.

"Now, if I could only get my hand on that bolt—"

He never finished this sentence. For as he was still groping about for the knob, the wind in a sudden rise sent the door flying from his grasp. There was a sharp, clanging sound, and the dull noise of some heavy object beating upon the roof; and, as the door, torn from its hinges, pulled the lightning-rod down from the cupola, Tom lost his balance, and was thrown backwards from his perch. Happily for himself, he was flung upon his bed, whence he rolled to the floor.

Two boys assisted him to rise, and gazed anxiously into his face.

On that occasion Tom, far from being stunned, was unusually awake to every impression. His senses had become sharpened; and as he rose to his feet he took in the whole scene. At the other end of the dormitory stood huddled together all the boys save Harry, Pitch, Alec, and Green. The prefect was just advancing from the group towards them. Tom could see all this, for the simple reason that a cassocked figure—he recognized the President of the college—had just entered with a lamp that lighted the whole room.

The two who had lifted him to his feet were Jones and Green. Upon the face of Alec there still dwelt that sweet expression, brought from dreamland, but softened and beautified in a new way by concern for Tom's safety. Green's face had strangely changed. All the roughness had gone out of it. Awe and pity—awe at the storm, pity for Tom— had touched it into refinement.

All this, I say, Tom took notice of, as they raised him to his feet.

"You're not hurt, old fellow, are you?" inquired Green earnestly.

"Not a bit."

"Thank God!" murmured Alec.

"I'm glad I went this morning," said Green.

"Tom," said Harry, "we'll help you pull your bed away."

"Oh, it's no use getting drenched the way I am."

"We don't mind that," said Green, and he and Alec sprang forward toward Tom's bed.

They had not taken two steps, when there came a dazzling flash of light. Tom fell violently to the floor, pillowed upon the body of someone who had fallen before him, where he lay motionless, yet conscious, and with a feeling as though every muscle and fibre of his body had been wrenched asunder—lay there gazing up into a sky now suddenly brilliant with stars, into a rainless sky with not a cloud to mar its tranquil beauty.

The storm was over.

And as he fell the President's lamp had

gone out, and in the dazzling brilliancy of that awful flash he had seen five boys standing under the cupola go plunging forward violently to the floor, while the smell as of burnt powder and of ozone pervaded the whole apartment. Then, almost simultaneously indeed, came a deafening noise. To the President's ears it sounded like the explosion of a powder magazine at his side. But he knew that it was not an explosion of powder; he knew too well that it was the thunder following the lightning flash which had stricken down his boys before his very eyes; and, in the dread hush and darkness that followed, the President's voice, clear and firm, filled the room with the words of sacramental absolution, as, raising his hand and making the Sign of the Cross, he said:

"*Ego vos absolvo a peccatis vestris in nomine Patris et Filii et Spiritus Sancti. Amen.*"

"I absolve you from your sins, in the name of the Father and of the Son and of the Holy Ghost. Amen."

The presiding prefect had, in the meantime, relighted the dormitory lamp (which had also gone out in the shock of the lightning stroke), and was now standing beside his superior.

"Boys," continued the latter, who in the dim light perceived several moving forms, "take your clothes on your arm, and leave this room quietly, one by one. Go to the infirmary; the storm is now over, and there's not the least danger."

On occasions such as this the panic does not immediately follow the catastrophe. Between the two there is always a lull—a time when the imagination of each is charging itself with the realization of what has passed, with the picturing of what may come. That done, the panic takes its course.

The president had taken the right time for speaking. Had he lost his head for one moment, there would have ensued, in all probability, a frightful scene. But his calmness gained the mastery over all. Quietly, noiselessly, with pitiful faces, the boys passed down the stairs. How eagerly he counted them. It was the most trying period of his long life.

Six passed.

Three more—nine.

Three more—twelve. The last was the prefect.

Then there was a silence.

His senses, then, had not deceived him. Five had been struck by lightning.

He had relighted his lamp, and now hastened to the other end. Tom, his eyes closed, lay with his head pillowed upon Green's body; near him Alec Jones, calm—so quiet! Beyond was Quip, breathing heavily with an ugly gash upon his face. Pitch was in a sitting posture, murmuring incoherent words.

"Tom!" cried the President, stooping down, and catching the boy's hand.

The eyes opened.

"Yes, sir; I'm all right; what's happened?"

The president made a slight gesture, and bent over Green. No need to listen for the breath that never would return. He moved over to Alec Jones, and a stifled sob burst from his bosom. Green and Jones had been instantly killed; had never heard the crash that followed the dazzling stroke; had been called suddenly before that God whom they had received at the morning Mass into their bosoms. It was the First Friday.

Tom's wet garments had saved him. The electricity had taken its way through his clothes instead of through himself. But he did not know at the moment that he had passed forth free from the jaws of death; for not one of those now remaining in the dormitory, save the President, was aware that the power which sent them stunned to the floor was the awful power of the thunderbolt.

Chapter XII

TOM'S MIDNIGHT ADVENTURE

"HARRY—are you hurt?"

Tom was bending over Harry Quip. But there came no answer. The president touched Tom lightly on the shoulder.

"Playfair," he said, "can I trust you to keep cool?"

"Yes, sir! if you just tell me what's happened. There was a queer feeling went through me just now, and something seemed to burn my right leg."

"The house has been struck by lightning, and you received a slight shock. Harry Quip got a worse one, and Green and Jones are seriously injured. You and Pitch might remove Harry to a bed over there; but don't tell him, when he comes to, what's happened to the others, and be sure not to show him a long face, or you'll frighten him."

"Catch hold of his head, Johnny," said Tom. With tender care, they conveyed poor Harry to the nearest bed; while the president, still cherishing a faint hope in his heart, eagerly sought to discover some signs of life in Green and Jones.

Harry, shortly after being placed upon the bed, gave signs of consciousness.

"Halloa, Harry," cried Tom, forcing a grin.

"Tom!" Harry gave a gasp.

"Yes; it's me; and you're all right, old boy."

"Wh—what's happened?"

"An electric machine got loose, or something," replied our ingenious hero, "and spilled itself on top of us. They let you have it at fairs for five cents a head."

But even this comic view of the situation failed to win a smile from Harry.

"Where's my leg?" he gasped.

"Both your legs are screwed on in the right place."

"No: my right leg's gone."

Tom caught the right leg and lifted it into full view.

"How does that strike you?"

"But I don't feel it."

"Well, catch hold of it, then; it won't come off. You gave me an awful kick with it just a moment ago."

"I'm choking," continued Harry.

"If you were, you couldn't talk."

"But I can't swallow. Oh!" And Harry looked more and more frightened.

"Who the mischief asked you to swallow? It isn't breakfast time yet, and there's nothing to eat round here, anyhow."

The infirmarian, who had entered at the beginning of this conversation, and who, having satisfied himself that Green and Jones were dead, had now come to Harry's side, here broke in.

"Playfair, we want the doctor at once. Run downstairs to the room on the next floor where the brothers sleep. They are dressing now to come up here and lend us help. Take the first one you meet, or the one that's nearest dressed, and tell him to hurry off after the doctor: we want him for Harry Quip."

Waiting for no second bidding, Tom, followed by Pitch, hurried from the dormitory. Luckily they met a brother who was just coming up the stairs: and as the house clock struck twelve, Tom delivered his message.

"I'll have the doctor here within half an hour," said the brother, turning about at once.

"I'm coming along, Brother George."

"No: you'd better go to sleep."

"I couldn't sleep now, brother. Oh, please let me go."

Brother George made no answer, and Tom, taking silence for consent, followed after him. As a matter of course, Pitch clung to his leader.

Once out of doors, they sped through the garden and took the high-road leading to St. Maure's. Suddenly their course was arrested, for a most unprecedented thing had come to pass. There was an insignificant creek flowing past the college and down to the river. Ordinarily it was very shallow, but the furious rain of the preceding day and the past hour had caused it to swell into a muddy torrent. Worst of all, there was no sign of the bridge.

"The bridge has been swept away!" cried Tom.

"I wish I could swim," said Brother George. "Boys, you remain here, and I'll go to one of the houses on this side and get help."

Scarcely had he turned his back upon them when Tom pulled off his shoes, stockings, and sailor shirt.

"What are you going to do, Tom?"

"Didn't you hear the brother say he'd swim it if he could. I can swim that far."

"Oh, but it's an awful current. You'll be carried down to the river."

Tom gazed at the swirling stream, appar-

ently some fifty feet wide, moving in all the
swing of a torrent at his feet.

"I'll bet I won't," he said presently. "Anyhow, I'm willing to take a risk for old Quip.
Here, Johnny, just lend me your scap'lers. I
haven't been rolled in them yet; but it won't
hurt me to wear 'em. I think I'd better start
higher up so as to land about here on the
other side."

Having put Pitch's scapulars about his
neck, Tom ran some distance upstream.

"Now, Pitch, good-by. Shake hands. It's a
risk, you know. If anything happens, you
send word to my father and my aunt that
I had the scap'lers on."

Tom was decidedly of the opinion that this
bit of information would make up for anything that might occur. So, somewhat serious, yet light and bold of heart, he slipped
into the water.

He took one step forward, and found himself up to his waist; another step, and caught
by the current he was whirled downstream
like a cork. But this cork had legs and arms,
and struck out vigorously for the shore. Vigorous as were his strokes, however, he felt
almost at once that he would in any event
be carried far downstream before reaching
the other shore. For all that, he struck out

bravely, beating the water with over-hand stroke. Tom, at this period of his life, was by no means an expert swimmer. He had attended a swimming school several times a week during the last summer, and had succeeded in learning to swim a short distance and to float on his back. But he knew nothing of swimming with the current, and, in consequence, quickly expended his strength. Before he had gone two-thirds of the distance across he was worn out. But his presence of mind did not desert him. Murmuring a prayer, he turned over on his back, and, moving his feet gently, he suffered himself to be carried along. He had not drifted far, when his body came in contact with something a few feet below the water. Turning instantly he secured a hold on it with his hands.

"Hurrah!" he shouted to Pitch. "I'm all right. I've found the railing of the bridge. It's only about two feet under water."

And clinging to this, Tom made his way hand over hand, as it were, to the opposite shore.

Dr. Mullan was not a little surprised when he opened his front door three minutes later upon a boy arrayed in the simplicity of undershirt and knickerbockers, who was battering away at his door with a log of wood as though he would burst it open.

"Oh, doctor, our college has been struck by lightning. Three fellows are badly hurt, and you're wanted there right off."

"John!" bawled the doctor, "saddle my horse at once. Come in, boy; you'll need a doctor, too, if you don't look out. How did you wet yourself?"

"I couldn't find the bridge, sir, and I tried to swim across. I found it then, or I reckon I'd be in the river by this time."

The doctor's wife, who had caught these words, now came forward, and kissing Tom in true motherly style—an action which Tom, in his state of excitement, took no notice of—drew off his undershirt, and threw her own cloak about him.

"That's just the thing, Mary," put in Dr. Mullan. "Now get him a small glass of brandy, while I put him to bed.

"Oh, I say," cried Tom. "I'm not sick: you go off and take care of the fellows that need you."

Returning no answer to this expostulation, the doctor pushed Tom into his own sleeping-room, and without further ceremony pulled off our young swimmer's knickerbockers, and proceeded to rub him down vigorously.

"Ouch," cried Tom, suddenly.

"Why, boy, you're burnt."

The doctor was gazing at a spot on Tom's right knee about the form and size of the human heart.

"I though there was something the matter where I pulled off my stocking: that's where the electricity took me."

"Were you struck, too?"

"I think so; I went tumbling over as if I was paralyzed. That burn isn't much."

"It's good it's no more." And the doctor, who had opened a medicine chest, applied an ointment to the spot, bandaged it, and had Tom wrapped warm in his own bed before his wife entered the room with the glass of brandy.

"Now, boy, these are your orders. You stay in this bed till nine o'clock tomorrow. By keeping quiet, you'll escape the consequences of over-excitement and over-exertion. You understand?"

"But, doctor, I can't sleep."

"You can, though. Mary, if this boy doesn't go to sleep in ten minutes, give him a teaspoonful of this. Now good-by."

The doctor, aided by the directions of Pitch and the brother, easily found the bridge, and made the college in a few minutes. Jones and Green gave him no trouble: they were beyond doctors' skill—had been from the moment the bolt touched them.

But for the rest of the night he was busy nursing and warming and rubbing poor Harry's legs into life.

Tom, meanwhile, under the influence of an opiate, slept a dreamless sleep, watched over with loving care by a gentle woman.

Chapter XIII

IN WHICH TOM TAKES A TRIP

AS this story concerns Thomas Playfair and only incidentally the history of St. Maure's, the reader will be spared the sad details concerning the night of the catastrophe, and of the ensuing days of mourning.

Tom, whom we have to do with, was conducted to the infirmary Saturday morning by the doctor in person.

"Brother," he said to the infirmarian, "here's a boy who's to get complete rest for the next seven or eight days."

Tom, who was standing behind the doctor and the infirmarian, smiled genially, raised his right leg, and, while balancing himself on his left, waved it spasmodically.

"Just look at him," continued the doctor, turning sharply and catching him in the act; "he's trying to knock his burned leg against something even now."

"No, I ain't," protested the discomfited acrobat, bringing his foot to the floor; "I'm not a fool."

Whereupon he resumed his smile: the rogue knew that Harry Quip would be his companion.

"Of course, brother," pursued the man of medicine, "you are to diet him."

Tom's face fell.

"Diet me! with what, doctor?"

"With a boat-hook," answered the grave practitioner without showing the least sign of a twinkle in his eye. He added in a lower tone to the infirmarian: "Three pieces toast and tea for breakfast, same for supper, with beef-tea instead of tea for dinner."

Tom overheard him.

"I say," he broke in, "I'm not sick. I want to go to school, and keep up with my class."

"You can't go out for a week, sir; and if you don't keep your legs quiet, I'll not let you out for two weeks. Now, remember, young fellow, no hopping over beds, no skipping, no jumping about the room, no running. When you have to walk, walk slowly. But the best thing you can do is to keep perfectly quiet."

"Oh, pshaw!"

Tom was disgusted. Even Quip, jolly as ever, though battered, could not reconcile him to his imprisonment. Nor did he become more reconciled as the days passed. After swallowing his toast, he was wont to seek out the infirmarian.

"Brother," he would say, "I think I'm ready for breakfast now."

"I just brought it to you."

"What! you call that a breakfast? Look here, brother, I'm paid for."

The brother would answer with a grin, and Tom would turn away growling.

On Saturday of the following week he received a letter which elicited a whoop from him.

"What are you howling about now?" asked Quip, who with the exception of a slight bruise and a touch of stiffness, was as well as ever.

"Read it yourself," cried Tom, tossing the letter to Harry, and hopping about the room in an ecstasy of joy.

Thus the letter ran:

ST. LOUIS, NOV. 6TH, 18—

MASTER THOMAS PLAYFAIR:

Dear Son.—Have just heard from president of college fuller details of calamity, and of your sickness. Hear, too, that you have been changing for the better—got more sense—more faithful to your duty—study harder. Glad to learn, too, that you are brave, tho' far too reckless. Best of all, I'm told that your company is good.

Although president pronounces you quite well, he thinks that a few weeks' rest and change might be safe, as nervous shocks are likely to leave after-effects.

As I wrote you last September, your uncle has gone to Cincinnati, where, as he says, he is studying law. In a few days I shall be compelled to go there on business, and your aunt has already made an engagement to see a friend there.

Start for Cincinnati at once. Will telegraph your uncle to meet you at depot. Have advised president to procure you through ticket, and enclose you twenty-five dollars for pocket money.

Goody-by till we meet, and God bless you.

Your father, GEORGE PLAYFAIR

At half-past two that afternoon Tom, standing on the platform of a car, waved his handkerchief to his playmates as the train shot past the college.

Kansas City was reached fifteen minutes after scheduled time; and Tom, who had been counting for the last three hours on a grand lunch at the railroad depot, was obliged to hurry from his car to the Cincinnati train in order to make connections.

But here his forced patience was rewarded.

"Ladies and gents!" shouted a fat little man, who seemed to be in a perpetual state of breathlessness, "a dining-car is attached to this train; and supper, with all the delicacies of the season, is now served."

"How much?" inquired Tom, catching the fat man's sleeve, and fastening upon him one of the most earnest gazes the fat man had ever encountered.

"Seventy-five cents cash without any chromo. Do you want to come in for half price? Do you take us for a circus?" The fat man was chuckling between each word.

"Pshaw! Is that all? Why, mister, I'd be willing to lay out five dollars on a square meal. You're going to lose on me this trip. I've got a whole week to make up for."

"Come right along, then," said the fat man.

And Tom needed no second bidding.

A negro with an austere face and a white apron moved a chair for Tom, and, handing him the *menu*, waited for the order.

Tom's brows knitted as he read the bewildering list—a sort of macaronic out of rhyme and meter.

"I say, couldn't you let me have a program in English of this entertainment."

The negro, changing his austere expression not one whit, rattled forth—

"Chicken roast or boiled, chicken salad; eggs fried, poached, boiled, omelette with jelly if preferred; beefsteak, lamb, mutton chops, veal, ham, sausages; potatoes, fried, boiled, Saratoga chips; tomatoes raw, egg-plant, baked beans, apple and custard pie, coffee, cream, tea, and bananas."

"That'll do, I think," said Tom: "fetch 'em in."

The waiter changed expression.

"Fetch in which?"

"Those things you were singing out."

The waiter scratched his head.

"Look here," said Tom, confidentially. "I haven't had a square meal for a week. A doctor's been practicing on me, till I'm nearly ruined. Now, you just go to work and get me lots to eat; get me a good square meal, and I'll give you fifty cents for yourself."

There wasn't a sign of austerity on the negro's face as he hurried away. Tom was served with a meal fit for a starving prince. And he did it justice.

The negro, stationed behind him, could scarce credit his eyes. Nothing equal to Tom's performances had ever come under his obser-vation. Tom, ignorant of the admiration he had excited, plied knife and fork in a quiet, determined way, wishing in his heart that the doctor and infirmarian could see him. It would be a sweet revenge.

"Come here," whispered the waiter to one of his fellows; "this young chap won't be able to get up. He'll bust."

However, after three-quarters of an hour's steady attention to the matter in hand, Tom arose quite calmly (whereupon four waiters, who had been viewing his performance from behind, and expressing their wonder in dumb shows, slipped quietly away) and, making a huge Sign of the Cross, returned thanks for his meal.

"I said my 'prayers after meals' three times," he remarked confidentially to the waiter as he gave him one dollar and twenty-five cents, "because I think I got in at least three suppers."

Tom ought to have been sick that night. He should have suffered intensely.

The doctors and story books are at one on this point. All the same, he retired early and slept a dreamless sleep which lasted for over nine hours.

And if the recording angel put anyone on the black list for gluttony on that particular day, I am inclined to think it was the doctor, and not the patient.

Chapter XIV

IN WHICH TOM GOES TO THE THEATRE

SHORTLY after six o'clock of the following evening the brakeman, throwing open the door of the Pullman car, bawled out what sounded like "Hydrostatic," but was really intended to convey the correct railroad pronunciation of Cincinnati.

Tom seized his valise and hurried through the car into the depot.

"Why, Tommy!" cried our old (or young) friend Mr. Meadow, rushing up and catching Tom's disengaged hand, "welcome to Cincinnati; glad to see you. And you look so well! You've grown, too, and you're improved ever so much."

"I'm real glad to see you, uncle," said Tom, returning the hearty handshake with no less heartiness, "indeed I am. You've changed, too. Your mustache is very plain now—isn't it? And you're dressed awful stylishly. I'm glad I've my new clothes on, or I'd feel ashamed to walk with you. How do you like Cincinnati?"

"It's a splendid place, Tommy," answered Mr. Meadow as they walked out of the depot and made toward a streetcar. "The people are very nice; and there's more amusement here than in St. Louis."

Tom took a stealthy side-glance at his uncle. Oh, these little boys! Some of them read characters with an intuition which humbles the widest experience.

"Yes! but I though you came here to study law."

"So I did; but I'm kept so busy that I haven't settled down yet."

"You look heavy round the eyes, as if you stayed up late, uncle."

"Yes; I suffer from insomnia a great deal," answered Mr. Meadow, puzzled to find that he was annoyed under Tom's innocent analysis. "How have you been doing since you left St. Louis?"

"Pretty well, uncle. I made a bad start; but now I'm doing better. You see, uncle, I'm trying to get ready to make my First Communion."

"Indeed!"

"Yes. I hope it will be the happiest day of my life."

A few earnest, sympathetic words from Mr. Meadow at this juncture might have raised their mutual relations to a higher level. But Mr. Meadow did not understand boys. His influence on Tom, in consequence, was bad. He said:

"Here's our car; jump on, Tommy."

His chance was gone. He noticed a strange expression on Tom's face; it was as though the boy had received a blow. Now, there was nothing in the words of the uncle to produce this effect; but in our mutual relations there is something more potent than words. Manner, expression, and sympathy, or the want of it, are the chief causes that go toward gaining or losing our influence upon one another. Mr. Meadow felt that a wall of separation had at once arisen between himself and his nephew; that their intercourse hereafter was to be on the surface.

He fell into a train of reflection suggested by this incident, and, while Tom, with the lively interest of a boy in a strange city, took note of everything in his new surroundings, the uncle maintained silence till, at a signal from him, the car stopped at a streetcrossing.

"Here we are, Tom; jump off, and we'll be just in time for supper."

Walking to an adjoining square, Mr. Meadow pointed to a cheerful two-story building.

"Is that your house, uncle?"

"That's where I board; all the rooms in the upper floor are mine."

As Mr. Meadow had remarked, they were in time for supper, at which meal, owing to the fact that two young ladies with their father and mother were present, Tom was content to eat little, and contribute his share to the conversation by an occasional "yes'm" and "no, mem," which, as he directed either reply indiscriminately to either sex, did not serve to set him at his ease, though it sent the young ladies into a series of giggles, till Tom, through sheer force of indignation, recovered both tongue and appetite, to the admiration of all present.

After supper, Mr. Meadow proposed the theatre. Tom was delighted with the suggestion, and an hour later both were seated in the pit of a close building, waiting for the curtain to rise.

Tom, it must be confessed, was somewhat astonished at his surroundings. The audience failed to impress him favorably; and the sight of waiters hurrying about with their trays did not suit his ideas at all.

"Is this a first-class theatre, uncle?"

"Yes; that is, it's a first-class variety. Would you like a glass of beer or soda before the show begins?"

"Naw," said Tom, his disgust entering into and distorting his pronunciation: and he wished at that moment that he were back at St. Maure's.

The curtain presently lifted, and for an hour or so he tried to enjoy jigs, comic songs, and what was announced on the program as a "screaming farce." But he found it weary work keeping amused. The atmosphere, too, soon gave him a headache. Mr. Meadow seemed to be perfectly happy. Tom glanced at him curiously.

"I'm glad I'm not made that way," he thought. "If this whole business isn't what Mr. Middleton calls unhealthy, then I'm pretty stupid. It's coarse and vulgar."

"Say, uncle," he resumed aloud, as the curtain fell upon the "screaming farce"—screaming actors would be truer—"I'm getting a headache, and, if you've no objection, I'll go outside and take a breath of fresh air for a while."

Now, Mr. Meadow was very dry, and desirous also of conversing between the acts with a few young men, whom he did not purpose introducing to Tom. So he caught eagerly at the opportunity.

"Certainly, Tommy. Here's a dollar to buy some candy. Don't go far; and come back soon."

"All right, uncle."

Tom went out; as the next chapter will show, he never entered the theatre again.

Chapter XV

IN WHICH TOM IS LOST

TOM was at last free to follow his bent. From the moment he had left St. Maure's to the present he had had "no fun," to use his own expression.

Now that he was rid of Mr. Meadow, he was determined to make the best of the opportunity. Nor did the question of ways and means trouble him. In the matter of amusement Tom, like every well-constituted small boy, was of unfailing resource.

"Say," he began to the ticket-seller, "I'm going out: how'll I get back?"

"You can take a carriage," said the facetious ticket-seller, "if you don't care about walking."

Tom returned his grin.

"I mean how'll I get back without paying over again?"

"Oh, here's a check, Johnny. How are you enjoying the performance?"

"It's made me glad to get out," and without waiting for the ticket-seller's retort, Tom, satisfied that he had squared accounts, sallied forth into the night, and cast his eyes about in search of a confectionery.

The street was brilliant with electric lights. Every variety of store seemed to be in the neighborhood of the theatre. Two saloons across the way sandwiched between them an oyster-house; and stretching to either side were shops of many kinds, all open and all seemingly driving a busy trade.

Tom took a long look at the saloons. He was impressed, not favorably indeed, with the number of men in each.

"Pshaw!" he muttered. "It makes me feel like taking the pledge for life."

He had scarcely made this reflection when his attention was arrested by the sight of a small boy, who, with a bundle of papers under his arm, passed one of the saloons, and, pausing in front of the oyster-house, stood gazing in through the large show-glass.

Tom was growing lonesome. With a hop and a bound he crossed the street, and noiselessly placed himself behind the newsboy.

The object of his attention was a lad of little more than eleven. He was neatly but scantily attired. The sleeves of his jacket and knees of his knickerbockers were patched, and his shoes were open at the toes. The face was quite beautiful, beautiful with some hint of refinement, all the more beautiful, perhaps, that it was touched and softened by sadness. But the eyes—large and black—how eagerly they looked into that window!

Tom was satisfied with the inspection. He put himself alongside the newsboy, and set to staring in himself.

"Paper, sir?" said the boy.

"What paper?"

"*Post* or *Times-Star*."

"How much?"

"Two cents for the *Star,* sir, and one cent for the *Post*, sir."

"You needn't talk to me as if I was your father," said Tom. "I'll tell you what I'll do, Johnny: I'll take a copy of each and give you a dime for 'em if you'll tell me your name."

"Thank you, sir: my name's Arthur Vane," and Arthur received Tom's ten-cent piece with unmistakable signs of gratitude.

"And my name's Tom Playfair; just drop that 'sir,' and call me Tom. I'm glad to meet a fellow my own size. I haven't talked to a boy for three days; and grown people are so tiresome!"

Arthur here smiled, and the twinkle in his eye evinced that for all his sadness he was naturally a merry lad.

"I think," he put in, "that it might be better if you could get boys of your own class in life to talk with you."

"Just listen to him," said Tom, apostrophizing the oyster shop, "talking to me as if I wasn't an American—why, Arthur, I'm a Democrat."

"But your mother and father mightn't like it," said Arthur, very much astonished with his new acquaintance.

"My father's in St. Louis," answered Tom, "and my mother's in Heaven. And what's more, you're just as well up in talk as most boys of your size; and it's my opinion that you haven't been on the streets very long, either. I took a good look at you before I came up, and I'll bet anything you're not used to taking care of yourself."

"You're right, Tom: I've been supporting myself and my little sister for only two months. Papa died when he came here, and left us only a little money."

"A little sister, too!"

"Yes, Tom; poor little Kate has been very sick, but now she's almost well. She's in charge of the kind Sisters."

Instead of continuing the conversation, Tom caught Arthur by the shoulders and bending down stared straight into his eyes.

"See here," he began after a pause. "Can you remember the last time you got a square meal?"

The lustrous-eyed boy with the pale, thin

face smiled again.

"I had a pretty good meal yesterday. But today I've had hard luck. This morning I was stuck."

"On the Latin verb or a pitchfork, or what?" queried Tom.

Arthur laughed again.

"That's a newsboy's term, Tom: we're 'stuck' when we buy papers and have a lot left unsold."

"Oh, that's it. So you didn't get a square meal today?"

"I had a plate of soup and two pieces of bread at noon."

"How much?" asked Tom.

"Six cents."

"Whew! think of a little boy going around with six-cents' worth of provisions—say, Arthur, do you like oysters?"

"Oh, don't I!" exclaimed Arthur with enthusiasm.

"I thought you meant something by looking in through that window. It's the same way with me," continued Tom, gravely. "I'm uncommonly fond of oysters myself, and so are all my friends. Now I'll treat. You go right in, and order all you want. Here's a dollar. Is that enough?"

"I'd like to take it," said Arthur, looking

wistfully at the money. "But I can't. It isn't fair."

"But it is fair," answered Tom. "You're worth a dollar to me, and more. O Arthur, you don't know how tired I am of hearing grown folks talking about elections and stocks and bonds. That's all I've been listening to for three days. It's terrible. It got so bad that I felt like praying never to grow up."

After further words, Arthur consented to take fifty cents. He was about to enter the oyster-house, when Tom snatched his bundle of papers.

"What are you up to now, Tom?"

"I'll keep the business going at the old stand: while you're eating I'll sell. And without waiting for remonstrance, Tom darted away.

"Here you are," he shouted, putting in his head at the saloon to his right; "all the evening papers with all the news about the elections and stocks and bonds."

"Elections! where?" exclaimed a portly gentleman, holding a glass in suspense.

"Don't know, sir. There's always news about elections in the paper."

The gentleman smiled, and, joining in the laugh at his expense, bought a paper, and insisted on several of his companions following his example.

Tom, richer by fifteen cents, repaired to the next saloon. Here he made the same announcement, and was sternly ordered out by a barkeeper all bang and jewelry.

Nothing daunted, he took a position at the nearest street corner, and exerted his eloquence on every passer-by. But he found this slow work. Five minutes passed, and he had disposed of but one more paper.

"I didn't get a fair chance in that saloon," he murmured. "I think I'll try it again."

He peered in cautiously this time, and, when the barkeeper's back was turned, rushed in.

"Last chance, gentlemen. Here are all the evening papers complete and unabridged."

The barkeeper, with an ugly word, sprang over the counter and made a rush at him.

Tom stood his ground, looking the enraged attendant squarely in the face.

"Which paper do you want, sir? *Times-Star* or *Post*?"

"Get out of here, you beggar," cried the barkeeper, pausing suddenly as he saw that Tom did not take to flight.

"You needn't call names: I'm not a beggar. I'm selling these newspapers for a little fellow who's half-starved."

The barkeeper glanced around and perceived at once that the popular sympathy was against him.

"Give me a *Star*, Johnny," he said, and presently every man in the room was buying a paper. Tom's pluck had caught their fancy, while his declaration had touched their hearts. In a few moments he had disposed of his stock, and resisting several offers to "take a drink," hurried away to rejoin Arthur.

He found his little friend seated alone at a large table with a plate of fried oysters before him.

"I'm hungry myself," observed Tom, helping himself liberally to Arthur's dish. "Order a dozen more, Arthur, and I'll help you eat them."

"Where are the papers?" inquired Arthur.

"Sold—every one of 'em. I didn't have a bit of trouble, though I thought that the big barkeeper next door would murder me. But he didn't: he bought a paper, and ended by asking me to take a drink."

"You don't mean to say that you got Clennam to buy a paper—the fellow to our right?"

"But I did, though; and I sold over fifteen papers in his saloon."

"Well, you're the funniest boy I ever met.

There's not a newsboy in the city dares go into his saloon. They're afraid of him awfully."

"I was afraid, too," said Tom. "But when I saw him rushing at me, I just braced myself up to see what he'd do."

"Tom, I'd like to live with you all the time."

"Glad you like me, Arthur. Go on and order more oysters."

"Thank you, I've had enough."

"So've I. How are you on ice-cream?"

"Let me treat this time, Tom. There's a nice confectionery right around the corner."

In this realistic age one must be careful not to tell the whole truth, lest one be convicted of exaggeration. So I pass lightly over the astonishing feats of Tom and Arthur in the ice-cream parlor.

As Tom paid the bill he glanced at the clock over the counter. It wanted twenty-five minutes to twelve.

"Arthur, I forgot all about him. Oh, gracious!"

"Who?"

"My uncle. I left him across there in the theatre."

"Why, the theatre let out half an hour ago."

"Then, Arthur, I'll tell you a secret."

"What, Tom?" cried Arthur breathlessly, for

he was impressed with his companion's grave face.

"I'm lost."

"Don't you know where you live?"

"No; don't even know the name of the street. Uncle Meadow will be the maddest man in Cincinnati. The fact is, we were having such a jolly good time that I forgot all about him."

"Well, you're the queerest boy I ever met."

"I don't see anything queer about it. I'm lost, and you've got to take care of me. That's all."

Arthur laughed musically; looking upon him now one would hardly recognize the sad-eyed boy of the previous hour.

"It's so funny, Tom, to hear you talking of being taken care of by me."

"Where do you sleep nights?" continued Tom.

"I haven't any regular place since we gave up housekeeping."

"Halloa! who gave up housekeeping?"

"My little sister and I. Till she got sick, we had two little bits of rooms in 'Noah's Ark.'"

"Noah's Ark!" ejaculated Tom.

"That's what the St. Xavier College boys call it. It's a great big tenement-house right across the alley from the college; and in fact it does look something like an ark. Well, little Kate and I were there and happy as larks. She was just the best sister, and kept the rooms so bright and cheerful that I used to be so glad to come home after looking around all day for work! She could cook and sew like a grown person, although she's only nine."

"Who paid for you?" broke in Tom.

"Well, in the beginning we had a little over twelve dollars left by poor papa. But after two weeks we had hardly anything left. Then I had to go to selling papers and taking up all kinds of odd jobs. And in spite of all, I could hardly scrape up enough money to pay the rent. After a while we had hard times getting anything to eat. I didn't mind so much for myself, but poor little Kate kept on getting thinner and paler."

"Didn't you have any friends?"

"No, Tom. We were strangers in the city."

"Then Kate took sick, didn't she?"

"Yes, Tom; and a good woman who lived in the tenement got the Sisters to take care of her, and now she's quite well. But I don't know what to do. I'm not able to support myself; and I can't bear to think of seeing Kate starving right under my eyes."

They were standing under a lamp-post during this conversation and Tom could observe the signs of tears upon his little friend's face.

"Well," said Tom, choking down his own emotion, "we'll hold a council of war tonight before we go to sleep. Do you know any good hotel around here?"

"There's a place across the street, the European Hotel."

Tom glanced at the building disdainfully. "No; we want something first-class. We'll put up at the best hotel you know of."

"The Burnet House is about four squares away."

"That sounds better."

I think Tom succeeded in astonishing more people on that eventful night than, within the same period of time, any boy that ever came to Cincinnati.

On the register of the Burnet House he wrote in a large, bold hand:

"Thomas Playfair, travelling student," and he gravely added to Arthur's signature "merchant."

"We want a first-class room, and breakfast at seven," said Tom to the clerk, who had become unusually wide-awake.

"Four dollars in advance for the rooms, sir," said that functionary.

"I didn't say rooms. We're not accompanied by our families. Here's a dollar for one room."

"Two dollars, sir," said the clerk, now as thoroughly wide-awake as he had ever been in his life.

"There's the other dollar; you needn't mind about sending up shaving water in the morning."

The clerk laughed, and summoning a bell-boy, directed him to show the "gentlemen" number eight, second floor. Hotel clerks are men of large experience in certain directions; hence, notwithstanding the late hour, and the fact that the guests were boys without luggage, the aroused official was so taken with the honest little faces before him that he allowed them the privileges of the house without further investigation.

I am bound to say, though, that our two friends availed themselves of a privilege not ordinarily accorded to travellers.

No sooner had the bell boy left them in possession of their room than Tom picked up a pillow from the bed and proposed a game of "catch." Stationing themselves at opposite corners, the two tossed the pillow gently at first, till, growing interested in their work, they threw with not a little energy. As an agreeable variety, Tom got the other pillow, and before long they came to a genuine pillow-fight, hurling their downy missiles, and dodging about in a manner that sent the blood to their cheeks and caused their eyes to dance with excitement. The boy who has no heart for pillow-fighting is fit for treasons, stratagems, and spoils; let no such boy be trusted.

The contest waxed fiercer—that is, merrier—each moment. Finally, Tom, pillow in hand, charged upon Arthur. There was a rapid interchange of blows, much movement and noise of little feet, and a swaying from side to side of the room, till at length with a well-directed blow Tom sent his antagonist sprawling upon the bed.

It was then they noticed for the first time that someone was gently knocking at the door.

"Oh!" said Arthur, turning pale, "we're in for it now."

Tom threw the door open and found himself facing a mild-eyed old gentleman, who seemed to be far more frightened than Arthur.

"Good evening, sir. Won't you walk in?"

"I beg your pardon, young sir; but I thought there was a murder or something going on in this room. I live next door, and I was awakened a few minutes ago by a noise as of people struggling for life."

"It wasn't that bad, sir. There was a struggle; but it wasn't for life. My friend over there on the bed," added Tom, wickedly, "is very noisy."

The old gentleman now understood the situation, the light that shot from his eye and the smile that curled about his lips evinced that he too had been a boy in the golden long ago.

"Well, young sir, may I ask you as a favor not to make any more noise tonight? We old people can't afford to lose our sleep."

"Certainly, sir; honest, I didn't think about waking people up. I'll behave till morning, sir; goodnight."

"Good-night, young sir," answered the gentleman smiling benevolently, "and God bless you!"

"What a pity," said Tom as the door closed, "that he's grown up! He must have been a jolly boy."

"Yes, indeed," assented Arthur.

"It's the old story, Arthur; folks get spoiled once they grow up. They haven't right ideas about fun. Now, if that old gentleman had been a boy, he'd have come rushing in with his pillow."

"Yes," assented Arthur; "and if all the people in the hotel had been boys, they'd all have rushed in with their pillows."

"Just so; and we'd have had a gorgeous time. It's a mistake for people to live long. It seems to me if a boy's good, the best thing he can do is to die when he's sixteen or seventeen. Of course, if he's a sinner, it's right for him to live and take his punishment like a man."

"Where did you get that idea, Tom?"

"I don't know, but I've thought about it lots the last few days. You see, if a boy doesn't do anything real bad, he's bound to be pretty happy; then he dies and goes to Heaven, where there's just no end of fun, and gets saved hearing all that stuff about elections and stocks and bonds."

"Some boys have awful troubles, Tom."

"Well, the sooner they get to Heaven the better. Just the same, I'm not anxious to die yet. I want to make my First Communion. There were two friends of mine, Arthur, struck down dead; but it was on the First Friday and both were speaking about having gone to Communion that very day. *They're* all right. Come, let's say our prayers, and then when we get to bed I'll tell you all about it."

And before these two lads went to sleep, they had built in the intimacy of an hour a friendship which we older folk find to be the work of many years.

Chapter XVI

IN WHICH TOM ENTERS UPON A CAREER OF EXTRAVAGANCE

WHEN Arthur awoke next morning, he stared in no little surprise at Tom, who was standing before a mirror and surveying himself with evident complacency.

"Why, Tom!" he called out, "are you a real boy? or is the whole thing a dream?"

"Yes," answered Tom, with his customary modesty, "it's a sure thing that I'm a real boy. What are you staring at?"

"But you've got my clothes on."

"Yes; don't I look fine in them?"

"You'd look well in anything, Tom. But in the meantime, how am I to dress?"

"Take mine," came the sententious answer, as Tom turned his back to the mirror and craned his neck in a vain effort to see how he looked from that point of view.

"No, I won't, Tom; you've been too good to me already. I'll not take another thing from you."

"All right; if you don't put those clothes on, you'll have to stay in bed for a while. I'm going to leave in about ten minutes."

"I won't put them on."

"You've got to. See here, didn't you tell me last night that you'd take my advice?"

"Yes; but then you know—"

"Never mind the rest. My first advice is to put on those togs of mine. They're a pretty good suit; but I've another suit along with me that's just as good."

Tom, as usual, had his way, and waxed enthusiastic over his new friend's appearance.

"My! Arthur, but you look splendid. You see, you're rather skinny, and your own suit made it plain to everybody. Now you look like a young swell."

Indeed, Arthur's appearance had really improved. Even his face had changed for the better. The eyes shone with a joyous twinkle; the lines of misery and distress had softened; the refinement and delicacy of expression were now quite noticeable.

Two months upon the streets! Who would believe it of that gentle boy? Doubtless Arthur's guardian angel could have explained the mystery, and into that explanation would have largely entered the sweet prayers and tender sympathy and elevating influence of a dear little sister's love.

Tom did not *hear* any guardian angel say this, but it came home to him, all the same, as he gazed upon Arthur, who was blushing under his scrutiny.

"Arthur," he added aloud, "I want your sister to see you in good form. It will do her more good than all the quinine and paregoric in the world, when you walk in on her the way you are now. We'll get breakfast right away, and then you'll bring me down to the depot, so's I can find my way to uncle's, and we'll shake hands for a while. Then tomorrow you'll come and pay me a visit."

"That's a nice plan, Tom; but you must come and see my sister first."

"Me!" exclaimed Tom, shocked into the objective case. "Why it would spoil the whole plan. There'd be no fun at all, when she'd see me rigged out in your clothes."

"I'll tell her anyhow, even if you don't come; and I'll fetch her round to see you, too. It's my turn now to have my way. You've got to come."

"But I never talk to girls. I don't even know how it's done."

"Pshaw! that's nothing. You know she's almost a baby."

"I don't like babies," said Tom, growing

eloquent. "One baby looks just the same as another; and if you don't say a baby looks just like its pa, its mamma gets mad. Then babies don't do anything but scream and eat. They've no hair and no teeth and no sense. The only thing good about a baby is that it doesn't stay that way forever. It grows into something: but it's tiresome waiting."

"Kate has a full head of hair, a set of teeth, and lots of sense for her age. Now, Tom, I'll feel really miserable if you don't come."

Tom sighed.

"She's only nine?" he inquired.

"Just nine a few months ago."

"Well, I'll go, Arthur."

Then Arthur wrung his hand and so beamed over with joy that Tom became fully reconciled to what he considered the coming ordeal.

And an ordeal it promised to be from the very start. For when, an hour later, the two, having finished their breakfast, entered the hospital, and were walking along a vast corridor, a little girl with streaming hair and shining eyes came running toward them.

"O Arthur," she cried, dashing straight at Tom, who ducked very cleverly, and looked as sheepish as it was possible for him to look, while the girl checked herself and sprang back, blushing, and Arthur shook with suppressed laughter.

"I—eh—eh—it's the other fellow, I think," blurted Tom.

And the "other fellow" with great tact put an end to the awkwardness of the situation by catching little sister and saluting her in true brotherly fashion.

"And now, Katie," he said archly, "let me introduce you to the boy you were throwing yourself at. He's the best——"

"Oh, I say," broke in Tom, "you needn't begin that way; it's bad enough. I'm Tom Playfair and you're Kate Vane. How d'e do, Kate?" And Tom shook hands with some return of his ordinary coolness.

"O Mr. Playfair——"

"Tom," interpolated the young gentleman in patched attire.

"Tom," she went on, accepting the correction; "but I really thought you were brother Arthur."

"Oh, it's all right now," said Tom. "I'm not used to being taken for a brother. You see I never had any sisters; and that's why I got so nervous."

And then, despite our hero's protests, Arthur insisted upon describing at length the adventures of the preceding night. It was an awkward time for Tom. But, as he sat in the neatly-appointed room into which Kate had conducted them, he bore it with what meekness he could summon for the occasion.

The little child who faced him was very like Arthur, with a beautiful and refined face, but so pale and thin! Sickness had stolen the rosy hue of health, and left in its stead a pallor upon the delicate features; sickness had worn away the rounded cheeks till the face, lighted by large, beautiful eyes, was such as lofty-minded artists dream and ponder, but fail to reproduce as angel forms.

"Tom," said Kate, when Arthur had come to an end, "I dreamed last night that St. Joseph was going to help me and brother Arthur."

"She carries his statue in her pocket," whispered Arthur, "and prays to him often."

"I wish you'd pray to him, Kate, to get me out of trouble. I'm lost—and I think my uncle will make it pretty hot for me. He gets mad so easily!"

"My dream has come true, like in a fairy book. Do you like fairy stories? I do. And, Arthur, you look so well now. And I've got some good news, too."

"What?" cried Arthur.

"Guess."

"A situation for me."

"Guess again. It's a letter."

"Who from?"

"From a lady in Danesville."

"Danesville! That's where our uncle Archer used to live."

"You're getting hot, Arthur. What do you think it says?"

"Come on and tell me."

While brother and sister were speaking, Tom drew a railroad time-table from his pocket, and began running his eye over it.

"It says that Uncle Archer is the nicest man, and oh, such a lot of things. Here, read it, Arthur." And Kate produced a letter.

"Why," exclaimed Arthur, glancing at the superscription, "this is a letter to Sister Alexia."

"You didn't guess that. Yes; she wrote without saying anything to me; and, and—why don't you read it?"

"Listen, Tom; you know our story.

"DEAR SISTER ALEXIA:
"There *is* a Mr. Archer in Danesville—a Mr. F. W. Archer."

"There, now! He isn't in California," exclaimed Kate, her eyes dancing.

"He is in comfortable circumstances, and as good as he is wealthy. Everybody esteems him. He is now past middle age, has an excellent wife, but lost his two beautiful children, a boy of three and another of five, two years ago on a trip to California. His wife is a very sweet woman and very affectionate. They had intended on leaving for California to remain there; but the loss of their two children brought them back to Danesville. Their residence is 240 Lombard St."

"Why, Kate," exclaimed Arthur, "This *is* news. It's almost too good to be true. Danesville is in this State, and—and—"

"Didn't mamma say that her brother was the best of men?" broke in Kate. "And now we're going to see him soon."

"Kate, I'll tell you a secret. When papa was dying, he told me to take you to our uncle in Los Angeles. But after the funeral we didn't have enough money, and I thought it awful hard. But now it's best we didn't go. I never told you papa's order."

"Halloa!" said Tom. "Here we are. Danesville is on the road between here and St. Mary's—one hundred and twenty miles from Cincinnati."

"How many days will it take to get there?" asked Kate, eagerly.

"Days! You don't expect to go there by streetcar, do you? It won't take more than six hours, and there's a train starts at half-past eleven this morning."

"O Arthur!" And Kate clasped her hands and looked anxiously at her brother.

"The next question," pursued Tom, "is, how much have you two got?"

"I've fifteen cents and a quarter with a hole in it," answered Kate.

"And I," said her brother, "have eight-five cents."

"Well, I happen to be well-off just now, and I really didn't know what to do with my money. Now, little girl, you just go and pack up your clothes and dolls and things like that; and if you don't hurry up about it you'll miss the train."

"Tom," said Arthur, "how'll you find your way to your uncle?"

"Oh, there'll be no trouble about that. Once I get to the depot where I came in, I can easily find my way to the streetcar uncle took, and I know just where he got off."

"But, Tom, where'll I write to you, to tell you how everything turns out?"

"Send your letter to the Burnet House; afterward I'll send you my address."

In due time preparations for departure were completed. Tom took possession of Kate's valise—it was very light; witnessed an affecting parting scene between the nuns and the little girl; and before brother and sister could fairly realize what a change had come in their prospects, he had made arrangements for their tickets and seats in the parlor car, and given the colored porter directions concerning the little travellers which rather astonished that functionary.

Kate and Arthur cried on bidding their protector good-bye, and our generous friend experienced a dimness about the eyes himself, as he stood at the passenger entrance and waved his hand in farewell.

Tom and Arthur were not to meet again for several years. But their friendship defied separation. Two days later Tom received a letter from Arthur, enclosing twenty-five dollars, and giving a glowing account of the cordial reception accorded them by his uncle. With this letter came a note from Mr. Archer himself, containing such warm expressions of gratitude as made Tom blush at every line. The correspondence thus begun continued for years, until Tom and Arthur met—well that belongs to another story.

So it was that our hero left the depot light of pocket and light of heart. He had but one dollar left of the twenty-five given him by his father. He took it out and gazed at it.

"Well, I've had fifty dollars' worth of fun; and now I'll go and buy a dinner, and after that I'll go back to Uncle Meadow; and for the rest of my stay here I reckon I'll have to be poor and honest."

With a sigh, Tom entered an oyster parlor; and when he came forth he had five cents left for car fare.

Chapter XVII

IN WHICH THE PRODIGAL RETURNS

IT is nigh upon four of the afternoon. Mr. Meadow is pacing up and down the front apartment of his suite of rooms, taking huge strides, occasionally striking his clenched hands upon an unoffensive table bordering the line of his route, and ever and anon stopping to glance savagely out of the window. Mr. Meadow mutters now and then, between his clenched teeth, words which are mostly profanity and severe criticisms of his lost nephew. In short, Mr. Meadow is very angry.

"I'll cowhide the wretched little brat within an inch of his life if I ever get my hands on him." This remark, with the adjectives a

trifle stronger than here set down, issued
from his lips as the last stroke of four came
ringing through the air from a neighboring
church, and Mr. Meadow made his periodi-
cal pause at the window front.

This time he gave a sudden gasp, his eyes
bulged from his head, as far as the economy
of his bodily frame would allow, and he *did*
stare.

He recovered himself by a strong effort,
made a remark which shall not be repeated,
then dashed down the stairway, threw the
front door open with vicious and unneces-
sary violence, and——

Could that be Tom? The figure walking up
the front steps look more like a young beggar, and a very disreputable young beggar
at that. Arthur Vane in his proper costume
looked like a gentleman in comparison with
Tom's present appearance. Arthur's hat on
Arthur's head had at least been in shape—
on Tom's it was crushed as though it had
been used as a substitute for a football. On
Arthur the clothes, though patched, had been
neat; on Tom they were splashed with mud,
while one patch on the knee was torn, and
a deep rent under the armpit revealed what
kind of a shirt Tom was wearing. But the
wretchedness of his appearance did not end

with his garb. His face was swollen and dis-
colored; and his upper lip was puffed out to
a ridiculous degree. Mr. Meadow had seen
Tom in many a sad plight, but the limit was
reached on this occasion.

"You brat! you vulgar little beggar," roared
the uncle, with an extra adjective, "come
right in, and I'll lash you with a cowhide."

Tom paused halfway up the steps, and
tried to smile. It was an *awful* failure. Probably he was willing enough to smile, but his
upper lip, the most important part of his
smiling apparatus, refused to do its duty:
and so instead of smiling he succeeded in
distorting his face still more.

"Thanks, uncle," he made answer. "But I
guess I'll not come in. I've been walloped
enough."

"Have you been fighting, you vulgar little
guttersnipe?" continued the enraged uncle.

"Yes, uncle," answered the "vulgar little
guttersnipe," backing down a few steps in
preparation to take to his heels should need
arise, "but I couldn't help it, honest."

"Who whipped?"

Mr. Meadow was a sporting man; his weakness asserted itself, and Tom was quick to
see his chance.

"See here, uncle, if you promise not to

touch me, I'll tell you all about it."

"You young beggar, what did you do with your own clothes?"

"Promise not to whip me, uncle, and I'll tell you all about it."

"Were you robbed?"

"No; but all my money's gone, seventeen dollars and a half."

"Were you robbed?"

"Promise not to whip me, uncle, and I'll tell you all about it. It's as good as a story."

Mr. Meadow took a step forward; Tom as quickly moved down to the foot of the steps.

"Stay where you are, uncle, or I'll run."

"Where did you go last night?" continued Mr. Meadow, less savagely, for the humor of the situation was making its impression even upon him.

"Promise not to whip me," answered Tom, firmly.

"I'll see about that after I've heard your story."

"Honest, uncle?"

"Yes, honest."

"You won't whip me till I tell my story?"

"I promise."

"Cross your heart, uncle?"

"Confound you!—yes."

"All right, then." And Tom ran up the steps

with his usual spryness.

"Now, uncle, let me wash first; I feel awful sticky."

Mr. Meadow deigned to supply the young gentleman with a basin of water. Tom threw off his coat, rolled back his shirt sleeves, and kept up a severe process of bathing for fifteen minutes without saying a single word.

"Well," snapped his uncle, impatiently, "who won the fight?"

"Oh, I've got to change my clothes yet. These things are spoiled from Cincinnati mud. Wherever there was a puddle, I was sure to step right into it. You see, uncle, I was chased."

"Who chased you?"

"Two dogs and—oh, wait till I change."

Mr. Meadow had to content himself for the next five minutes with grinding out remarks between his teeth, which, through a sense of decency, he did not wish to find way to Tom's ears.

At length Tom was apparently ready for his recital. With the exception of his face, he looked like the boy of yesterday and the day before.

"Well, now, let's hear your story."

Tom took a sponge from his valise, wet it and put it to his lip.

"Ah!" he sighed in relief; "that's just the thing."

"Did you hear me, sir?"

"Oh, I beg your pardon. You want the story?"

"That's what I said."

"And you remember your promise, uncle?"

"Yes, you brat!"

"You needn't call names. Well, uncle, I'm not going to tell you my story; then you can't whip me." And he removed his sponge and smiled hideously.

Mr. Meadow bounded from his chair; Tom made for the door.

"Will you keep your promise?" he asked with his hand on the knob.

"Yes; come in; I'll not touch you. Go ahead with your story: I promise not to whip you in any case."

"Ah! that's a bargain. You know, uncle, papa doesn't want you to whip me; so I thought it was fair to get ahead of you. Well, last night——" and Tom then narrated his adventures up to the moment of his leaving the oyster-house with five cents for car fare.

"And then, uncle," he continued, "I thought how I could best please you."

"What exquisite consideration," growled the auditor.

"Wasn't it, uncle? I knew you wouldn't like me to come back without a cent in my pocket; and besides I was afraid you might call me a lot of names, and lose your temper—and you did, uncle. You swore dreadfully, and you said——"

"Go on with your story," growled the affectionate young man. "Tell me about the fight."

"I'm coming to it, sir. Well, then, I started to walk home along the street where those cars ran that we took yesterday. You see, uncle, I'd made up my mind to save that nickel."

"You've wonderful ideas of economy," snarled Mr. Meadow, in parentheses.

"Well, when I'd walked about two squares I came to an alley. It was an awful rough-looking place, uncle. There were three fellows leaning against a house on the alley corner when I came along; and before I knew where I was, they'd got on the outside of me, and shut me into that alley. I never saw three rougher-looking boys since I gave up going to fires."

"And did you knock 'em all down?"

"Huh!! The wonder is they didn't knock me down first thing. The middle fellow seemed to be the ringleader. He was the smallest, about my size. He had two teeth that stuck out so's you could count 'em without trying. They were his higher teeth."

"Upper, you barbarian," corrected Mr. Meadow.

"Exactly. They were large teeth; larger than yours, uncle, I really do——"

"Go on, will you?"

"Why don't you give me a chance? This isn't a grammar class. Well, the fellow with the big teeth said, 'Say, gimme chaw terbacker.'"

"And did you hit him?"

Tom looked at his uncle reproachfully.

"Do you think I'm a fool? I said that I couldn't speak French, and the other two giggled. Then he looked so that I could count *five* teeth, and said in an awful savage way— just the way you were talking to me a minute ago, when——"

"What *did* he say?" burst in the excited listener.

"He said 'Gimme chaw terbacker.' And then he used some words something like what you——"

"Go on—what did you do?"

"I said, 'I don't talk German either,' and then before I could guess what he was up to he gave me an awful whack on the lip, and he struck out again. I dodged the second blow, and I got so excited that like a fool I struck back with all my might, and he went sprawling. I struck him on the mouth, uncle, and when he got up he was spitting and coughing, and I could only count one tooth."

"And what did you do then?"

"I couldn't do anything, uncle. The other two grabbed me tight, and while the fellow who used to have a loose tooth was choking and hopping round, and swearing whenever he could get his breath, the other two went through my pockets and got the silk handkerchief Aunt Meadow sent me on my birthday, a small magnet, a pocketknife, a lot of string, a broken jew's-harp, and my last nickel."

"And didn't you make any resistance?"

"I squirmed and wriggled round, and when they'd emptied all my pockets, I ran as fast as I could till I turned the corner. And then I began to feel awful bad about that nickel. It was real hard to have to come home without it, so I turned back quietly, and walked into a drugstore on the opposite side of the street. I sneaked in while they weren't looking that way. The drugstore had a big window looking out so's you could see into that alley for a whole block. I told the drugstore man that I felt sick, and that I'd like to sit down in his store for a while. He laughed when he looked at me, and said, 'All right.' Then I pulled a chair over to the window, and watched those three fellows for over fifteen minutes. They were fussing just awfully about the handkerchief. The fellow with the tooth didn't get that. Then they had a row about the knife, and the fellow with the tooth came near having it knocked out and *he* didn't get the knife anyhow. They gave him the string and the jew's-harp; and then they had an awful row about the nickel. They tossed it up and yelled 'Heads' and 'Tails,' and shouted, and I don't know what all, till somehow or other the fellow with the tooth got that. You ought to have seen him. He jumped into the air and knocked his heels together three times, and started out of the alley, just as proud as though he were a millionaire."

"And what did you do?"

"I followed after him quietly; and when he'd got off about a square from the alley on a big crowded street, I caught up with him, and touched him on the shoulder. He gave a little jump, but he didn't knock his heels together this time. 'See here,' I said, 'give me back my nickel or I'll yell for a policeman.' He put on a savage look, and said, 'Don't yer fool wid me, or I'll fetch yer one on de ear,' and I said, 'If you do, I'll loosen your other tooth, and yell for the policeman too. Now hand over, or I'll shout.' He looked around, and sure enough there was a policeman turning the corner. He got pale, and handed over that nickel."

"That wasn't bad," commented Mr. Meadow, forgetting his resolution to be stern and uncompromising with the young scapegrace. "Then, of course, you started to find your way back."

"No, uncle; I began to think how bad Aunt Meadow would feel when she learned what had become of her pretty Christmas present, and how bad you'd feel about that old knife which you gave me the time you bought a new one."

"Don't be sentimental," growled Mr. Meadow, in disgust.

Tom stared.

"So I thought I'd go back, and see what were my chances for the old knife and the pretty handkerchief. When I got there, it all seemed to be arranged just the way I wanted it. The two fellows were squatting down on a board about twenty feet in the alley, playing at mumble-peg with my knife; and the fellow who was farthest had my nice handkerchief flying round his neck. They were bigger than I; but I saw a good chance. I didn't stop to stare, but came running up softly while both had their heads down watching their game, and grabbed that handkerchief, and kept running right on through the alley without stopping to say anything."

"Good!" said Mr. Meadow, unable to contain his enthusiasm. "Go on."

"Well, they gave a yell, and before I'd got halfway down the alley there was a rushing out of people from back gates, and two dogs came flying at my legs, and a billy-goat got right in my way and would have broken my neck if I hadn't jumped over him, and the dogs barked and snapped, and the boys kept yelling, and the people kept crowding out, and just as I got to the corner of the alley, a lot of stones and things came sailing after me, and a pebble or something hit me on the leg, and then I went into an awful puddle, and came plump against a boy with red hair, and sent him sprawling."

Here Tom lost his breath.

"I don't know how I ever got out of that alley alive. The last thing I did was to kick a bull-pup in the ribs; he howled like he was crazy, and then I was halfway up the street. I looked round then, and found that they weren't chasing me. Then I got off some of the mud and started for home. And now, uncle, I'm sorry and awful hungry."

And Tom looked at Mr. Meadow pathetically.

"Hand over that nickel, young man." For the first time since his return, the prodigal lost countenance.

"I haven't got it, uncle."

"Oh, you spent that, too."

"No, sir, I—er—I gave it away."

Tom had become very nervous and awkward.

"Whom did you give it to?"

No answer.

"Did you hear me?"

"To a poor fellow I met. Come, uncle, and get me something to eat."

Tom did not reveal the whole story; there was some modesty in his composition.

When the "boy with the tooth" had surrendered the nickel to its proper owner, Tom had noticed the sullen face of the poor wretch lengthen in disappointment. In a flash the words recorded in the sole entry in his diary, "Vinegar never catches flies," recurred to him. He ran up to the boy, who, with his shoulders raised and his head depressed, was creeping away, and touched him lightly again.

"Keep off," cried the fellow, with a snarl:

"you and me's quits."

"No, we're not," said Tom. "Old fellow, you need this nickel more than I do," and he pressed it into the lad's hand. "It's all I've got with me; but I wish it was more, and I'm sorry about that tooth of yours."

As Tom turned away, he left the poor little wretch gasping, mouth and eyes wide open, and the little brain within pondering over the only sermon that had ever came home to it.

Tom walked on, light of heart and happy.

"It can't do him any harm," he reflected, "and maybe it'll do him good."

Then someone touched his shoulder.

"Say," exclaimed the toothless one, almost out of breath, for he had had some trouble in picking Tom out of the crowd, "say, Johnny, I'll never act dat way again—never. Do ye catch on?"

It was in order for Tom to improve the occasion by saying something pious and edifying. But Tom didn't follow the traditions of the book. He merely grinned, gave his penitent a hearty hand-squeeze, and said not one word.

This part of the story, as I said, he concealed from Mr. Meadow. But that gentleman inferred something of it, and was so pleased with his inference that he gave Tom but a quarter of an hour's scolding which he salved with a twenty-five-cent piece and a good dinner.

Chapter XVIII

*IN WHICH TOM ASTONISHES AND
HORRIFIES HIS AUNT*

IT is ten of the night. Tom has just arisen from his knees, and seems to find some difficulty in divesting himself of his sailor shirt. He is gazing very hard at Mr. Meadow through a sort of lattice-work formed by the bosom of his shirt, which is now concealing his little head. In this dramatic attitude he stands till Mr. Meadow gets into bed. Then Tom with a jerk brings the shirt back to its normal position on his shoulders, and says:

"Uncle, you've forgot something."

"What?"

"Why you forgot to kneel down before going to bed. You didn't used to do that when we lived in St. Louis. Hop out and kneel down."

"Mind your business, young man."

In answer to which Tom sat down on a chair and began to whistle softly.

"Stop that noise and come to bed."

Tom ceased his whistling, arose, walked over to the sofa, and, throwing an overcoat about himself, lay back with his eyes fixed upon Mr. Meadow's astonished face.

Then there was a long pause, during which the recumbent uncle and nephew looked at each other steadily.

"What are you staring at?" growled Mr. Meadow, raising his head and leaning upon his elbow.

"I'm taking in your night-cap, uncle. It makes you look so funny."

"Get off that sofa and come to bed."

"Not in that bed."

"Why not?"

"You didn't say your prayers. Suppose the Devil were to come round tonight: he might get things mixed up, and take me for you. Then there'd be a pretty how-de-do."

Tom was not entirely in earnest, but he spoke with funereal gravity.

"If you don't come to bed, sir, I'll report you to your father."

Tom sighed. Mr. Meadow had hit upon the best means of subduing him. He arose form the sofa, slowly undressed, then going to his valise took out a bottle containing holy water, which he proceeded to sprinkle over the bed, incidentally dousing the astonished countenance of his uncle.

Then with another sigh he retired. He intended to sigh for a third time once he had composed himself for slumber, but he fell asleep before the time came for carrying out this pious intention.

Tom was unusually docile on this occasion. But Mr. Meadow's threat was not an idle one. That very day a telegram had reached them, announcing the coming on the morrow of Mr. Playfair and Aunt Meadow. The one person in the world whom Tom feared was his father; and he still remembered, vividly too, their painful encounter, touched upon, or rather glossed over, in Chapter II.

Next morning, accordingly, Mr. Playfair and Miss Meadow arrived.

Mr. Playfair unbent so far as to give his little boy a paternal kiss; but his aunt's greeting was so warm as to disarrange her toilet very considerably. Then holding her darling nephew at arm's length, she anxiously scanned his features.

"Tommy, dear," she exclaimed at length, "you must have received an awful shock."

"No, I didn't, aunt, it was just nothing at all. I fell down all of a heap, and picked myself up as good as new."

Tom made light of the matter; he knew his aunt from of old, and he had no intention of being plied with family medicines for a week.

"Roll down your stocking, Tommy, I must see where you've been burnt."

"Do you take me for a tattooed man?" exclaimed the young gentleman indignantly.

"Pull down your stocking," said Mr. Playfair.

And when Tom with commendable promptness exhibited the red mark, as of a branding-iron, upon his calf, Miss Meadow pulled out her handkerchief and began to cry. Poor, gentle lady!

"Oh, I say, Aunt Jane, don't," exclaimed Tom, earnestly. He was a warm-hearted little fellow, and under a boyish mask of levity concealed the great love he bore his aunt.

In answer to this remonstrance, she threw her arms about him again, and renewed the kissing and hugging till he blushed as a red, red rose.

"Why doesn't somebody take notice of me that way?" queried Mr. Meadow, who felt that he was being ignored.

"I think I'll pull up my stocking," said Tom, now really embarrassed. "There's no use in making such a fuss about it. People that cook get burnt a lot worse, and don't say a word."

"Tommy, dear," resumed Miss Meadow, who, having had her cry out, was now, after the manner of her sex, thoroughly renewed, "you're not quite well yet; you've lost color."

"Gracious!" exclaimed Tom, turning his face to a looking-glass. "Aunt calls me pale, when my face looks for all the world like— like—"

"A ham, or better still, an Indian in his war paint," interpolated the agreeable young man of the party.

"George Playfair," Miss Meadow went on, after bestowing a withering glance upon her only brother, "just look at your boy."

"I have been looking at him these last five minutes, Jane."

"Can't you see that he's badly shaken?"

"He was pretty badly shaken when you got hold of him. But if you mean to say he's sick, I must give it as my opinion that he never looked better in his life."

"Men have no feelings," exclaimed Miss Meadow with unusual bitterness.

"They can see through a millstone, though, when there's a good-sized hole in it," said Mr. Meadow, grinning at his own wit.

"Now, Tommy, tell us all about that dreadful night. By the way, Charles," she continued, addressing Mr. Meadow, "are there any lightning-rods on this house?"

"Two."

"Is that all?"

"I should think that's enough."

"You can't have too many," continued Miss Meadow.

"We might attach a lightning-rod to Tom," suggested Mr. Playfair dryly. "He'd present an interesting spectacle, going round with a lightning-rod sticking out of his hat."

"George Playfair," exclaimed Miss Meadow, arising from her chair, "if you had any heart in you, you wouldn't go jesting on that subject, after such a terrific visitation!"

"Oh! if you wish, my dear, we'll have both lightning-rods removed from this house."

Miss Meadow gave him a look—such a look!—then turned to Tom, and, with many a question, succeeded in extracting from her tortured nephew some account of the calamity.

"Wasn't he brave! she exclaimed, when he had detailed his experiences in crossing the creek. "He might have been drowned." And Miss Meadow caught Tom to her arms again.

"If the boy had had any sense at all," said the practical father, "he'd have felt around for that bridge to begin with, instead of risking his life."

"Yes, Tom," added the genial uncle, "you

were a fool. By the way, that swimming adventure of yours reminds me of—"

Mr. Meadow was about to relate how he had once saved a drowning companion by reaching him a long pole from the bank, when he was interrupted by Tom's extraordinary gesticulations. For Tom had at once raised both hands in air, and set his fingers wriggling in a way that was little short of dazzling.

"What's the matter?" exclaimed the narrator.

"Ten times," answered Tom. "You've told us that story ten times in the last ten months. Give us something new."

Tom intended to be facetious, but his impertinence offended his uncle, who forthwith proceeded to narrate Tom's adventures in Cincinnati.

During the recital Mr. Playfair's brow clouded.

"I don't like it," he observed at the end.

"Don't like what?" cried the aunt. "Indeed, sir, you don't know what a treasure you've got. Few boys would give all their money and their best suit of clothes in charity."

"Yes, and few boys who are supposed to be gentlemen would stay out all night, and run into saloons to sell papers."

"I forgot, Pa."

"And," continued the stern father, whose very love for his son made him a severe judge, "it's very charitable to give away clothes and money, but whose were they?"

"You gave me the money, Pa; and, besides, I only loaned it."

"And then," Mr. Playfair was resuming, but Miss Meadow came to the rescue.

"Now, George, the idea of scolding your heroic little boy after a separation of three months! You know you'd have been sorry if Tom had acted any way else."

"No, I wouldn't, Jane. Tom should have gone back to his uncle in the theatre—"

"It wasn't much of a theatre, anyhow," put in Tom, getting in return a savage scowl from his uncle.

"And Charles would have taken care of the boy without all this paper-selling and staying out all night."

"Well, Pa, I meant to do right."

"What's that place they say is paved with good intentions?" asked Mr. Meadow.

"I'm sure you meant right, Tom, but you must be careful. Remember you're getting ready for your First Communion."

Mr. Playfair, it may be remarked, was somewhat Jansenistic in his ideas. All during

Mr. Meadow's account of Tom, he had been deliberating whether the boy were of a fit age and disposition for receiving the Blessed Sacrament. He loved his boy, but did not understand him.

"By the way, Jane," he said, turning to Miss Meadow, "if you wish to see your former schoolmate before dinner, we'd better start at once. Of course you'll come with us, Tom."

"Hurrah!" cried Tom, regaining his spirits.

But at this point Miss Meadow failed him.

"Mr. Playfair!" she exclaimed dramatically, "will you please look out that window?"

"I'm tired looking out that window, Jane."

"And do you mean to say that you are willing to expose your son's precious life in the face of a blinding snowstorm?"

Miss Meadow was carried into exaggeration by her anxiety for Tom's welfare. It was snowing quite briskly, but by no means in such a way as to merit her strong epithet.

"Pshaw!" cried Tom. "I ain't a girl."

"I don't see any particular risk," said the father.

"In his present debilitated state," continued Aunt Jane firmly, "it would be absolute suicide to let that boy put his foot beyond the threshold."

"Do you take me for a wax doll?" growled Tom.

But, despite all protests, Miss Meadow had her will.

Presenting her nephew with a box of candy and the "History of Sandford and Merton," and cautioning him to avoid all draughts and keep his feet warm, the good little lady departed with Mr. Playfair and her amiable brother, leaving behind her a very discontented young man indeed.

Tom spent fully half an hour munching candy and reading the initial chapters of the story; then he closed the book with a snap.

"Those English boys must be queer fellows, if they go round preaching sermons the way that Sandford does.* I'm glad he doesn't go to St. Maure's; he makes me tired."

That was the last of Sandford and Merton for Tom. He presented the precious volume, before leaving Cincinnati, to the house cook.

The ensuing hour passed very slowly. He gave most of the time to gazing ruefully out of the window, with his nose flattened against the pane. The snow continued to fall, and

---

*Tom did the English boys injustice. Master Sandford, I am told, exists in fiction, not in England.

the street below had become carpeted in white. Tiring even of this, he at length took to standing on his head and turning somersaults; and he was thus putting himself into a happier frame of mind, when there came a ring at the door.

Thinking that it was his father and aunt, he hastened to admit them himself; but instead of finding his relations standing without, he opened the door upon a very small boy, with a very weazen face and a very large snow shovel.

"Halloa!" said Tom.

"Would you like to have the snow shoveled off your pavement, sir?"

"It isn't my pavement; and, besides, I'm not the lady of the house," explained Tom. "But, if you like, I'll go and ask her."

"Thank you, sir," said the very small boy.

Tom returned presently, with the news that the lady of the house would put her hired man at it, later on.

"Thank you, sir," and the little boy touched his cap and sniffled.

Tom was touched.

"I say, little chap, won't you take some candy?"

"Thank you, sir." The small boy received the handful of caramels with a smile.

"How much do you charge for shoveling snow?" pursued Tom.

"Twenty-five cents is the regular charge, I think, sir."

"What's your charge?"

"I don't know, exactly. I never tried before."

"How does fifty cents suit you?" continued Tom, spreading his feet and with his arms akimbo.

"That's too much."

"Not for you, though. You're not used to the work, and it'll take you twice as long to do it as a fellow who is used to it. That's why I'll pay you twice as much."

This was Tom's first expression of opinion in political economy.

The very small boy was presently working away with a will, while his smiling employer, standing in the doorway, looked on with undisguised interest.

"Where's your gloves?" asked Tom, after a silence of at least five minutes.

"I ain't got any, sir."

"Here," cried the employer, returning from the hat-rack with his own, "come up here and put these on."

"Please, sir, I don't want them, thank you."

He was a modest boy, this weazen-face.

"Who asked you whether you wanted them

or not? You're in my employment now, and
you've got to do what you're told. Hop up
here and put 'em on. What's your name?"
continued Capital, as he handed Labor the
gloves.

"Fred Williams, sir."

"Call me Tom, or I'll discharge you. I like
your name. I knew a fellow named Fred once,
and he wasn't a bad sort of a chap, though
he was an awful blower."

Fred smiled in an ancient way and,
descending the steps, resumed his work. One
moment later, a snowball took him on the
back of the head. He turned his face to the
door, but Tom, who was grinning behind it,
was out of sight.

"I did it," said the honest but undignified
employer, after a judicious interval, as he
came running down the steps. "Say, you're
tired, aren't you?"

"No, sir."

"Yes, you are; let me catch hold of that
shovel. I'll bet I can manage it better than
you."

Aghast, the employee yielded, and Tom put
himself to shoveling till his back ached. He
had completely forgotten Aunt Meadow's
injunctions.

"There!" he exclaimed, throwing a last shovelful into the gutter, "now that's done for. Here's your fifty cents, Fred."

"Thank you, sir," said Fred simply. "It's for mamma."

"Take some more candy," said Tom.

"No, thank you. Good-bye, sir."

"Hold on; let's have some fun."

Fred grinned.

"Just stand at that corner," continued Tom, "and we'll peg at each other. You ought to get a chance at me, because I hit you when you weren't looking, you know."

"I'd like to, but mamma's sick and I want to help her."

"If I had any more money," said Tom, "I'd get you to clean off some more sidewalks; but I'm dead broke."

The little boy was about to speak, when a sound not unlike a scream startled the two lads.

"Why, Tommy," continued Miss Meadow, turning the corner with her brother-in-law, "you'll catch your death of cold. Go into the house this very instant. Aren't your stockings wet?"

"Of course they are; I've been shoveling snow. Say, aunt," he added in a low tone, as he brought his mouth to her ear, "this little chap's got a sick mother. Give him a dollar and I'll do anything you like."

"You will? Then I'll give him two."

Tom's promise cost him a hot mustard bath, but he bore it bravely for sweet charity's sake.

After supper, our hero actually did become ill.

He felt an uneasy feeling somewhere within, and didn't know what to make of it. Like the young Spartan with the fox gnawing at his vitals, he tried to bear his misery with unchanged demeanor. Poor boy! a week's feasting following hard upon a week's fasting had been too much for him.

Miss Meadow, who had been watching him all day with the eye of a detective, noticed a change in his color. There was no imagination this time.

"Tommy, tell me the truth," she said, "you *are* sick."

"It's here, aunt," said Tom, laying his hand pathetically upon his stomach.

Whereupon Miss Meadow put him to bed, placed a mustard plaster upon the place indicated, and, seating herself beside her boy, held a watch before her to time his misery. In ten minutes he began wriggling.

"You've got to bear it, Tommy dear."

"I prefer the belly-ache," growled the impatient invalid. He attempted to move his aunt by groans, but she was obdurate. Then he begged for a glass of water, determined, once his aunt had left the room, to fling the wretched plaster out of the window. But Miss Meadow, with her eyes watching his every motion, backed over to the door and called out for water.

"I think, aunt, you'd better take that rag off," implored Tom, when the watch had gone seventeen minutes. "I'm perfectly well, honest; and that thing's burning awfully."

But Miss Meadow mounted guard till twenty-five minutes had elapsed.

He was cured. His aunt, bent on making assurance doubly sure, now produced a box of pills; however, when he protested, almost with tears in his eyes, that he never felt better in his life, Miss Meadow gave in.

When she returned to the room rather suddenly, a few minutes later, she was horrified to find the darling boy dancing about the room, apparently in an ecstasy of joy.

"Tommy! you reckless boy! What are you doing now?"

"I was celebrating," he answered, somewhat discomfited at being discovered, and highly astonished at seeing that his aunt had a coil of rope in her hands.

"Celebrating what?"

"That old mustard plaster. I feel so good that it's off. But I say, aunt, you're not going to tie me down, are you?"

"No, Tommy; but get into bed, and I'll tell you all about it."

Curiosity gave Tom's obedience a generous amount of promptness.

Then Miss Meadow gravely tied one end of the rope to the bureau.

"It's a heavy bureau, Tom; and it will stand the strain."

The astonished lad began to fear that his aunt was losing her mind.

"What strain?"

"Tommy, pay attention to me; if the house catches fire, or gets struck by lightning, drop this rope out the window and climb down. You're good at climbing, you know."

"Do you really think, aunt, that the lightning is chasing me round the world?"

"We don't know what may happen," said the little woman. "There are storms and fires all over the country. Now, good night, dear!" and she kissed the unromantic youth.

Miss Meadow had not been gone five minutes, when she remembered that Tom's water-pitcher needed replenishing. She hastened back, and, as she entered his room, gave a gasp. He was not there.

"Tommy!" she called.

"Yes'm."

The voice was from without. Ah! she saw it all now, as with a suppressed scream she hurried over to the open window, following the course of the rope.

Tom was halfway down.

"You wretch—God forgive me!—my dear Tommy, what on earth are you doing?"

"Testing your fire-escape, aunt. It's immense!" He delivered this opinion as he touched foot in the yard. No sooner had he relinquished his hold on the rope than Miss Meadow hauled it up into the window with feverish haste.

"I say," he protested, "how'll I get back?"

"I'll open the door for you, Tommy."

"But you've spoiled all my fun; it would be jolly climbing up again."

Master Tom, nevertheless, re-entered by the side door; and slept without a fire-escape that night.

Chapter XIX

*IN WHICH TOM AND KEENAN
HOLD A COUNCIL OF WAR*

"HEY! you fellows over there; you needn't try to dodge work; come on, now, and haul snow. Harry, for goodness' sake, go and show Conway how to roll that snowball of his here. If he goes on that way he won't have it here in time for next Christmas. I say, John Donnel, stir up John Pitch, won't you? There he is fooling around in a puddle of water with his old rubber boots, when he ought to be hard at work."

Such were the quick and various remarks that came from the mouth of Tom Playfair, some few days after his return from St. Louis, whither he had gone with father and aunt to spend his Christmas holidays.

The events of the November night had made Tom extremely popular among his playfellows. All boys are at bottom generous hearted. Selfishness is the crust of years; and the countless mean acts of certain boys are in nine cases out of ten the result of thoughtlessness, and in the tenth case, the fruit of false ideals and defective training. So, in the general chorus of praise for Tom, there was not a single dissenting voice.

For some days past there had been talk in the small yard of building a snow fort, and of inviting the boys of the large yard to attempt its capture. Various details had been discussed, until finally, with the rejection of some and the acceptance of others, it was resolved to carry the matter into effect.

"Who'll be captain?" queried Conway.

"Keenan!" suggested Pitch. "He was captain last year."

"Not this time," said George Keenan. "One turn is good enough for me. I like to play second fiddle now and then. It seems to me that our captain for this year ought to be Tom Playfair."

"Playfair! Playfair!" was re-echoed on all sides, and with the least little touch of a blush on the part of Tom, and wondrous unanimity on the part of his playfellows, our hero was installed as captain of the small boys' snow fort.

With his usual energy, Tom set about constructing the ramparts of snow; his orders went flying right and left. He was an active superintendent; he inspected everything personally; and in doubtful points consulted the experience of Donnel and Keenan.

"I say, John," he said, addressing Donnel,

when matters were well underway, "how long did you fellows hold the fort against the big boys last year?"

"About eleven or twelve minutes. They stole a march on us last year. Before dinner, we had got over five hundred snowballs ready. While we were in eating, some of the big boys stole them. That took all the spirit out of our fellows. By the way, we ought to get even with them for that trick. I'm going to try to think out some scheme. Yes, Tom; last year they put us to rout in eleven minutes."

"Pshaw! That won't go. We're not going to allow them to clean us out in that style this year."

"Aren't you, now? I don't know about that," put in Keenan. "Some of those big chaps are just awful at throwing a snowball. Once Carmody pegged a snowball that took me square on the nose. It came in so hard, that I thought at first that my nose was driven through my head, and would come sticking out on the other side."

"Yes," chimed in John, "and once last winter when Ryan hit me in the eye, I saw so many moons that I thought I was a lunatic."

This excellent classical pun—excellent because so extremely bad—was lost upon Tom. It was lost upon George, too, who at that moment was seemingly absorbed in thought.

"Tom," he said suddenly, "I've an idea. Come over by the playroom; I think you're just the boy that can carry it out."

There was inspiration in George's face.

The two walked away together, and held a long, animated, but whispered consultation. Presently they returned to John's side.

"Now, the question is," began Tom, "to find out who are the best throwers in the big yard."

"Let's see," said Keenan. "There's Ryan and Carmody and McNeff and McCoy (he uses ice balls, too; he's a mean fellow) and Drew and Will Cleary and Ziegler. That's all I can remember." As George enumerated each name he checked it off on his fingers and blinked his eyes.

"You left out two of the best," put in John Donnel—"Miller and Arthur."

"Just nine," said Tom, as he walked away.

Donnel perceived that something was on foot; his curiosity was aroused.

"Say, George, what scheme are you and Tom hatching?"

"We're going to steal all the snow in the big yard, so's to deprive the big fellows of ammunition," was George's grave reply.

"Oh, come on! what's the idea?"

"We're going to make a bonfire in the fort, so's to keep the boys warm and prevent the snow from freezing too hard."

John aimed a blow at George, which would have taken that young wag in the ribs, had he not ducked promptly. With a growl on the part of John, and a laugh on the part of George, the conference ended.

Meantime, the work went on with ever-increasing energy; so that, as the sweet notes of the Angelus bell announced the hour of noon, and the boys with bared heads paused from their work to renew the angelic salutation—one of the sweetest memorial customs of St. Maure's—they bowed their faces and breathed their words in the presence of a fort graceful in its way, and strong as boyish skill could make it.

It had been arranged that the storming of the fort should begin precisely at one o'clock. Contrary to the general custom on holidays, there was much talking and little eating at dinner; and even the advent of the favorite pie aroused but little enthusiasm.

Truth compels me to say that not a few of the boys shortened their customary after-dinner visit to the Blessed Sacrament on this occasion—we are dealing with boys, not with angels.

While twenty or thirty of the stronger lads busied themselves in inspecting and strengthening the fortification, the others gave themselves to the manufacturing and storing away of snowballs.

These they placed within the entrenchments, which, I forgot to mention, were situated in the angle formed by a wing and a portion of the main body of the "old church building."

Precisely at fifteen minutes to one o'clock, Tom, assuming an air of coolness which belied his real feelings, presented himself to the second prefect of the large yard.

"Mr. Beakey," he said, politely raising his cap, "could you please tell me who is the captain of the big boys?"

"Captain!" repeated Mr. Beakey, banteringly. "They don't need a captain to rout out you little fellows."

"Maybe they *think* they don't, Mr. Beakey; but I hope they'll change their minds. Well, if there isn't any captain, couldn't I please have a talk with some of the leaders?"

"Certainly—not the least objection," answered the prefect, in an encouraging tone; for he perceived that Tom was strangely timid and embarrassed.

"And eh—eh, Mr. Beakey," continued Tom,

blushing and hanging his head, "could I please have the key of your classroom, so's we can go up there and fix our plans? It won't take more than two minutes."

The prefect handed Tom the required key. "Oh, thank you, Mr. Beakey! and please, sir, will you ring the bell for the assault to begin as soon as I come down?"

"Yes; anything else on your mind?"

"Yes, sir; just one thing more. I want to see Carmody, Ryan, McNeff, McCoy, Drew, Will Cleary, Ziegler, Arthur, and Miller."

"Are those the leaders?"

"I think so, sir," answered Tom modestly.

"You have their names pat; probably you'll find most of them in the reading room, and a few in the playroom."

Tom sought them out at once. They were not a little amused at his proposition to hold a meeting; but good-naturedly yielded, and followed him over to the classroom building.

"I say," said Tom, as they trudged up the stairs, "how long do you expect us to hold the fort?"

"If you hold it five minutes, you'll be doing well," volunteered Miller, with a grin.

"Perhaps you may hold out fifteen minutes or so," remarked Carmody, with a view to encouraging the young captain.

"Well, I'll tell you what," said Tom; "if we stand it out half an hour, will you agree in the name of the big fellows to give up the fighting, and allow the victory to us?"

"Of course." "I should say so!" "Yes, sir," came the general chorus; and as they spoke Carmody winked solemnly at Ryan, Will Cleary put his finger to his eye, and a general grin passed from face to face.

"Well," said the object of this subdued and ill-concealed merriment, as he unlocked the door of Mr. Beakey's class-room, "if you'll walk in, we'll settle everything in less than no time."

Tom stood holding the door open, with the key in the lock, waiting in all innocence and politeness for the wily leaders of the large yard to enter. All entered, still grinning. Suddenly, Tom sprang from the room, and the door banged after him, while coming close upon the slam grated the ominous sound of the key turning in the lock, followed by the quick patter of light feet down the stairs.

The hard-hitters of the large yard were prisoners.

Chapter XX

*STORMING OF THE SNOW FORT—MR. BEAKEY TALKS
AT CROSS PURPOSES WITH THE SENIOR STUDENTS*

"**O**H, Mr. Beakey," shouted Tom a few
moments later, "ring the bell, please—
we've got everything fixed the way I want
it. And—I came near forgetting it—won't you
please time us? The fight isn't to go beyond
half an hour. If we last it out half an hour,
we win, you know." With which words, Tom
started off at break-neck speed for the fort;
and such progress did he make that he was
within a few yards of his entrenchments
when the college bell gave the signal for the
beginning of hostilities.

The sound of the bell, coupled with Tom's
appearance, drew shrill, hearty cheers from
the little boys, as standing, snowballs in
hand, they impatiently awaited the onset.

By way of echo, a hoarser, deeper sound
came from the large yard; it was the battle
cry of the large boys, confidently moving to
victory.

Scarcely had these raucous cheers been
fairly heard, when their authors, thus far
screened from the eyes of the small boys by
the intervening building, appeared in full

view, as they came rushing round the corner of the "little boys' dormitory."

Forthwith, a few balls began to fall harmlessly about the fort.

"They might as well send off sky-rockets," remarked Conway.

"Boys," said Tom, "don't throw a single ball till I give the word. Be sure not to forget. All you have to do for the present is to keep your eyes open and dodge every ball."

Thicker, swifter, oftener, straighter, came the snowballs; nearer and nearer the attacking party.

"Hi! hi! Come, clear out of that, little chaps!" shouted Fanning, who was well in the front of his party. "Come and put us out!" came the answer from Conway.

"Come on, boys," continued the energetic aggressor, "let's charge 'em."

Inspirited by Fanning's advice, the large boys gave a rousing cheer.

"Now, give it 'em," bawled Fanning, as he came within about fifty feet of the fort.

In prompt obedience to this order, a shower of snowballs made the air white; and two of the small boys, each holding his hand to his nose, marked their way to the infirmary with a trail of crimson.

"Whoop-la! Now's our time," cried Tom, as

the large boys stooped for a fresh supply of snow. "Fire!"

As ball after ball whizzed into the ranks of the besiegers, their expressions of enthusiasm, so multitudinous before, shaded off into blended expressions of astonishment and uneasiness. Presently, however, astonishment pure and simple stamped itself on their faces; for before they had fairly begun to dodge the well-directed balls of the small boys, the shrill cry of "Charge!" came from the fort upon their startled ears, and presto! there issued at a run twenty-five of the small yard's chosen sharp-shooters.

Whiz! whiz! whiz! whiz!

This was too much. Amidst the shouts and taunts of the small boys, the crash of cymbal, beat of drum and blare of trumpet—all purloined from the music room by the ingenious Conway—the large boys of St. Maure's turned tail and fled! Not all, however.

In the confusion of onset, Fanning and a few of the unterrified resorted to a manœuvre. Quietly slipping aside they allowed pursued and pursuers to pass, then suddenly advanced upon the fort.

But the smaller boys inside were thrilled with the martial spirit of their leaders; they fought bravely. Still, the issue could hardly be looked upon as doubtful. Slowly but inevitably the hope of the large yard advanced. Fanning's voice was becoming "hoarse with joy." He hoped that in a few moments the works of the enemy would be his. But he reckoned without his host.

He was still urging his men on, forgetful of the sharp-shooters in his wake, when Tom's voice rose above the din.

"Hold the fort, for we are coming," bawled the young Sherman; and as he spoke he laid his hand on Fanning's shoulder.

"Do you surrender?" continued Tom.

Fanning with his contingent turned, only to find that he was hemmed in by twenty-five warriors bold.

"Never!" shouted Fanning, as with a vigorous shove he tumbled Tom over into the snow. "We'll die first."

"Then die!" said Keenan; and forthwith twenty-four small boys fell upon the unterrified—outnumbering them, I must say, three to one—brought them to the earth, bound them, dragged them behind the entrenchments, oblivious in the meantime of the galling fire of the main body of the enemy, who were content to remain, however, at a safe distance.

From that moment, the fighting on the

part of the large boys was tame. Deprived of their most skillful throwers, whose absence they had not noticed at the beginning of hostilities, and without the leadership of Fanning, they displayed a "masterly inactivity."

Whenever the junior students issued forth for a charge, they had a capital opportunity of observing the elegance and variety of the senior students' coattails.

In the meantime, the prefects and several of the professors stood looking on. Among them was Mr. Beakey. He had a quick eye, and it struck him, presently, that a number of the large boys were absent. Where could they be?

His suspicions were aroused. Perhaps they had taken advantage of his being a new prefect—he had arrived in St. Maure's but a few weeks previous—to slip up to the village. Perhaps—dreadful thought!—they might come back to college intoxicated. Mr. Beakey was familiar with stories of boarding-schools, and he remembered some sad cases of youthful intemperance.

He gave a sigh, took out his notebook, and ran over the list of the boys. His face grew longer as he read and compared. Yes, all the leaders, the very boys whom Tom had asked for, were missing.

"This is too bad," he muttered to himself.

"They are the last boys I would suspect of acting underhand. I do hope they won't do anything to disgrace the college. They're all good boys, and it would be a pity to have even one of them expelled. It's a pity I don't know the boys better. But perhaps they're about in some corner or other. I'll make sure of that point first."

Just then, Tom, on a grand triumphant charge, came sweeping past him. Regardless of the flying missiles, Mr. Beakey caught up with him.

"Playfair," he cried, raising his voice above the din, "do you know anything about Carmody, Ryan, and those other boys you asked leave to speak to? Where are they?"

Mr. Beakey's face as he spoke was clouded. Tom judged the expression to be one of vexation, and inferred, boy-like, that the prefect was not at all pleased at seeing his boys routed.

"I'll tell him the story," thought Tom, "after the battle, when he's not so excited. If I tell him now he'll give me a big scolding."

So he replied demurely:

"Mr. Beakey, won't you please excuse me? But, really, I'd rather not tell."

This answer confirmed Mr. Beakey's worst suspicions.

"There's no doubt about it," he muttered, as he made his way out of the thick of the fight. "These boys have stolen away to the village. But I do hope they'll not drink anything."

Mr. Beakey took out his watch. He started; it was two minutes beyond the half hour agreed upon. Hastening to his own yard, he rang the bell.

A great scream rose from the throats of a hundred small boys, as, in the full flush of victory, they charged their vanquished seniors for the last time. It was a disgraceful rout.

No sooner had the bell sounded than Tom quickly pattered to the classroom building, stealthily hastened up the staircase, and under cover of the cries of victory without, and the growling of the prisoners within, unlocked the door. He then hurried away, entrusted Mr. Beakey's key to the care of a large boy, and returned to his proper yard—there to receive congratulations and fight his battles o'er again.

In the classroom which he had just left, however, there were no congratulations exchanged. Carmody and Ryan were sulking in a corner; Ziegler was elaborately writing "sold again" on the blackboard; Will Cleary was whistling the "Last Rose of Summer," after the manner of a dirge; while Miller paced up and down between the benches like a caged tiger.

"Confound it!" burst forth McNeff. "I was never so badly taken in since I came here."

"You haven't been here so long; you're young yet," was Ryan's consolatory reflection.

"This is a pretty how-de-do," growled Cleary. "Every mule in the yard will have the laugh on us."

"I'll paralyze the first fellow that laughs at me," said McCoy.

"Just imagine the grin on Fanning's face," muttered Carmody.

The task of imagining Fanning's grin seemed to be attended with some difficulties, for it induced a silence that lasted for several minutes.

"Isn't that little wretch ever coming back to unlock this door?" cried Arthur, at length. "The fight's been over nearly an hour. Hasn't anyone got a button-hook?"

There was a sullen silence.

"Well, come on," continued Arthur, "let's go to the window, and catch some fellow's eye, and get him to open up for us."

"For goodness' sake!" cried Ryan, "don't. There'll be laughing enough at us as it is. But if the fellows once know we're here, they'll march up in procession to let us out."

"Well," said Ziegler, "I don't propose to stay here forever. I wonder, couldn't I squeeze through the transom?"

"You might try," said Carmody encouragingly. "And who knows but the key is still in the lock? It would be just like that brat of a small boy to leave it there, and forget all about it. Small boys are nuisances."

While Carmody was speaking, Ziegler had taken off his coat and vest.

"Now, boys, give me a lift," he said.

Eager hands came to his help—a trifle too eager, perhaps; for Ziegler was hurried through the aperture in such wise that he came down on the other side on hands and knees.

"You're a lot of lunatics!" he volunteered as he arose, "you'd think I was insured for a fortune, and had two or three necks to break. There isn't any key here."

"Try and break the door in," suggested McCoy.

"All right! Get away from the door, then," returned Ziegler.

He stepped back a few paces, and then made a violent rush at the door, catching and turning the knob as he threw the whole weight of his body against the woodwork.

The door flew open, and Ziegler flew in. His flying progress was arrested by Cleary, who was rendered breathless and brought to the floor with his friend on top.

While the two unfortunates were ruefully picking themselves up, the others broke into a ringing laugh.

"Shut up!" roared Ziegler, when he could command his breath. "You're a lot of fools! You might have known that door was unlocked."

"That's a fact," assented Carmody. "It's funny it didn't occur to you. You're a pretty sharp fellow, you know."

"Aw! tell us something new," snarled Ziegler.

"Oh! why doesn't somebody hit me hard?" apostrophized Ryan. "We've been mooning in here over an hour and a half, and that door's been open over a century."

Slowly and sadly they went down the stairs, each one trying to get behind the other—a feat in which all, of course, did not succeed. On emerging into the yard, they breathed more freely when they perceived that no one was outside but Mr. Beakey, who had been anxiously scanning the four quarters in hope of discovering their whereabouts.

"Boys," said the prefect, whose suspicions were confirmed by their sheepish looks and blushing faces, "you're caught—there's no getting out of it."

"Well, that's so, Mr. Beakey," said Carmody, trying to be easy and failing; "we might as well acknowledge it. We've been stupid."

"So, you don't offer any excuses?" exclaimed Mr. Beakey, in astonishment.

"Oh!—well—it was only in fun, sir," said Ryan, whose sheepishness had now grown intense.

"Only in fun!" gasped Mr. Beakey. "Fun! fun! that's not my idea of fun."

"Why, it's not so very serious, Mr. Beakey," said Cleary, in a conciliatory tone. "And I hope," he continued, "you won't punish Playfair on account of it."

Mr. Beakey remembered Tom's embarrassment.

"What!" he exclaimed. "Do you mean to say that that little innocent was concerned in it?"

"Why, he was at the bottom of the whole matter," broke in Carmody, in astonishment at the prefect's obtuseness. "And let me tell you, he's not so innocent, either; he's up to more tricks than any boy twice his size in this college—confound him!"

"Really," said the prefect, in a troubled voice, "the case is far worse than I thought.

Boys, I didn't expect it of you. I thought you had more sense."

General sheepishness at its maximum. Some grinning helplessly. Majority gazing at their feet.

"Frankly," he continued, "I am very sorry on your account."

"Oh, don't bother about us, sir," put in Cleary; "we can stand being laughed at."

"Laughed at!" echoed the prefect in dismay; "do you mean to say that such things are matter for laughter to the students of this college?"

"Why, certainly," said Ryan, no less puzzled than the prefect. "And, in fact, I guess we'll have to laugh the thing off ourselves."

"There, now, that'll do," said Mr. Beakey sternly. "I see that not one of you is in a condition to talk sense. You will repent your words tomorrow, when you regain the proper use of your reason."

The boys exchanged glances of perplexity. For the first time, they began to suspect that they were talking at cross purposes.

"Come, now," continued the prefect, "tell the exact truth. How long were you up?"

(Mr. Beakey meant uptown; the boys thought that he had reference to the class-room.)

"Over an hour," said Carmody.

"And how much did each one of you take?"

The boys again looked at each other.

"Do you mean chalk, sir?" ventured Ziegler. "I took a small piece, but meant no harm," and he produced from his pocket a bit of blackboard chalk.

Mr. Beakey flushed with anger.

"There wasn't anything else to take but ink," continued Ziegler, "and none of us wanted any."

This made matters worse. Mr. Beakey now felt confident that the boys were quizzing him.

"Enough of this nonsense," he said. "You need not make your case worse than it is by untimely joking. You have already acknowledged that you are fairly caught. I missed you from the yard before you were gone five minutes—and you have shown some signs of sorrow; you have acknowledged that you were "uptown" for over an hour; your shamefaced expressions and flushed faces show the effects of your indiscretion—there's a clear case against you. So, now, you may as well out with the whole thing, and tell you how much you took."

The astonishment that deepened on each one's face with each remark of Mr. Beakey culminated in a look of comic amazement;

the misunderstanding was too ridiculous. Mr. Beakey's last question was the signal for a hearty burst of laughter.

"Boys! boys!" implored Mr. Beakey, "for goodness' sake don't create a scene!"

Restraining his mirth, Ryan explained the misunderstanding; and as he spoke, it was delightful to see how the wrinkles and frowns disappeared from the prefect's brow, and how the firm-set, stern lines about the mouth softened into the brightest of smiles.

"Well, boys," he said, when Ryan had detailed their adventures, "I acknowledge that I've made a big blunder, and I ask your pardon. I don't know the ropes yet, you see. But sincerely, I am glad that I am in the wrong."

There was a whispered consultation among the boys; then Ryan spoke:

"Mr. Beakey, we want you to do us a favor. You and that Playfair boy are the only ones that know of the way we were taken in— we'll make him keep quiet, if you'll promise to say nothing to anyone about it."

"You can trust me," answered Mr. Beakey, "not a soul shall hear of it from my lips."

"Thank you, sir," came the general chorus.

Tom was easily induced to hold his tongue on the subject; so, too, was George Keenan (who had suggested the plot to Tom); and so the "true inwardness" of the big boys' failure to take the snow fort now becomes public for the first time.

Chapter XXI

IN WHICH TOM MEETS WITH A BITTER TRIAL

IN the events I have narrated as happening after the night of the first Friday in November, I have purposely avoided enlarging upon the grief and horror of that dreadful accident.

One would think, judging from what I have related of Tom, that our cheerful little hero had been strangely unimpressed by the tragic incident. This, however, is a wrong inference. True, Tom, by being sent to the infirmary, was wisely spared the sad sights incident upon the burial of his two friends. After leaving the dormitory, he never saw the face of Green again—face more beautiful and composed in death than it had ever been in the years of college life. Nor did he ever again see the face of the gentle boy who had asked his prayers. Had he seen it, he would have recognized the same beautiful expression which had thrown a halo upon the countenance when the boy had uttered "Sweet Heart of Jesus, be my Love."

Nevertheless, the accident had deeply affected Tom. He knew that his own escape from instant death had fallen little short of a miracle; and every night from his inmost heart he thanked God that he had been spared to make his First Communion. That Green had been taken away just as he had conquered his passions and made a start for the better, and that Alec had been called to God on the very day he had completed his ninth First Friday, seemed to Tom to be a wondrous manifestation of God's mercy. It was a lesson, too.

It filled his little heart with a burning desire to receive Our Lord in the Sacrament of His love. Among Catholic boys—as I have known them—such feelings and affections show themselves outwardly in a somewhat negative manner. They do not manifest themselves in deed and conversation, save by increased carefulness in avoiding anything sinful.

Joke and jest, play and study, may go on in all seeming as before. But the change, for all that, may be radical and life-long.

It was a happy day for Tom when on the fifteenth of February the First Communion Class was organized. I dare say that no small boy who ever attended St. Maure's set about the work of preparation as Tom did. Each day he had his catechism lesson prepared with a thoroughness that was beyond criticism. Nor, in the meantime, did he neglect his other studies. Indeed, owing to his long absence, it became necessary for him to apply himself very hard, in order to put himself on a fair footing with his classmates. Unfortunately, the semi-annual examinations were upon him before he could repeat all the class matter he had missed, and when, on the 22nd of February, the class-standing was published, Tom stood at the foot of his class, with but sixty merit marks out of a hundred.

"I hope my father won't get mad about it," he remarked to Harry Quip; and as he spoke he looked quite serious.

"Oh! I'm sure he won't mind it," said Harry. "He knows you've missed several weeks."

"Yes, but Pa's getting mighty strict. He thinks I'm awful careless. The fact is, we like each other immensely, but Pa doesn't know what to make of me."

In these few words Tom had set down their relations quite clearly. Mr. Playfair loved his boy; but as for understanding him, that was another question. Clearly, if Mr. Playfair had ever been a boy himself, he had either forgotten that circumstance or he had been cast in quite a different mold from his son. The wall of misunderstanding had been rising higher between them ever since Tom reached the age of reason. Such relations between father and son are not uncommon.

Tom's forebodings on this occasion were not without foundation. Several days later he was summoned to the President's room. On entering, he saw at once from the reverend Father's face that something had gone wrong.

"Ah! Tommy; how are you studying?"

"Pretty hard, sir."

"And how are you getting on with your teacher?"

"I like him very much. If he's got anything against me lately he hasn't told me anything about it."

"Are you sure you've had no trouble lately?"

"Yes, Father; I'm getting ready for my First Communion."

"Well, Tom, I've very bad news for you."

"Anybody sick at home, sir?"

"No; it regards yourself. Your father is very much displeased with your bulletin."

"Oh, I got low notes because I missed a lot of classes. Mr. Middleton says I've caught up already."

"Your father knew you had been absent, too, but there must have been something more in your bulletin—some remark which indicated that you were not giving satisfaction; for your father sends me imperative orders to take you out of the Communion Class at once."

A strange expression came over Tom's face. Every nerve seemed to be a-quiver. Till that moment, Tom himself had had no idea of the ardent desire with which he looked forward to his "day of days."

"Don't take it too much to heart, my boy," continued the President, both touched and edified at the way in which Tom received the news. "I have a hope that further examination will discover some mistake. You mustn't give up hope yet. I'll inquire about your bulletin, and find out just how things stand, as soon as possible."

"Thank you, Father," said Tom.

"In the meantime, offer your trial to God, my boy. It comes from Him. His ways are not our ways. And when He sends us trials, He wishes us to bear up under them cheerfully."

"I'll try to swallow it, sir. But it's rough."

Tom went directly to the chapel, prostrated himself before the Blessed Sacrament, and there prayed fervently. When he entered, he was dazed, bewildered; when he left, three minutes later, he was comparatively calm. There is no sorrow that prayer cannot soothe; and children's sorrows, God be thanked for it, are quickest to yield their bitterness to fervent prayer.

No one observing Tom playing at "foot-and-a-half," within that same hour, could imagine that the nimble lad, all gayety and motion, had just met the second great sorrow of his life. The death of his mother had been the first.

A week elasped before he was again summoned by the President.

"Well, Tom, things are looking a little brighter. There's been a grave blunder. Report was sent to your father that your conduct had been 'highly unsatisfactory.' Now those words were put in your bulletin by some clerical error. They belonged to some other boy's. I have just written your father how matters stand, and I'm quite sure that all will be right within a week."

Tom grinned excessively, and, finding some difficulty in keeping both feet upon the floor, hastened to leave the room; whereupon he danced all the way back to his yard.

And till news came from Mr. Playfair, Tom was in great glee. How eagerly he hastened to the President's room to hear the final word! He entered all aglow and smiling, but the glow gave way to ashen whiteness and the smile disappeared instantaneously. Something there was in the President's face which warned him that his troubles were not yet over.

"I've been a little surprised, Tom, by the tenor of your father's letter. He says he is glad to learn that your conduct is so satisfactory, and that you are doing so well in your studies; but he adds that he has been doubting for some time about the propriety of your making First Communion, on other grounds."

"I used to give lots of trouble at home," explained Tom humbly. "I guess Pa thinks I need more time to reform."

"He is acting through love for you, Tom; he wants to make sure that you are well prepared. He suspects that your levity of disposition is a sign that you are too young."

"Yes," assented Tom sadly, "I'd be better off if I could go around with a long face."

"However," added the President, suppressing a smile, "he leaves the matter in my hands."

Tom brightened at once.

"Judging from the drift of his letter, though, I think that he would prefer you to wait."

Tom's face fell again.

"Now, my boy, you have your choice. If you insist, I shall allow you to rejoin the Communion Class."

Tom thought for a moment, then suddenly a light flashed from his eyes—the light of an inspiration.

"Father, I'll tell you what I'll do. I'll give it up for this year."

He did not explain his reasons, but for the Father no explanation was needed. Tom had taken the side of strict obedience and of sacrifice.

"God will bless you for that resolution, my boy. Your Communion, when it comes, will be all the happier; and even if you have been disobedient at times, the act you have now made will more than atone. You have chosen wisely, and God's blessing will be upon the choice."

Tom departed happy. But the pain and struggle were not over. At times an intense longing would come upon our little friend.

On the feast of St. Joseph's Patronage,

when sixteen little lads knelt at the altar to receive for the first time their divine Master, Tom's eyes became very moist. One tear trickled down his honest face, and with the dropping of that tear all his sadness was gone.

There was no relaxation in his studies, meantime. Looking foward to his First Communion, he consecrated every day to preparation; and so, when the last examination came, Tom won highest honors in his class, with ninety-nine merit marks after his name.

Poor Tom! Between him and his Communion another tragic experience was to intervene. Upon this roguish little boy God seemed to have special designs.

Chapter XXII

*IN WHICH TOM WINS A NEW FRIEND
AND HEARS A STRANGE STORY*

IT must be said in justice to Mr. Playfair that Tom's record during the last half of school pleased him very much.

Indeed, he expressed his pleasure in such terms on their meeting again that Tom blushed to the tips of his ears.

"Say, Pa, what about my Communion?"

"You can make it, my boy, just as soon as the President allows you next year. Perhaps I was a little severe on you, but it has done you good."

And, indeed, there could be no doubt about Tom's improvement, though truth compels me to add that he made things very lively indeed at home during the two months of vacation.

On returning to college, he had a long talk with the President, the issue of which was, that Tom should prepare under the reverend Father's personal direction to receive his Lord at Christmas.

That Christmas was to be the turning-point in our hero's life.

September passed quietly. Towards the end of the month Tom came upon a new friend.

He was sauntering about the yard one bright afternoon, when his attention was caught by the following dialogue:

"He's homesick!"

"He wants his ma!"

"Give him a little doll, in a nice gold-paper dress!"

These were a few of the remarks from John Pitch and a few others of the same ilk, addressed to a timid-looking lad, around whom they had rudely gathered. Just then Tom and Harry chanced to be passing by.

"What's the matter?" inquired Tom of the victim.

"He wants his ma, but you'll do, Playfair," volunteered John Pitch.

"You're a mean set, to be teasing a poor newcomer, who hasn't got any friends," exclaimed Tom, his eyes flashing.

"Mind your business, Playfair," said Pitch.

"Yes, and you mind yours, and let the poor new kid alone. Come on, Johnny What's-your-name, and have a game of catch. Here, take some candy."

Tom's new friend, James Aldine, said very little, but his eyes spoke volumes of gratitude. He was a quiet, olive-complexioned boy. His eyes, dark and heavily shaded, had a trick of passing from an expression of gentle timidity to one of marked fear. Tom, who at once took a liking to the newcomer, soon came to notice this change of countenance, and as the days slipped by and their intimacy increased, Tom's wonder grew. He was puzzled, and, being an outspoken boy, was only waiting a favorable opportunity of satisfying his curiosity. At last the occasion presented itself.

It was the second week of October, when

he and James found themselves alone on the prairie, fully two miles from the college. The average boy can make an intimate friend in something under a week. The intercourse of these two had already gone beyond that period, and Tom felt himself fully justified in remarking:

"What makes you look so scared, Jimmy?"

"Do I look scared?"

"Just as if you had been training a large stock of ghosts, and hadn't succeeded."

Jimmy shivered, and his face paled.

"Halloa! now, I say," cried Tom, clapping him heartily on the back; "what *is* the matter, anyhow?"

"Oh, Tom," and Jimmy's long-pent emotions escaped in a flood of tears, "I'm afraid of being murdered."

"What?" gasped Tom.

"Just listen. You know where I live, about sixty-five miles from this place, on a large farm. Last year a newcomer moved near us, named Hartnett. He was a short, dark, ugly-looking man, with bristling black whiskers. He lived all alone, about a mile from our folks, and seldom said a word to anybody. One night, about a month ago, I happened to pass by his house, when I heard a noise inside, as if someone were trying to shout, but couldn't; then I heard a tremendous hub-bub, as if there was a scuffle; then the crack of a pistol, and then all was still again. In spite of my fright, I crept to the window, and, oh, Tom, how I was frightened! On the floor lay a man in a pool of blood, and over him stood that dark man, looking still darker. I was so frightened that I couldn't stir, and there I stood with my face against the window-pane. Somehow, I couldn't move. Then my heart gave a great jump, when suddenly Hartnett's eyes met mine. At first he turned deadly pale, then he swore a dreadful oath and made for the door. As he moved, my strength came back, and I tell you I ran down the road at full speed; yet not so fast but that I could hear his heavy breathing as he followed. Oh, it was awful—that run through the dark woods! I don't think I'll ever be as frightened again, not even when I come to die. Even as I ran, I could tell that he was gaining on me; and I called to God to help me, and prayed as I had never prayed before. At last his hand was on my collar, and he had me tight. He pressed me to the earth with one hand, and with the other pulled a knife from his bosom. I shut my eyes and said what I thought was to be my last prayer. Suddenly his grasp loosened.

I opened my eyes and saw he had changed his mind. 'Boy,' he said, in a tone that froze my blood, 'kneel down.' As I took the position, he held me closely. 'I know you,' he said, 'and you needn't fear I'll ever forget your face; now swear never to tell what you saw in my house.' Then he put me through a dreadful oath, and swore that if ever I opened my lips about what had happened that night he would kill me with most awful tortures." Here James paused, and trembled in every limb.

Tom put his hands in his trousers' pockets, and stood with his legs wide apart. It was his method of expressing astonishment.

"Gracious!" he said, "but he's a bad man! You oughtn't to be afraid of him, though."

"But I am; it is not so much fear of him as of my conduct that worries me. Sometimes I wonder whether I have to keep such an oath. Do you think I have?"

"I haven't got that far in my catechism yet," said Tom; "but I can ask my teacher. Why, what's the matter?"

As Tom was speaking, a look of horror had come upon Jimmy's face.

"Oh, Tom, *I've broken my oath.* I've told you the secret without thinking of it."

Tom was startled. His hands went deeper

into his pockets and his legs spread wider.

"Well," he inquired, after a few moments' reflection, "you didn't mean to break your oath, did you?"

"Honor bright, I didn't," protested James.

"Well, then, it isn't any sin; because you can't commit a sin unless you mean to—that's what we are told in catechism. But if I'd been in your place I wouldn't have taken that oath. I'd have died first."

"Well, do you think I'm obliged to keep it?"

"I don't know about that. I'll tell you what: I'll ask the President about it, so's he won't know that I mean any particular boy. What do you say to that?"

"I think it's a good idea."

Before night, Tom had inquired of the President and learned that an oath taken under compulsion was not binding.

"But," said James, when this news was imparted to him, "what shall I do about it? Do you think it my duty to tell on him?"

"I don't know, Jim; you'd better think about it. Come on, let's play catch"; and Tom produced a Spalding league from his pocket. They were hard at it, when Harry came running up in great excitement.

"I say," he began, "have you heard what

the Red Clippers have done?"

"No; what?" inquired both in a breath.

"They have put up, as a prize, a fancy baseball bat and a barrel of apples to any club in the yard that plays 'em a decent game inside of a month."

The "Red Clippers" was the banner baseball club of the small yard, and the players were the strongest, hardiest, most skillful and most active of the junior students. They were the constant theme of admiration among all the little boys—an admiration not unmerited, inasmuch as the Red Clippers had over and over again defeated the best middle-sized nine of the large yard. A challenge, consequently, from their nine, was, in the eyes of all, an opportunity to win glory.

"I'll tell you what," said Tom, "let's get up a club to beat 'em."

James Aldine smiled, and looked at Tom as though he doubted the seriousness of this offer.

"Get out!" said Harry in disdain. "We'll have to grow several inches, and swell out in every direction, before we'll be able to beat them."

"That's what you say," retorted Tom. "But we'll see about that. Now, look here! Harry, you can curve, can't you?"

"A little," was Harry's modest reply.

"Very well; you'll pitch and I'll catch. We'll practice together and fix things so as to fool some of those fellows. Joe Whyte may hold down first base; he's a good jumper, and isn't afraid of anything you can throw at him. Willie Ruthers can play second base, and you, Jimmy, can try short stop. Harry Conly seems to be a pretty good little chap, and he can hold down third. Then, we can put Harry Underwood in right, he's a gorgeous thrower; Frank McRoy in center, he's got long legs and can cover a great deal of ground; and Lawrence Lery in left, he's a good fly-swallower."

"Pshaw!" grumbled Harry. "All those fellows you've named are little tads. Do you expect to beat the Red Clippers with them?"

"That's about it."

"Beat the Red Clippers!" reiterated Harry.

"That's just what I said, if we take a few weeks for practice."

"Hire a hall?" said Harry.

"Just wait, will you? Now, you and Jim go round quietly and get our fellows together, without letting any of the other boys know what's going on."

With but little delay, the boys in question were brought together; whereupon Tom in a low voice unfolded his plans. At first his hearers received the idea of beating the Red Clippers as a bit of unintentional pleasantry, but as Tom went on, they settled into earnestness in such wise, that when he came to a pause, all yielded the readiest assent to his wishes, and despite Tom's modest disclaimer elected him captain, manager, and trainer of the new club.

From that time on, Tom saw to it that his men were practicing constantly; and yet their training was so unobtrusive, so "hidden under a bushel," as to excite no comment among their playmates.

After breakfast and supper, for instance, McRoy, Underwood, and Conly would take extreme corners in the yard and give the whole recreation-time to the catching of "high flies"; the basemen would practice the stopping of "grounders" and the catching of line balls; while Tom and Harry, with the prefect's permission, would go behind the old church and employ their time at "battery work." Tom was a plucky little catcher, and even if he failed sometimes of holding a ball he was not afraid to stop it. His main idea in regard to practicing with Harry was to initiate that young pitcher into such tricks as Tom's small experience could supply.

Whenever half-holiday came he and his men, instead of going out for a walk, remained in the yard. Then, when the playground was fairly well cleared, he would put his basemen on the bases, his pitcher in the box, and his three fielders in turn at the bat.

It was a pleasing sight to see how deftly these knickerbockered lads handled the ball. See the pitcher, bending his fingers into almost impossible positions round the ball! He is preparing to deliver an "in-curve." Whiz! there it goes, right over the plate, whack! into Tom's hands; and the boy with the bat wonders how he came to miss it. From the way Tom throws it at the second baseman, you would think it was a matter of life and death. But it is thrown too high; however, Ruthers seems to think the catching of it to be likewise a matter of life and death, for he springs into the air, brings it down with one hand, and without stopping for applause passes it on a low line to the first baseman. The first baseman is familiar with the short bound; he makes a neat scoop, then sends it daisy-cutting across the diamond to the short stop, who secures it on a dead run, jerking it into the hands of the third baseman. How quick they are! how eager! The one week's practice has been magical in result.

"Good gracious!" exclaimed Willie, "but we can play ball a little bit."

"You're right," said Joe as he walked in. "Say, Tom, I think we can play 'em any time, now—right away."

"Not much!" said Tom emphatically. "There's a big thing we've got to look out for yet; if we fix that we'll be all right."

"What's that?" was the general query.

"We've got to get used to their pitcher's delivery, so's to bat him easy. If we can't do good batting, they'll beat us badly. Now, I'll tell you what; I've got a scheme to bring the thing the way we want it. It's this: I'll bet any boy here the cakes for the next two weeks, and the apples too, that I can hold his delivery for half an hour."

The "cakes and apples," also the "pie," were favorite stakes at St. Maure's. By these terms was understood the daily dessert.

"I'll take you," said Harry, whose twinkling eyes gave evidence that he understood Tom's plan. "And I'll give Keenan half the cakes if I win."

"Done," said Tom, clasping Harry's hand, and holding it till Joe kindly "cut" the bet. "And I'll go halves with George if I win. And what do you say, Harry, if these boys here, who have heard us make the bet, do the batting to see whether they can bluff me?"

"I agree to that, too," answered Harry, with a solemn wink.

All now perceived the ruse and were delighted with their parts. No matter who should win the bet, it would be a splendid opportunity for studying their pitcher, and for getting some practice in batting.

After supper George Keenan was somewhat astonished to find himself waited upon by a delegation of yard-mates.

"What are you fellows up to?" he exclaimed.

"Look here, George," Tom began, "I want you to do me a favor. You see I made a bet today, while these fellows were standing around, that I could hold your hottest balls for half an hour. Now if you pitch your best and I win, you'll get my dessert for a week; if I lose, Harry'll give you his for a week."

Most model boys, if we can believe the story books, are rather indifferent in regard to cakes and pie; but George was a model boy on lines of his own—he jumped at the offer.

"Why of course I'll pitch to you; that's fun for me."

"Thank you," said Tom gratefully. "And I say, George, these boys will bat your pitching so as to make it more real."

"Oh! that's all right," answered George,

taking off his coat, and stepping into the pitcher's box.

A referee was then appointed to time the carrying out of this novel bet; and the proceedings began. For some time Tom contrived to hold George's hottest balls with apparent ease, while the witnesses improved their batting abilities. Strange to say, however, Tom, at the end of twenty-five minutes, began to show signs of weakening; and presently called time. Harry had won the bet.

Tom then protested that he was sure he could win the wager some other time; and, as before, offered to bet on the result. Forthwith, Will Ruthers took him up, and it was agreed that on the following day the test should be repeated.

In a word, Tom, by a variety of devices, succeeded in getting his men an opportunity of studying and "solving" George's curves three or four times each week.

Nor was he satisfied, once they had caught the knack of hitting Keenan. He went further; he insisted on their batting so as to send it toward third base. He had a good reason for this, as the issue will show.

Thus, giving himself to study and to play with equal zest, and never losing sight of the sacred Christmas that was approaching, the month passed quickly and pleasantly for Tom; and almost before he could realize it, the day for the great baseball match was at hand.

———————————

Chapter XXIII

IN WHICH THE "KNICKERBOCKERS"
PLAY THE "RED CLIPPERS"

HIGH Mass on All Saints' Day had just ended. In one corner of the small yard a knot of boys had gathered together, and were indulging in a hearty laugh.

"O Jupiter!" Pitch exclaimed, "won't we do 'em up!"

"They're pretty cool for little fellows," remarked Harry Jones, the field captain of the Red Clippers. He was holding in his hand a note.

"What's the fun?" asked George Keenan, who had arrived late on the scene.

"The best joke of the season, George," said Conway. "Go on; read it to him, Henry."

"Listen to this," said Henry, with a smile.

ST. MAURE'S COLLEGE
NOV. 1st, 18—

MR. HENRY JONES—

Dear Sir: We, the Knickerbocker Club of St. Maure's College, do hereby challenge the Red Clippers to a game of baseball to be played on the afternoon of All Saints' Day.

Respectfully,

THOMAS PLAYFAIR, captain and c.
HENRY QUIP, p.
JOS. WHYTE, 1b.
WM. RUTHERS, 2b.
JAS. ALDINE, s.s.
HENRY CONLY, 3b.
HENRY UNDERWOOD, r.f.
FRANK MCROY, c.f.
LORENZ LERY, l.f.

But George did not laugh.

"Those fellows," he said gravely, "may be little, but they are no slouches. As for ourselves, we have not played a game the last three weeks, and some of you fellows need practice badly."

"Oh, pshaw!" said Pitch, "we need no practice for them. I batted against Quip's pitching last year, and I can knock him all over."

Despite George's doubts, the Red Clippers decided to play their opponents without preparation.

Soon after dinner, accordingly, all the small boys hurried from the yard to the baseball field beyond the blue grass, where they were presently swelled in number by the arrival of the senior students, who, having heard of Tom as an "exorcist," and known him as captain of the snow fort, were anxious to study his methods in the national game.

At five minutes to two, Henry Jones sent a five-cent piece spinning in the air.

"Heads!" said Tom.

Heads it was, and the captain of the Knickerbockers chose the "outs."

"Time! Play!" bawled the umpire, as George Keenan stepped up to the bat.

The ball that came from Harry's hands seemed to be in a great hurry. It fairly crossed the plate, but was too high.

"One ball."

Then came another ball, swift and low.

"Two balls."

The third ball was tempting, and just where George wanted it. But it was one of those deceitfully slow balls, and almost sailed over the plate some little time after George struck at it. The batsman had lunged vigorously, and as the resistance of the air was mild, he whirled round and was within an ace of losing his balance. Before he could recover himself, another ball shot by, straight and swift.

"Two strikes," cried the umpire.

The crowd laughed; George tried to look easy, and Tom stepped up behind the bat.

George struck at the next ball, but he was too slow, and walked away wearing the hollow mask of a smile; while the crowd, always in favor of the smaller boy, applauded lustily.

Shane next came to the bat, only to go out on a foul, captured on the run by Henry Conly. Pitch followed with an easy bounder to the pitcher, and, amid lifting of voices and casting of caps, the Red Clippers took the field.

Harry opened the innings for his side by popping up an easy fly back of the pitcher, and before reaching first base, changed his mind and went for a drink of water. Tom now advanced to the bat and, after two strikes, knocked a sharp grounder to Pitch, who was covering short. As the ball went through Pitch's legs, Tom ran to second. Then arose a shout of triumph from the crowd, as Joe Whyte drove a low liner straight over third, earning second for himself and bringing in Tom. Willie Ruthers gave variety to this stage of the game by striking out. Aldine followed with a high fly toward short. Pitch, and Conway, who played third, both ran for it; a collision followed, and ball, third baseman, and shortstop rolled in three several directions.

"You idiot! What did you do that for?" Pitch blurted.

"Who? me?" inquired Conway, as he picked himself up and began rubbing his head.

"Yes, you!"

"Oh, I thought you were talking to the ball! *I* couldn't help it. I wouldn't strike against *your* head for a fortune, if I could help myself."

Taking advantage of this altercation, Joe, who had stolen third, ran home. The next batter, Harry Underwood, knocked a vicious grounder between first and second, but John Donnel was there and threw him out with ease.

My baseball readers must have already perceived Tom's motive in training his men to turn on the ball. The weak points of the Red Clippers were third and short.

In the second inning, after a three-bagger by Donnel, Conway made a clean hit, and sent John home. Presently, Conway saw a good chance to steal second; the baseman was playing far off his bag. Just as soon, then, as the pitcher delivered his ball, Conway made a bold dash for second and thereby fell into one of Tom's snares. The shortstop of the Knickerbockers was there, caught the ball from Tom, and touched the runner out.

In their half of the second inning, Tom's nine covered themselves with honors, and their opponents, especially Pitch and Conway, with errors. The third and fourth innings brought two runs on each side.

In the fifth, Pitch, who had lost his head, let several slow grounders pass him, while Conway dropped a fly and muffed two thrown balls—errors which, coupled with two base hits, yielded the Knickerbockers four runs. In the sixth inning, consequently, these two worthies were ordered to take positions in the outfield.

"If that's the way you treat a fellow, I won't play," growled Pitch, putting on his coat.

"And I want plaster for my head," added Conway, putting on his.

"Let's not play any more today," said Donnel, at this juncture. "We're done up and we might as well give in gracefully, before we begin fighting among ourselves."

The suggestion was good; the Red Clippers, beaten in the field, outwitted at the bat, and jeered at by the crowd, were indeed in no condition to continue. Jones perceived this, and wisely concluded to follow Donnel's advice.

Thereupon he held a short whispered consultation with Tom, apart, and, turning to the scorer, called for the score.

"Knickerbockers, 7; Red Clippers, 3," roared the scorer.

Tumultuous applause from the sympathetic audience, handsprings and handshakes from the victorious players.

"Playfair," said Ryan, the captain of the senior club of the college, "I've been here four years, and, honestly, I've never seen a club better trained than yours. You little fellows deserved to win that game, you went about it so neatly."

Ryan's words voiced the general opinion.

Tom's training had indeed been successful. On one occasion during the game, the umpire called Will Ruthers out at second when he was manifestly safe; but not by the least word or look did Ruthers or anyone of his side show dissatisfaction. So it was during the entire contest, while Jones and Pitch and Conway made it disagreeable for the umpire by constant quibbling and growling, the Knickerbockers, to a man, cheerfully accepted his every ruling. This is but one point of their training; but it is a point which I enlarge upon for the simple reason that so few college teams set any importance upon it. And yet this point, if attended to, makes baseball a training-school for wondrous self-command, and gives the game a dignity well befitting a nation's choice.

Chapter XXIV

TROUBLE AHEAD

TOM'S improvement was not limited to baseball. In class and out, he advanced steadily. Nothing, perhaps, had so helped him as his choice of friends. From among all the boys of the small yard, he had selected as his chums Harry Quip, Willie Ruthers, Joe Whyte, and James Aldine.

Harry Quip, mischief-loving though he was, had a great amount of practical, common-sense piety. No one enjoyed a joke or a laugh more heartily than he, but he knew where to draw the line. he was easy of disposition; in fact, a superficial knowledge of him might bring one to think he was easily led. In regard to indifferent matters this was quite true. Harry would rather yield than quarrel. But when it came to a choice between right and wrong, he was firm as a rock.

One instance will give an idea of Harry's method on such occasions.

During the preceding vacation he was thrown in with the boys of his neighborhood.

Shortly after his return from St. Maure's, he was conversing with some of them, when one began narrating what he considered a very good story indeed.

Harry saw the drift of it. "I say, boys," he interrupted, "the air is getting too strong for me around here. I guess I'll take a walk."

To his gratification, three of the little lads mustered up courage to leave with him. The joke was left unfinished, and whenever Harry Quip joined the boys the conversation was entirely proper. Indeed, before vacation had ended, the ethical standard of his companions had risen by many degrees.

Willie Ruthers and Joe Whyte were bright, pleasant little lads, reflecting the virtues of their heroes, Harry and Tom.

James Aldine was something more than an ordinarily pious boy. The younger students of St. Maure's College actually revered him, and called him the "saint." He was remarkable for gentleness. But his gentleness was made of stronger stuff than the term usually implies. His meek little ways wrought wonders upon

Tom and Harry. They seemed unconsciously to catch his gentleness, and soon joined with him in little devotions that touched and refined their lives into spiritual beauty. Tom was often overawed by Jimmy's piety.

"Say, Harry," he remarked one day, "that Jimmy Aldine's got more praying and piety in his little finger than you and I have in our prayer-books and whole bodies put together. Did you notice him last Sunday after Holy Communion? His face was as bright as—as—anything, and I watched him till he looked like a saint in a picture; and I expected every minute that a pretty gold crown would shine around his head and a pair of spangled wings would crop from his shoulders, and he'd go off sailing up to Heaven, leaving you and me to fight it out, and even then find it hard to behave half decently."

Evidently Tom had an imagination. Had he been older, he would have put his idea into verse and published it.

One of the first friendly secrets that Tom imparted to James Aldine was the story of his deferred First Communion. James took as much interest in Tom's preparation as Tom himself; and on recreation days, when they walked out together over the lonely prairies, he would speak so lovingly of Our

Saviour in the Blessed Sacrament, that his companion, like the disciples on the road to Emmaus, felt his heart burning within him.

On November the eighth two things came to pass, both bearing closely upon the fates and fortunes of our five little lads.

On that morning a cheering fire lighted up the windows of Mr. John Aldine's home, on the outskirts of the village of Merlin. Within, a pleasant-featured woman was busily setting the tea-table. Beside the fire, a child, who had just emerged from babyhood, was critically and dispassionately examining into the merits of a picture book.

A brisk step was heard without, the door opened, and a man entered.

"Papa! Papa!" screamed the child, clapping his little hands with glee and running toward the newcomer.

"Well, little Touzle," said Mr. Aldine, raising the child in his arms and kissing him, "and how are you, Kate?" he continued, affectionately greeting his wife. "We must be happy tonight. I have succeeded well today in my law matters; and, best of all, I have a letter from James."

"Hurrah!" cried Touzle, dancing about his papa's legs, to the no small inconvenience of that gentleman, who was trying to divest himself of his greatcoat, "letter from Dimmy! how's brudder Dimmy? Tell Touzle all about it, Papa."

Mrs. Aldine, though not so demonstrative as Touzle, was no less anxious to hear the contents of the letter.

"Sit down, my dear, by the fire," she said, "and when you feel perfectly cozy, let us all together hear what our darling has written."

Mr. Aldine, be it observed, never opened the letters from his boy but with his wife beside him. It was a delicate attention, and a very small thing, it may be, but take the small things out of life, and we have little left but murders and bank robberies.

"Well, here goes!" said Mr. Aldine, as he opened the envelope and spread out the letter.

ST. MAURE'S COLLEGE, November 4th

Mr. and Mrs. John Aldine

MY DEAR PARENTS:—

A knock at the door, so sharp, so vicious, as to cause Mrs. Aldine to start violently, and Touzle to jump with great alacrity from his father's knee, here interrupted the reading.

"Come in," said Mr. Aldine.

Touzle took refuge behind his mother's

skirts, as a short, dark, ill-featured man, with bristling black whiskers, entered the room. For a moment Mr. Aldine gazed at the stranger in some perplexity.

"It's Mr. Hartnett, who has called several times in your absence to inquire for James," whispered Mrs. Aldine.

"Oh, pardon me, Mr. Hartnett," cried Mr. Aldine, advancing and shaking his visitor's hand. "I ought to know your face by this time. Sit down."

"Well," Mr. Hartnett made answer, as he seated himself, "I can't blame you for not knowing me, for although I have called on you several times I have always missed you."

"I thank you, sir, for your goodness," cried Mr. Aldine, "and especially for the interest which I understand you take in my boy."

"Won't you take tea with us?" asked the wife.

"Thanks, with pleasure; it's chilly outside, and a cup of tea isn't such a bad thing in this weather. By the way, have you heard from the boy lately? You can't imagine what an interest I take in him. I met him once or twice and am convinced that he'll one day make his mark."

"We have just received a letter from him," said Mr. Aldine, highly pleased—as what father would not be?—at these praises of his boy, "and, perhaps, if I read a little of it to you, you may not take it amiss."

"My dear sir," said Hartnett with much warmth, "you are too good; I shall be delighted. Touzle, you little rogue," he said to the child, "come here and look at my pretty watch."

But Touzle, who had thus far persistently clung to his mother's skirts, was not to be tempted from behind his entrenchments. With his great, round eyes staring severely on Mr. Hartnett, he neither spoke nor moved. It is said that little children have an instinctive knowledge of good and bad people. Whether this be true or not, it is certain that Touzle had decided views relative to Mr. Hartnett, and by no means favorable to that person.

"Here's the way the letter runs," said Mr. Aldine:

My Dear Parents:—I am so glad to learn that you are well, and that dear little Touzle is happy—

"Hurrah!" cried Touzle in parenthesis.

—I am very happy here, and like the boys very much. Most of them are very good and kind, and only a few are mean. I like my prefects very much—my professor is just splendid. I think he can teach more in a week than most other teachers in a year. And now, my dear parents, I want to tell you something I have long kept secret.

"Halloa! what is this?" said Mr. Aldine, knitting his brows, and reading what followed to himself. He did not notice that Mr. Hartnett's face changed color, and that his right hand was quickly thrust into his side pocket and remained there. For a moment there was silence, an awful silence—had the little family but known the thoughts of their visitor!

"Why, this is strange!" said Mr. Aldine, at length. "He says that he is the only witness of a crime which he had sworn never to confess."

"What crime?" asked Hartnett.

"He doesn't say; but promises to tell me about it when I come to see him Christmas."

Mr. Hartnett's hand returned from his pocket, and with a forced laugh, he said:

"Oh, indeed! Perhaps it'll turn out to be a regular romance." At the harsh merriment of the visitor, Mrs. Aldine could not refrain from shuddering. Touzle hid himself entirely from view.

"Well, it's drawing on late," resumed Hartnett, hastily drinking his tea, "and I'd better be going." Awkwardly enough he took his departure.

"Dear John," said Mrs. Aldine, as the door closed upon him, "I don't trust that man. Somehow I fear he means us no good."

"You think so?" said Mr. Aldine, in surprise.

"I do, indeed."

"He's a *bad, bad* man," said Touzle, stamping his foot.

"Well, I'll keep my eyes open; that's all I can do," said the strong-nerved husband.

Their suspicions would have been confirmed had they seen Hartnett standing a few yards from their door, his clinched hands raised in imprecation upon their happy home.

About midnight, Hartnett issued from his lonely house, valise in hand, and set off rapidly down the public road. He was never again seen in Merlin.

At St. Maure's, on this same day, Tom was made the happiest boy at college—and that is saying a good deal—by receiving from home a box containing, among other things, a rubber coat, a pair of Ice-King club skates, and a fine breech-loading shotgun for hunting purposes. Luckily it was recreation day, and Tom, having obtained permission of the prefect of discipline, joined the customary hunting party, of which James Aldine was a member. Under his friend's direction Tom learned very fast. His eyes were good, his nerves strong. To his great joy he brought down a duck on his fourth shot. Tramping through the woods and over the prairies, stealing cautiously up to game under cover of tree and bush, and creeping along the margin of lake and river, the day passed quickly indeed; and Tom, with three ducks in his hunting pouch, returned to college jubilant. Before retiring, he had arranged with Harry, Willie, James, and Joe to go on an all-day hunt that day a week.

Chapter XXV

A JOYOUS GOING FORTH, AND A SAD JOURNEY HOME

A MID-NOVEMBER morning, cold, blustering, gloomy, the day of the great hunt. Shortly after breakfast, five little lads scampered to the gun room, and arming themselves according to the hunting traditions of St. Maure's, set out across the prairie in the direction of Pawnee Creek.

"Well, I'm glad it's cold," Tom remarked as

they got clear of the college premises. "A boy enjoys walking more in this kind of weather. He doesn't feel like standing around doing nothing."

"And I'm glad it's cloudy," said Harry Quip, "because we aren't in any danger of spoiling our complexions."

"Every kind of weather is good," said James.

"Yes, even hot weather," remarked Willie Ruthers. "Dear me, there'd heaps of folks be drowned if it wasn't for hot weather, because no one would ever learn to swim."

"Yes," said Harry, his eyes twinkling, "and on the same principle I reckon there would be heaps of folks frozen to death in winter, if there was no cold weather, because folks wouldn't learn how to keep themselves warm."

Suddenly James Aldine stopped walking.

"What's the matter?" asked Tom, who was immediately behind him.

"You are, Tom. Do you think I'm going to walk in front of your gun, if you hold it with the muzzle pointing where my brains are supposed to be?"

"Oh, what's the difference? It isn't loaded."

"That's not certain. And, besides, I object to it on principle. My father has often told me never to hunt with anyone who handles a gun carelessly. Here, now, hold it this way, resting on your arm; now, should it go off, you may bring down a cloud, if your gun carries that far, but you won't hurt any of us."

"Pshaw!" growled Tom, as he complied with the request, "I thought a fellow who knew as much about a gun as you wouldn't be afraid!"

"Just the opposite; the more you know about a gun, the most respect you'll have for it. A child, if he knows how to use a gun, is the equal of the strongest man. It is a dreadful weapon. One little load in it may carry death to the bravest."

James spoke earnestly; his words made a deep impression on Tom.

At this point the conversation was cut short by the appearance of a rabbit, which James despatched with a skillful shot. Game was plentiful that day, and before noon Tom succeeded in bagging his first rabbit, along with a plump quail, while James secured three rabbits and several birds.

Thus wandering along the banks of the Pawnee in the direction of the river, they stopped shortly after midday at the skirts of the woodland which sweeps along, perhaps a quarter of a mile in width, on either side of the river, and partook of a homely but hearty repast.

The boy who, after being on his feet half the day, can sit down to a meal without appetite is not worth writing about. Our little party *are* worth writing about, indeed! Cold beefsteak, ham, bread, cakes, and apples disappeared with wondrous rapidity.

"My!" said Tom, "I wish we'd brought more!"

All echoed this sentiment.

"I tell you what: let's fix up a rabbit," said Harry; "we can build a fire easily, and I'll cook."

The suggestion was favorably received, and in a trice James was preparing the rabbit which Tom had brought down; Harry was lighting a fire, while the others collected sticks and dry leaves. They had hardly put themselves to their interesting task, when snow began to fall.

"Hurrah!" cried Harry, jumping to his feet, and dancing about the fire, "we'll have a snow fort in the yard tomorrow."

"Hurrah!" shouted the others, and all began dancing about the fire. There is an inexpressible charm in the first snowfall of the year, which glorifies a boy; every tiny little messenger falling radiant, white-robed from the skies seems to whisper a tale of glee to his responsive heart. Round and round the fire the lads danced, faster and faster, while thicker and larger fell the flakes. Their dancing might have been prolonged indefinitely, had not the embers given warning that more fuel was needed.

"Hold on, boys!" cried Tom, who had just failed in an attempt to execute a handspring, "we want more wood, Jimmy; get your rabbit ready quick," and off they danced in different directions.

By the time the rabbit was cooked, the ground was hidden from view.

"We'll have plenty of fun going home," remarked James, as they again fell to.

"How's that?" asked Joe.

"Why, we can track rabbits over the snow."

"Hurrah for King Winter!" shouted Tom with fresh exhilaration.

"I wonder when we'll have another meal as jolly as this?" queried Harry.

"Who knows?" This from James Aldine.

"I say," said Tom, who was too healthy a lad to indulge in conjecture, "I'd rather be here eating this old rabbit, with the snow getting into my ears, than at a turkey and ice-cream dinner in the most stylish house."

No one seemed inclined to gainsay this statement; and a few minutes later, having done full justice to their fare, they resumed their hunt, each one peering in every direction to discover rabbit tracks.

As they pushed along, Tom noticed that James, who was lightly clad, shivered occasionally.

"Say, Jim, aren't you cold? Here, take my coat, I'm too warm for any use."

"No, no!" remonstrated James; "I'm used to being out in the cold."

But Tom whipped off his garment before James had fairly entered his protest, and with his grandest air of authority made his friend put it on. Then, clad in his sailor jacket and knickerbockers, the sturdy young Samaritan trotted on as comfortable in his light attire as though he were in the heats of mid-summer. Genuine kindness is warmer than any coat.

They were about two miles to the northwest of the college (two and one-half from the village of St. Maure beyond) when to their great joy they came upon the long-looked-for tracks. On they ran with new energy, but coming to the road, over which many vehicles must have passed, they were brought to a sudden halt. The prints had become confused with the impress of wheels and horses' hoofs.

It may be observed, that the road lay between the woods skirting the river and a long strip of land known as the valley, which, stretching on either side of the railroad track, changed gradually into the wild, rolling prairie.

Tom was for following the road, Harry for moving through the valley on toward the prairie, while James favored taking to the woods. By way of compromise, they agreed to scatter, each following his own plan.

So Tom, followed by Willie and Joe, trotted along briskly some ten or fifteen minutes, when Joe, out of breath, begged him to slacken his pace. Tom paused, and suddenly, from right beneath his feet, a rabbit which had been concealed in the brushwood scampered forth.

Bang! went his gun; the rabbit fell dead.

"Ain't I getting to be a great hunter!" roared Tom in undisguised admiration at himself. "Wait one moment, boys, till I load up again. Here goes for a deadner!" and he inserted his loaded shell. "There's five fingers of buckshot in that—enough to kill six rabbits standing in a row."

"I say, Tom," said Willie, "it's getting dark!"

"So it is," assented Tom, taking out his watch. "Why, halloa! it's near four o'clock.

We'd better get ready to start for the college, or we'll come late for supper and get fifty lines each from Mr. Middleton. Come on, we must find the other boys."

Vigorous shouting soon brought Harry to their side, but shout as they might, James Aldine gave no sign of being within ear-shot. Some minutes passed—darkness was coming on apace. Joe Whyte began to betray signs of nervousness, and Willie Ruthers caught the feeling. Suddenly—it was an accidental circumstance, but nonetheless awkward—all ceased shouting, and the hush of the evening seemed to take grim possession of each. Tom was the first to break the silence.

"Well, I suppose we'd better take a trot into the woods," he observed.

"Isn't it gloomy and silent under these trees?" said Joe, as they picked their way among the trees.

"Isn't it, though!" said Willie. "I feel as though I had the nightmare."

As they plunged into the woods they became more and more solemn; their shoutings had ceased entirely, and, indeed, they hardly spoke above a whisper. The gloom and grim silence of the white-armed trees had exercised a spell upon them. Suddenly they heard a sound that made their blood run cold; it was a groan.

"Good God!" whispered Tom, crossing himself, "but that sounded like Jimmy's voice. Come on, boys—softly. Don't step on any twigs, but pick your steps. I'm afraid Jimmy's in danger, and I have reasons you don't know of;" and Tom, as he moved forward, followed tremblingly by the others, held his gun at full cock.

Another groan was heard. Tom's face became pale as death, but his whole expression was nonetheless determined. Bending low, and partially protected from view by the bushes, they moved on till Tom paused, his face alive with horror, staggered, but recovered himself and raised his hand to the others in warning.

Judge of their terror, as, in obedience to Tom's gesture, they ranged themselves beside him and gazed on the sight that had so stricken him.

In a pool of blood, its bright red color contrasting so frightfully with the white snow, lay James Aldine. Above him, a stained dagger in his hand, stooped a man—dark, sullen, villanous, with the unholy light of murder in his sinister eyes. He seemed to be examining the poor child's features, as though to make sure that he was dead.

As Tommy gazed, his expression changed from horror to determination. Making a slight gesture to his companions to remain quiet, he drew up his gun and covered the stranger. Then, advancing stealthily to within a few feet of the villain, who was facing in the opposite direction, he said in a clear, ringing voice:

"Drop that knife, or I fire!"

So sudden came the shock upon the stranger, that, as he turned, his nerveless fingers let the dagger fall to the earth, while his face assumed a look of the most extreme terror.

"Raise your hands above your head, at once, or I fire," continued Tom, in the same inflexible tones. The gun, pointed direct at the man's breast, was as steady in the child's hands as though it were held by a statue.

The determined face of the boy utterly cowed the man. Up went his hands without delay.

"Now, sir, take that path right behind you and go straight on at a steady walk till you come to the road leading to St. Maure's; and I give you my word that if you attempt to move from the path, put down your hands, or turn around, I will shoot you at once. I know you, Mr. Hartnett [at the name the man's face put on new terror], and I know that this is not your first murder. Now, turn round and walk straight on."

"Take down that gun," chattered Hartnett; "it might go off accidentally."

"It *will* go off if you don't do what I tell you."

Completely mastered, the man turned and moved forward, keeping Tom's directions to the letter. Boy though his captor was, Hartnett perceived that he was dealing with a man, as far as determination went, and a very determined man at that.

As Tom, preceded by his captive, moved toward the village, Harry, Willie, and Joe raised James from the ground, wrapped him in their coats, and tenderly bore him toward the college.

It were vain to attempt portraying adequately the state of Tom's mind as he tramped steadily on after the murderer. His imagination never wandered; his whole being was fused into the determination to bring that man to justice. The road was lonely and deserted; not a sound smote the stillness; the minutes passed on into the quarters, but the steady tread of captor and captive beat equal and silent upon the yielding snow; the heavy gun covered its object as though supported by muscles of steel; sensation, fear, hope—all were kept in abeyance to Tom's present purpose. The blinding snow dimmed not his eyes, the cold stiffened not a limb. Whether it was a minute, an hour, or a day that the stern tramp lasted, Tom could never have told. His senses, concentrated to a single purpose, were dead to all else till the village was reached, and crowds of men came thronging around him and his prisoner.

Then speech and his normal activities returned.

"Arrest this man," he said; "he is a murderer!"

Strong hands were laid upon Hartnett; Tom's gun slipped from his grasp, a mist swam before his eyes.

"My brave boy," said a gentleman, catching his hand, "you must be cold, and worn out too. Let me put my coat about you."

"Thank you, sir," said Tom.

Then he staggered, blood issued from mouth and nose, and he fell into the gentleman's arms senseless.

Chapter XXVI

SICKNESS

D R. MULLAN's face was graver than usual as he issued that evening from the college infirmary in the company of the reverend President.

"Both are critical cases, Father, and, indeed, I have more fears for that brave little Playfair than for the other. Aldine's wounds are not necessarily fatal; a good constitution will probably bring him through. But the little hero is in danger of something worse than death. The strain upon his mind, the force of his emotions, the terrible ordeal to which his most remarkable will-power has subjected him, have thrown him into a high fever. He may recover, but, even then, his mind may be impaired or his nerves shattered for life."

"God forbid!" said the President. "Do you consider it advisable to write for the relatives of either?"

"Well, it would be no harm to send for Aldine's people; but as for Playfair, there's time enough. We had better wait till we see how his case turns."

Both little sufferers were in a private room, removed from the common ward of the infirmary. James Aldine, weak, pale, hardly conscious, was lying on his uninjured side—now and then giving forth a feeble moan of pain. In another part of the room lay Tom, his cheeks flushed with fever, his eyes bright and wild. Harry sat beside him and occasionally bathed his forehead. Whenever the infirmarian approached, Tom would shiver with horror, and would beg Harry, whom he called by the name of some former acquaintance, to take that man away, for he was a murderer, there was blood upon his hands— could they not see the blood?—there was murder in his every look.

About seven o'clock in the evening, when the college boys had been safely housed in their respective study rooms, Mr. Middleton, Tom's teacher, prefect, and dear friend, entered the room, and, strangely enough, Tom recognized him at once.

"Oh, Mr. Middleton," he cried, "will you help me?"

"Certainly, my dear boy," said the prefect, grasping the fevered hands entreatingly extended to him, "what can I do for you?"

"Come close to me," said Tom, "I don't want them to hear it. See them all watching me," he cried, pointing around the room. "They are all in the crime. Stoop down, Mr.

Middleton, I want to whisper to you."

The prefect bent low.

"They want to kill Jimmy, and they've poisoned me, so's I can't help him; but you'll take my place, won't you?"

"Yes, yes, Tommy; rely upon it, no one shall touch a hair of his head."

"And, Mr. Middleton, I'm going to make my First Communion tomorrow. It's Christmas, you know, and I've waited—oh, so long!"

"Not tomorrow, Tom."

The fevered patient took no notice of this answer.

"Where is Jimmy now?" asked Tom, presently.

"There he is, lying on that bed."

Tom raised himself and looked in the direction indicated. Then a strange, perplexed expression came upon him, as though the true ideas of what had so lately happened were striving vainly to square with the wild vagaries of his fever. Exhausted by the mental conflict, he fell back and, still holding tightly the prefect's hand, closed his eyes.

Toward nine o'clock that night, as Willie Ruthers was sitting beside the other sufferer, James recovered from his stupor.

"Willie," he said, "how did Tommy come to be sick?"

Willie told him the story of Tom's heroism, and of the high fever which the exposure and mental strain had brought on him. The listener's eyes filled with tears of gratitude to his brave companion, but on hearing of Tom's great danger, his face grew troubled.

"Tom is a real hero," he said, "and I shall pray for him night and day, that he may get well."

Next morning all the students were unusually subdued. Gathered together in knots, Tom's bravery was the subject of universal panegyric; while all, even the most flighty, were concerned at his danger.

At all times, Harry, Willie, and Joe were at the side of their friends. Nothing could exceed their devotedness. Ever and anon Aldine's face quivered with pain, but there constantly dwelt upon it a gentle expression of resignation. The doctor was satisfied with his symptoms. Tom's case seemed to trouble him more.

Toward evening of the second day after the hunting expedition, a lady entered and, kneeling beside James, covered his face with kisses.

"Don't be troubled, Mamma," said James, holding her hand tenderly, "I am not suffering much, indeed I am not. Tom is in danger, and you must pray for him."

Mrs. Aldine, who had heard the whole story, presently went over to Tom. The poor child, who had been tossing restlessly all day, started up on seeing her, his face softened with joy.

"Oh, Mamma," he cried, "why didn't you come to me before? Come to me, Mamma, and stay with me always." He tenderly embraced Mrs. Aldine—his mother, poor child, was in Heaven. "Mamma," he continued, "there's something I'm so anxious to tell you. I'm to make my First Communion Christmas, and you must pray for me that I do it well. I used to be very wild at home, but I think that I am not quite as I used to be. I've worked hard to change, and it is partly on your account, Mamma. I know that you've been praying for me ever since you went to Heaven; and I remember what you said to me just before you died. They want to poison me before I can make it. But poison doesn't hurt me. I'm used to it now. I'm glad I'm sick. You can't fool me; I know I'm sick; and it's just as easy to keep from sin if you're in bed as it is anywhere else. Easier; I'd commit murder, maybe, if I were out. I'd shoot—shoot—shoot—" and Tom ended this strange monologue with jumping up into a sitting posture and clinching his hands, while his eyes flashed in fury.

About sundown he changed for the worse. He shrieked and cried, and could hardly be held down in his bed. Toward midnight the doctor was summoned.

"If his delirium lasts above twenty-four hours, his case, I fear, is hopeless."

On hearing this, James called Willie, Joe, and Harry to his bedside.

"Boys, I want you to join me in prayer," he said. "I have made God a promise if He cures Tom. It may not be His holy will to cure him; but let us unite in prayer."

Led by James, the boys, in low, fervent tones, recited decade after decade to the Blessed Mother; while Tom, hanging between life and death, was soothed and restrained in his paroxysms by the kind hands of Mrs. Aldine and Mr. Middleton.

Chapter XXVII

DEATH

IT was ten o'clock of the following day Tom's raving had gradually lessened. As the hours wore on he became quiet, till at length, for the first time since the eventful Thursday, he fell asleep.

"His life is saved," said the doctor; "but the danger to his mind is not yet over. All now lies in the hands of God."

"So much the more reason for our praying," said James. "Come on, boys," he continued, addressing his three friends, "let us take Heaven by storm!"

Morning waned into afternoon, afternoon shaded into night, and still Tom slumbered. Standing about his bed, Mr. Middleton, Mrs. Aldine, and the three boys anxiously watched the face of the sleeper.

A little after eight in the evening Tom's breathing changed. He opened his eyes. All stood with bated breath, awaiting his first words.

After gazing about vacantly for some seconds, he stretched out his arms, gave a low sigh, and said, "Good gracious! I'm all broken up!"

There was a smile upon every face; the tone was so natural, so like Tom.

"Tom, old boy, don't you know me?" cried Harry, unable to restrain himself.

"I rather think I do. Why shouldn't I? But what's the matter with you all? I'm not a museum, am I? You're all staring at me so!

And where in the world am I, and what's the matter with my head? It feels as light as a balloon!"

"Do you know, Tommy," said Mr. Middleton, "that you've been sick for several days? Very sick, indeed?"

"Let me think," said Tom, passing his hand over his brow. "We were out hunting, and when we came to the place where poor Jimmy was stabbed—we—we—what did we do, anyhow? Did I fall down? And did that man try to murder me? And what's become of Jimmy?"

"Here I am, Tom," cried James, who was sitting up in his bed and literally brimming over with joy. "I'm all right, and so are you. You brought that murderer to jail. Don't you remember?"

"What—what did I do?" Tom inquired.

"Listen," said Harry, and with no little astonishment Tom heard his famous adventure narrated.

"Well, well, dear me!" he said at the conclusion, "it may be all true, but there's one little question I'd like to ask."

"Ask away," said Harry cheerfully.

"Well, I'd like to know if I was there when I did all that?"

All laughed at the serio-comic way in which Tom put this query. In truth, his question, under the circumstances, was not extraordinary; nor is Tom the only one who has been puzzled by the mystery of his own identity.

"Tom," said Mrs. Aldine, when the invalid had heard a full account of his recent doings, "don't you know me?"

"No, ma'am," he answered, with a blush, as he encountered the sweet eyes of a refined lady fixed upon his.

"While you were sick, you took me for your mamma; and, indeed, if the love and gratitude of one who has not the sacred name of mother can supply her place, I shall do it. I am the mother of James Aldine, whom you so bravely rescued." And stooping down, Mrs. Aldine tenderly kissed the little boy, as though, indeed, she were his mother.

To say that Joe, Harry, and Willie were happy, is the mildest possible way of expressing their sentiments; they were beside themselves. Their joy was threatening to develop into uproariousness, when the infirmarian very wisely ordered them to their respective dormitories.

From that night Tom's improvement was rapid. He soon outstripped James in the race for health. While Tom bustled in and out of the infirmary, James kept his bed, his wound healing, but his cheeks growing thinner and paler day by day.

"I say, Jimmy," said Tom, about one week from the date of the crisis, "why don't you eat a decent meal?"

"I'm not hungry, Tom."

"That's no way to do; eat, anyhow; you're getting thinner all the time."

"I know it, Tom; and, what is more, I believe I shall never be well again."

"Nonsense! Humbug!" said Tom sturdily, though his cheek blanched as he spoke.

"I do believe it, Tom, and I have reason. The doctor of late looks troubled. He complains that the wound isn't healing fast enough. And Mamma knows that I am in danger; for her face grows very sad when she thinks I am not looking at her; and once, after she had spoken with the doctor, I saw her cry. But don't think, Tom, that I am anxious to live; I had rather die, for I am ready. Should I live, dear Tom, the day might come when I should fall into some mortal sin. So far God has been so good to me; He has given me a holy, pious mother, and very dear, good friends," he pressed Tom's hand as he said this, "and, by His grace, has kept me out of all dangerous occasions. So I am happy at the thought of dying now."

"Well, Jim," said Tom, with the tears starting to his eyes, "I know you are ready, and I do wish I was as good as you. You've got the makings of an angel, but you mustn't die; I should lose my dearest friend."

"No, no; indeed you won't," answered James earnestly. "Please God, I shall be your friend in another world. I would be of little use here; but there I am sure I could help you far better. And, Tom, I am not sorry to die, for another reason. I don't think I could ever be happy here below. I fret about things so easily. The least thing worries me."

"Yes, that's so," admitted Tom, "you do fret about things. I'm not that way myself."

Toward evening Mr. Aldine, who had been East on business, arrived at the college, bringing with him Touzle.

Touzle entered the sickroom dancing with joy, but on seeing his brother so pale and thin he sobered very much.

"Poor Dimmy is sick," said the child, running his fingers through James' hair. "Where's the wed on your cheeks, Dimmy?"

"Somebody whitewashed me," was the answer; but Touzle was not convinced.

In December James was so weak that he was unable to leave his bed. Tom had been about his class duties for several weeks, but whenever he was free he spent his time at the sufferer's side. As the boy drew nearer the grave, his spirit seemed to draw closer to God. At times the light of sanctity flickered upon his face—such a light as nothing but exquisite purity and exalted holiness can enkindle.

Nor was Tom idle. Christmas was to be the day of his First Communion. With all his resolute will he applied himself to prepare for this august moment. Many an hour would he spend with James, speaking of the dearest of all miracles, the miracle of Our Saviour's ineffable love. At night, too, he would kneel long by his bed praying for love and grace; and the boys began to remark that instead of the dying saint Tom had arisen in his stead.

It was the eve of the great day. Just before retiring for the night Tom repaired to the infirmary to pay a last visit to his friend. The wan face of James almost glowed with joy at his approach.

"Oh, Tom, I'm so glad to see you," he said, "for I want to tell you the news. Tomorrow, Tom, as you go to Holy Communion for the first time, I shall be receiving the Last Sacraments of the Church."

Tom was not dismayed; he had long expected this news.

"That is good," he said; "and I shall offer up all my Communion for you."

"Thank you, Tom; you are too good. But I wish now to tell you something else. Do you know why I expected to die from so long ago?"

"Why?" asked Tom.

"Because when you were so sick I prayed and prayed, night and day, that, if it might be, God should take my life and spare yours. I knew you would be of some use in the world, Tom, but I would do little. So, Tom, you must try to do your work, and mine too; and that, you know, is little enough."

Tom was weeping.

"I am very glad to die," pursued James. "At first, when I prayed to God, I was a little afraid of being heard; for I had hoped, Tom, to live long enough to be a priest, and to touch with my poor hands Our Saviour Himself. I intended to give my life to God; but God has come to take it before I can give it."

Tom was still weeping.

"Mamma," said James, as his mother came up and laid her head beside her darling boy's cheek, "I know you do not refuse to give me up to God."

"No, my darling; if I loved you a thousand

times more, He should have you."

"I'm so glad, Mamma; tomorrow will be Christmas. Wouldn't it be nice were I to die then? Then you would give me to God on the very day God gave Himself to you."

Tom was returning from the Communion table, his heart beating in unison with the heart of his sweet Master, his radiant soul in the life-giving embraces of her Spouse. How the minutes flew, as he knelt in earnest commune with his loving Jesus! He was a saint that morning—one of those little children whose souls are the glory of the Sacred Heart. How long, how fervent, had been his preparation! But Tom now thanked God for the delay. His soul had been purified by trial. And now that the probation was over, Tom felt that he had been in God's hands. It was truly his day of days.

Thanksgiving over, he hastened to the infirmary. As he entered the room, Mrs. Aldine's sobs broke upon his ear. He hastened to the bedside, but the gracious eye of welcome was closed forever. A sweet expression, ineffably sweet, lingered upon the child's face, as though the body itself had, for one last moment, shared in the happiness of the liberated spirit.

"My God," murmured Tom from the fullness of his heart, as he threw himself on his knees beside the body, "Jimmy offered himself for me. Let me take his place in life. If it be your will, my God, I from this day give myself entirely to your work."

Chapter XXVIII

AN ESCAPE FROM JAIL, AND THE BEGINNING OF A SNOWSTORM

STILL Christmas morning! In a narrow room, lighted by one close-barred window, was Hartnett, worn no less by confinement than by anxiety. His face had grown darker, his fierce eyes had become bloodshot; while his beard, nails, and hair, long neglected, imparted to his appearance an increase of loathsomeness.

Like a caged tiger, he was fiercely, doggedly pacing up and down the room. Occasionally he would pause to catch the interchange of greetings from the passers-by without. They were merry words; words beautiful in themselves, but colored into beauty more gracious than the dawn by the infinite Peace and Love that gave them birth; words that brought back again that undying song of the angels, that song of gladness, which, ringing down the ages, will move the glad echoes of the human heart till this world shall have passed away. "Merry Christmas! Merry Christmas!" The words few, the meaning simple. Yet, link them with the glad smile, the bright eye, the look of love, the warm pressure of the hand—and what a wealth of meaning there is in the expression! It is the full-hearted utterance of human sympathy, kindness and love, raised into priceless value by the benediction of Bethlehem's Babe. But upon the prisoner's heart, long since attuned to the chords of anger and hatred, these words grated harshly. Muttering maledictions upon the authors of these cheery greetings, he resumed his weary tramp—not blessed on this thrice-blessed day by so small a gift as one kind thought. By and by, a key from without rattled in the lock, the door swung open, and the marshal entered the room.

"Well, Hartnett," said the marshal, "your game's about up."

"What's happened now?"

"The boy you stabbed died this morning. So tomorrow you're to be removed to the jail at the county-seat, if you're not lynched before you get there."

This prisoner wiped his brow with his sleeve, his breathing grew short, and an expression of abject fear started upon his face.

"What do the people say about me?" he gasped.

"There's not much said; they're rather quiet. But their way of looking makes me reckon that you won't get out of this jail more'n six foot before you're in the hands of a mighty mad crowd. But I guess we'll come a game on them. We'll take you off tomorrow before folks know what's what."

"When are you coming for me?"

"Oh, about four in the morning. Anything I can do for you?"

"No; I'll be ready when you come."

"Ain't you sorry that boy died?"

No answer from Hartnett.

"Won't you feel nervous-like tonight, with that boy's face before you in the dark?"

"See here, now," said the murderer, "don't try that on me. You needn't try to get me frightened. The boy is dead, and that's an end of it."

The prisoner spoke with vehemence.

"'Well, I can't wish you a merry Christmas, but I do wish that you may come to realize what an awful thing you have—"

"Go away! Get out! Leave me!" shrieked Hartnett, his bloodshot eyes growing hideous with rage, and his fingers working in impotent passion.

"One moment," said the marshal, producing a pair of handcuffs; "here's a pair of bracelets you might as well try on."

"Now?" exclaimed Hartnett, aghast.

"Why not?"

"Can't you wait till tomorrow?" he exclaimed, drawing back.

"Come on; now's the time!"

"Marshal, I haven't asked you many favors since I've been here. Please let me go free till we start tomorrow; it's an ugly matter to have those affairs on, and I'd like to put it off as long as possible."

"Let's see," said the official dubiously.

"Why, I can't escape, man. Look at these bare stone walls—four ugly walls and a wretched, barred window; and that dismal low roof that I can almost touch with my hand."

"Well, all right," said the marshal; "but remember, on they go the first thing in the morning. I'll leave them here for you to admire." And, carelessly tossing the handcuffs on the prisoner's bed, the marshal locked himself out. Had he seen the lurking smile of triumph on Hartnett's face, he might have reconsidered his favor.

Hartnett listened intently till the retreating footsteps had become inaudible; then, going to his bed, he turned up the mattress, and inserting his hand into a small opening, drew forth a slender, steel, saw-like instrument. After pausing to assure himself that no one was near, he climbed up one of the stone walls of the prison, by means of hardly perceptible holes made for his feet, till his hands could reach the wooden roof. His first act was to jerk from the ceiling three strips of black cloth, which, on being removed, discovered three long, narrow chinks, plain in the sunshine, and needing only a fourth chink to make a hole abundantly large enough for his escape. The work already done had cost him days and nights of patient labor, his instrument being small and, in appearance, unsuited for the purpose. He put himself to work now with redoubled energy. Presently the beginning of the fourth narrow slit appeared. Half an hour passed; hardly a quarter of an inch was done, and two feet to be cut before three o'clock of the next morning. Hartnett grew nervous at the thought, and pushed his makeshift saw up and down with all his strength. Suddenly there was a sharp snap—his instrument had broken. In the agony of the moment Hartnett forgot himself, lost his hold, and fell heavily to the floor, where, with a smothered curse still lingering on his lips, he lay for some minutes stunned and helpless. But the sound of footsteps without soon brought him to his feet; and with an agility wonderful under the circumstances, he again clambered up the wall, deftly covered the betraying chinks with cloth, then lightly dropped to the floor.

For the rest of the day he passed his time brooding and sullen, now traversing his cell with hasty, impatient strides, now tossing restlessly upon his couch. Darkness at length came; the sounds of the day died away. Toward midnight, perfect quiet reigned. Hartnett's time had come. With the handcuffs in one hand he again mounted, with all his strength beat them against the part he had partially cut away. One, two, three heavy blows and the wood yielded a little. Another strong blow, and another; and his escape was secured. A moment later, he had gained the roof, leaped to the ground—then skulked through the village, across the railroad track, out into the great undulating, deserted prairie beyond.

Whither he was going he knew not. But, strange as it may seem, no sooner was he free of his prison walls than an overpowering sense of terror came upon him. Did he seek the lonely prairie of his own choice? That was a question he could not have answered himself. He seemed to be fleeing from some pursuing evil. It might have been the bitter wind of the chilling night; but there seemed to ring in his ear a dying groan; there seemed to dance before him a knife, dripping with blood; and the wild angry jargon of many voices haunted him as though a horde of demons were at his heels. The very sky was dark and threatening; and strange, weird shapes, clad in the sable vesture of the dead, sprang up at every step before his startled eyes. Hour after hour passed away, and still he pushed wildly, madly on, his face quivering with fear and horror. With the first streak of dawn his strength, thus far supported by terror, deserted him; and coming upon a lone tree standing amid the vast solitude of the prairie, he threw himself beneath its shelter, and losing his night's terror in the splendor of the dawn, fell into a deep sleep.

Let us turn from this wretch to the side of the dead child. His delicate, fragile hands clasped upon his bosom and intertwined with the beads he had so loved in life, his face calm and serene and telling a tale of beatitude immortal, he lay in his white coffin, surrounded by father, mother, and little playmates, subdued into unwonted gentleness as they entered the chamber where death had dealt his kindliest stroke. It was the morning after Christmas, and James, it had been decided, was then to be buried.

"Not," said Mrs. Aldine, "that I am tired of gazing upon the dear face of my angel boy, but because death in a house where so many boys are together would keep them in a sadness not suited to the time."

Mr. Middleton, who had been James Aldine's teacher, spoke a few last words.

He told the students of the child Jesus; of His hidden youth, and of His love for little children. Then he narrated, almost in the beautiful language of the Gospel, the story of how Jesus, when He was asked by the Apostles who was the greatest in the Kingdom of Heaven, took a child and set him in their midst. "And," he continued, "when I consider the little I have seen of our departed brother's life, when I recall how earnestly, how devoutly, he sought to love and imitate the Sacred Heart of Jesus, it seems to me that such a one as this must our Divine

Lord have chosen to stand in the midst of His Apostles."

Slowly and solemnly the students, in ordered ranks, devoutly reciting the Rosary as they moved, walked from the college toward the graveyard, which lay a mile or so out upon the prairie. As they neared the newly-made grave, snow began to fall in large flakes. Before the burial services had concluded the storm became blinding in its intensity. Mr. Morton, the prefect of the large boys, was alarmed.

"Boys," he said in a loud voice, as the grave-diggers were completing their task, and the students were about to start for the college, "I warn you, on peril of your lives, not to disperse on the road back. This promises to be a terrible snowstorm, and were you to lose your way, death on the prairie might be the result. Form into ranks as before and I will put two boys who know the prairie best at the head."

It was very happy of the prefect to have taken this decisive measure. At first some of the youthful wiseacres grumbled, but when, with difficulty, all had arrived safely at the college, it was generally acknowledged that any other course might have led to the loss of life.

Chapter XXIX

END OF THE SNOWSTORM

WHEN Harnett awoke he found himself covered with snow, and, hastily rubbing his eyes, discovered with dismay that he was alone on the trackless prairie in the face of the fiercest and most blinding snowstorm that had ever come under his experience. Starting to his feet, he pushed vigorously ahead. But whither was he going? He could not tell; mortal eye, were it ever so strong and steady, could not have pierced the snow-veil which stretched from earth to sky. Yet he must go on. To stand in such a storm were to perish. As he started out upon this enforced tramp, the snow was already ankle-deep; after an hour's weary walking it had deepened several inches. But it was a tramp against death, and as the echo of the last night's horrid voices rang in his memory, he pushed on as though the whole demon-world were at his back. Several hours passed, and finally the wanderer came to a lone tree. One look, and he perceived that it was the tree he had started from.

The wild, horrid explosion of curses that burst from his lips fell idle upon the dreadful solitude, but to his distorted fancy they seemed to be re-echoed by a million hideous tongues; and more affrighted than ever, he set forward again. Travel had now become very difficult. At times he would fall into a snowdrift, and on one occasion he was almost suffocated before he could free himself. As the afternoon advanced, a feeling of languor stole upon him; his senses were losing their sharpness. This but terrified him the more, for he knew that, should he give way to this weakness, he was lost. On he went, then, with the desperation of despair; on, on, till darkness closed about him; on, on, till the rude wind rose and howled and hooted after him, and threw itself against him; on, on, till the voices of the night were changed into groans and shrieks and dirges; on, on, till, weary, frightened, hopeless, with his stubbly beard and hair encrusted with ice, his face numb with cold, he fell and stumbled over some earth slightly raised above the level— fell in such a manner that the raised earth served as a pillow for his head. The feeling of languor had now become a positive force; he would not rise again—let Hell or Heaven do its worst, he cared not. Again there rang in his ears a wild shout as of demon tri- umph. Despair forced him once more to open his eyes. Looking straight before him, he saw—could it be?—a little child, clad in white and standing looking down upon his face. Hartnett's eyes started in terror; an expression as of the damned came over his features, and with a low groan he fell back senseless.

The day following the storm Tom with his friends obtained permission to visit James Aldine's grave. As they approached, Harry observed:

"Look at that tombstone standing up right beside Jimmy's grave. It stands there all in white, like the ghost of a child."

"If I were to see that in the dark," observed Joe, "it would almost scare me to death."

"My God! look here!" cried Tom.

Tom had just removed a layer of snow from Jimmy's grave, revealing to all the head of Hartnett, pale in death, but horrible, despairing, ghastly—resting on the grave of the child he had murdered.

Chapter XXX

CONCLUSION

THE early history of Tom Playfair is told. On the day he made his First Communion, he may be said to have "made his start" in life. All the events dating from his first introduction to the reader—delay, disappointment, sorrow, disaster—all had converged into the shaping and perfecting of that "day of days," into the molding of a noble character.

Tom had met with two tragic experiences beyond the lot of most boys of his years and condition in life, and he had borne them bravely.

He had suffered, moreover, a bitter trial—nonetheless a trial that it was in part self-imposed—and his act of obedience had purified and strengthened him.

But he was still deficient; the evil effects of his unequal home-training had not been entirely effaced. About him there still lingered a touch of forwardness, and the shadow of a boyish irreverence toward his elders. Mr. Meadow's influence had woven itself into his very texture. To borrow a schoolboy's expressive phrase, he was somewhat "fresh."

He united in his character great physical and great moral courage, but the sweet modesty and gentleness which impart a lustre to perfect bravery were yet to come. He was a manly boy; the manliness was rough at the edges.

On the last day of the school year Tom tapped at Mr. Middleton's door to exchange a few words of farewell.

"Ah, Tom; I'm glad you've come! You're always welcome, but now—So you're going?"

"Yes, sir; and I've come to ask your pardon, Mr. Middleton, for all the trouble I've given you. You know, sir, I can hardly help wriggling; and it's so hard to keep quiet four hours a day, when there's such a good chance for a little fun sometimes; and then, sir, I've got to talk sometimes—I can't hold in."

"Well, Tom, *I* haven't complained, have I?"

"No, sir; that's the way you make me feel mean. You're so patient. If I were in your place, I'd raise a row, sure."

"If I have been patient, I have had my reward; for I'm glad to tell you, Tom, that your improvement in conduct and in application has been so steady that it could be noticed almost each week."

"Thank you, sir," said Tom, blushing.

Like most generous, noble-hearted boys, he

was a hero-worshipper; and from the time of the memorable interview between himself and Mr. Middleton, on the day that Tom and Pitch smoked together, his professor had been his hero. Tom had been conquered by kindness—a conquest, it is scarcely necessary to say, no less creditable to the victor than to the vanquished.

He had issued from that interview Mr. Middleton's disciple; and a faithful disciple he had been. No wonder, then, that his chubby cheeks colored with pleasure at these kindly words of commendation.

"You remember, Tom," continued Mr. Middleton, fixing an earnest look upon the little lad, "you remember that letter I sent your father, nearly two years ago?"

"I shall never forget it, sir."

"Well, I ventured on a bold prediction in it, and I have not been disappointed."

Tom could have kissed the hand extended to him; in our American way, he squeezed it heartily.

"I must add, though," continued Mr. Middleton, "that you've lost a friend you could ill spare."

"Jimmy Aldine?"

"Yes; he had a gentleness and sweetness of disposition which exerted a marked influence upon you for good. He was a true friend; you needed such a friend; so did Harry Quip. You and Harry have helped each other, too; but James Aldine had an influence that stepped in where yours and Harry's stopped short. He was in a manner a visible guardian angel to you both."

"He was like the fairy prince I read about the other day when I was alone in the infirmary with a sore throat and didn't know what to do with myself," sighed Tom. "I got thinking of him when I was reading. I miss him very much, sir. He was the nicest boy I ever met."

"Ah, Tom, if you could find another friend like him!"

"Well, sir, I'm young yet, and there's no end of good boys in the world, if a fellow could only find them out. Maybe there'll be lots of nice new boys here next year."

"Pray, Tom, pray for another James Aldine."

"I will, indeed, sir."

And with a swelling heart he bade his teacher farewell.

On that very day a Baltimore gentleman was bidding farewell to his daughters and an only son, the "fairy prince," who were departing for Cincinnati, to reside there with their aunt while their father was to spend the summer in Europe with his invalid wife. This was the beginning of events which bore closely upon the conversation just recorded and upon the after-life of Tom.

Knowing nothing of this, Tom prayed all vacation for the new friend; and in September his prayer was heard.

Those of my readers who are interested in Tom will learn in "Percy Wynn; or, Making a Boy of Him," how and under what circumstances he met with his "fairy prince."

The End

Spread the Faith with . . .

TAN·BOOKS

A Division of Saint Benedict Press, LLC

TAN books are powerful tools for evangelization. They lift the mind to God and change lives. Millions of readers have found in TAN books and booklets an effective way to teach and defend the Faith, soften hearts, and grow in prayer and holiness of life.

Throughout history the faithful have distributed Catholic literature and sacramentals to save souls. St. Francis de Sales passed out his own pamphlets to win back those who had abandoned the Faith. Countless others have distributed the Miraculous Medal to prompt conversions and inspire deeper devotion to God. Our customers use TAN books in that same spirit.

If you have been helped by this or another TAN title, share it with others. Become a TAN Missionary and share our life changing books and booklets with your family, friends and community. We'll help by providing special discounts for books and booklets purchased in quantity for purposes of evangelization. Write or call us for additional details.

TAN Books
Attn: TAN Missionaries Department
P.O. Box 410487
Charlotte, NC 28241

Toll-free (800) 437-5876
missionaries@TANBooks.com

TAN·BOOKS

TAN Books was founded in 1967 to preserve the spiritual, intellectual and liturgical traditions of the Catholic Church. At a critical moment in history TAN kept alive the great classics of the Faith and drew many to the Church. In 2008 TAN was acquired by Saint Benedict Press. Today TAN continues its mission to a new generation of readers.

From its earliest days TAN has published a range of booklets that teach and defend the Faith. Through partnerships with organizations, apostolates, and mission-minded individuals, well over 10 million TAN booklets have been distributed.

More recently, TAN has expanded its publishing with the launch of Catholic calendars and daily planners—as well as Bibles, fiction, and multimedia products through its sister imprints Catholic Courses (CatholicCourses.com) and Saint Benedict Press (SaintBenedictPress.com).

Today TAN publishes over 500 titles in the areas of theology, prayer, devotions, doctrine, Church history, and the lives of the saints. TAN books are published in multiple languages and found throughout the world in schools, parishes, bookstores and homes.

For a free catalog, visit us online at
TANBooks.com

Or call us toll-free at
(800) 437-5876

More recently, AM
sunder of baited
s bibles screened
or income Common
s term

edia 1960-s

... new boy that
... has grown ...
... himself. His man-
... school, and he has
... skating, boxing, bob-
... brain's courage
... and his buddies at St.
... such a great time as they
... all-American Catholic

TOM PLAYFAIR

The story opens with 10-year-old Tom Playfair being quite a handful for his well-meaning but soft-hearted aunt. (Tom's mother has died.) Mr. Playfair decides to ship his son off to St. Maure's boarding school—an all-boys academy run by Jesuits—to shape him up, as well as to help him make a good preparation for his upcoming First Communion. Tom's adventures are just about to begin. Life at St. Maure's will not be dull!

PERCY WYNN

In this volume, Tom Playfair meets a new boy just arriving at St. Maure's. Percy Wynn has grown up in a family of 10 girls and only 1 boy—himself! His manners are formal, he talks like a book, and he has never played baseball or gone skating, boating, fishing, or even swimming! Yet he has brains, courage and high Catholic ideals. Tom and his buddies at St. Maure's befriend Percy and have a great time as they all work at turning Percy into an all-American Catholic boy.

HARRY DEE

Young Harry Dee arrives at St. Maure's thin and pale from his painful experiences involving the murder of his rich uncle. In this last book of the three, Tom and Percy help Harry recover from his early trauma—which involves solving "the mystery of Tower Hill Mansion." After many wild experiences, the three boys graduate from St. Maure's and head toward the life work to which God is calling each of them as young men.